THE WIDOWS' GUIDE TO LAST ORDERS

AMANDA ASHBY

Storm
PUBLISHING

To request permissions, contact the publisher at rights@stormpublishing.co

Ebook ISBN: 978-1-83700-442-3
Paperback ISBN: 978-1-83700-443-0

Cover design: Emily Courdelle
Cover images: Shutterstock
Map design: Yopi Kwb

Published by Storm Publishing.
For further information, visit:
www.stormpublishing.co

ALSO BY AMANDA ASHBY

The Widows' Guide to Murder
The Widows' Guide to Backstabbing
The Widows' Guide to Skulduggery

Domestic thrillers
The Stepmother
The Ex-Wife
I Will Find You
Remember Me?

Romance – adult
Once in a Blue Moon
What Were You Thinking, Paige Taylor?
Falling for the Best Man
Dating the Wrong Mr. Right
You Had Me at Halo

Romance – young adult
How to Kiss Your Enemy
How to Kiss Your Crush
How to Kiss a Bad Boy
The Heartbreak Cure
The Wedding Planner's Baby

Middle Grade – paranormal adventures
Midnight Reynolds and the Phantom Circus

Midnight Reynolds and the Agency of Spectral Protection

Midnight Reynolds and the Spectral Transformer

Wishful Thinking

Under a Spell

Out of Sight

Young Adult – paranormal adventures

Demonosity

Fairy Bad Day

Zombie Queen of Newbury High

ONE

Sunday, October 11

'You had better keep walking. That's right, buddy, off you go. And make sure the door doesn't hit you on the way out.'

The voice sounded from somewhere deep in the pub and Ginny Cole, who had been on the point of standing, turned to discover the speaker was the sweet man who ran the plant stall at the local market.

Ginny had once caught him putting a knitted blanket over a peace lily because he worried it would get cold, yet here he was yelling abuse at Detective Inspector James Wallace. It made no sense. Why risk trouble with the police? Then again, not everyone shared her lifelong fear of getting arrested.

'Cheat. How could a copper know the number of tributaries coming off the Amazon River?' a second person chimed in. 'I demand a recount.'

A chorus of voices cheered in agreement.

This wasn't good.

At sixty-one, Ginny considered herself wise in the ways of the world, but she hadn't expected such an angry response to what she thought would be a quiet Sunday quiz night at the local pub.

An uneasy shiver went up her spine as she studied the makeshift stage in the other corner of the taproom, where DI Wallace was standing. The detective was also her next-door neighbour, which meant she knew him reasonably well, and she doubted he appreciated the comments. However, Wallace, who was in his mid-thirties and had a resting scowl face, didn't flinch as he accepted the handmade winner's certificate and a twenty-five-pound gift card on behalf of his quiz team.

Maybe Wallace hadn't heard the abuse?

Or was he simply taking the high road?

Ginny frowned and looked around her. The Lost Goat was usually a cosy pub with dark emerald-green walls, well-polished wooden tables and a welcoming atmosphere, but right now it felt anything but welcoming. She and her three friends were sitting at one of the round tables at the far end of the room, and she turned to them now, hoping to find out what was going on.

She had met JM, Tuppence and Hen when she moved to Little Shaw fourteen months ago. Like her, they were widows, and she was grateful every day that they'd taken her under their wings. Especially when it came to navigating the complicated customs of the small Lancashire village.

She made a mental note to add controversial pub quizzes to the growing list.

'How dreadful. It's not Wallace's fault that his team has won it for the last three weeks.' Hen's warm brown eyes filled with worry as she retrieved the knitting that was never far from her side. Her knitting bag was floral, as was the collar of the Laura Ashley blouse that peeked out from under the heavy navy argyle jumper she was wearing.

'Quizzing brings out the worst in people.' JM finished her drink and leaned back in her chair. Despite turning seventy-one last month, she was as stylishly dressed as ever, in an olive-green jacket and dark navy jeans that covered her long legs.

'I warned Mitch and Heather this would happen.' Tuppence ran a hand through her wild curls which sprang out in defiance. 'It was the same with the all-night Jenga marathon the golf club tried to start. It ended with a broken window, several fist fights and more trash talking than a boxing match.'

As if to prove the point, two punters made a jeering noise as Wallace and the other three members who made up the May the Force be With You quiz team left the stage and returned to their table, while Mitch, the new co-owner of The Lost Goat, valiantly took photographs of their retreating backs.

Next to him, his lovely wife Heather was ushering the young barman to safety, as the heckling continued.

JM, another latecomer to Little Shaw, frowned. 'What's made them so upset? It can't be the prize.'

'It's the bragging rights,' Tuppence explained. 'Doesn't matter if it's winning something at the spring fete or being first through the door at the hardware store's fertiliser sale, people here like to boast.'

Ginny wasn't convinced. She couldn't imagine her team, The Merry Widows, bragging about winning. Or using the gift certificate, which was for a water park ten miles away.

'The fact that the quiz was so difficult only adds to the appeal.' Hen paused from the intricate jumper sleeve she'd been working on. 'Ginny, we would have done ever so badly if you hadn't known the answers to those history questions.'

'Excuse me, am I invisible?' JM demanded with a growl. 'I'll have you know I came very close to guessing the answer to that fiddly question on space. Who knew the Boomerang Nebula was so cold?'

'You did much better than me,' Hen quickly amended, colour brightening her cheeks, just like it did whenever she worried about offending anyone. 'I meant Ginny did well in a category that wasn't her speciality. We'd better hope no one tries to poach her for next week.'

'I'm sure that won't happen,' Ginny quickly said. And it was true.

Despite doing the crossword every day, she had struggled with many of the questions and now understood why the entire village had spent the last month trying to recruit members for their various teams to celebrate The Lost Goat relaunching their quiz nights.

Not that she would ever consider another team. For her, friendship came first.

Speaking of friendship... it was her turn to get in a round of drinks, which was what she'd been in the middle of doing before the rudeness started. She gathered the four wine glasses and got to her feet.

'You're a duck,' Hen said. 'Usually, I'd say no because it's past my bedtime, but after seeing all the fuss, I want to support Mitch and Heather. To think that after working here for so long they now own it.'

'I'm happy for them,' Tuppence agreed before glaring at several of the nearby hecklers. 'I just wish they didn't have to put up with cranky punters who use quiz night as an excuse for bad manners.'

'Heckling is the lowest form of wit and I have no time for it,' JM announced before Ginny wove her way through the crowded taproom and over to the gleaming wooden bar.

'How did you get on?' Mitch appeared from the cellar. He was in his mid-thirties and after suffering the painful loss of his fiancée several years ago, he had found happiness with Heather.

'Not as well as Wallace and his team,' Ginny said diplomatically and gave him the order. 'But it was lots of fun. You and Heather are doing a great job.'

The worry left his eyes and he grinned. 'Thanks. It's hard to believe that a year ago my life was such a mess. Back then I couldn't see a way to fix it.'

'I know the feeling,' Ginny admitted, thinking of her own grief when she'd first moved into the cottage where she and Eric had planned to retire to. His death meant she'd made the journey alone, and never imagined she would find new friends, a new job, and most importantly, a new belief in herself.

Well, most of the time.

'Seems we're both doing better for ourselves these days.' He opened a bottle of white wine. Then he frowned. 'Poor Nathan. I hope the locals don't give him a hard time.'

'I think the bigger worry is how much they will try to bribe him before next Sunday,' Heather said in a dry voice as she joined them. Her purple hair hung over her shoulders and a wedding ring glittered on her finger.

'Surely not.' Ginny followed their gaze to where the quizmaster-slash-barman ducked his way through the crowd as several people waved five-pound notes in his direction.

'Come on, mate,' a tall man called out. 'You could at least have a category on the top ten UK rhythm bass guitarists from the years 1971 to 1978.'

'Bollocks,' someone else yelled. 'No one cares about music. We need more questions on cricket. There was only eight. What kind of rubbish is that? Let me give you a tenner. And plenty more where that came from if you consider a section on the Ashes.'

'They could at least try to hide the cheating.' Mitch planted a kiss on Heather's forehead and finished making Ginny's drinks. By the time he had passed over the change, Nathan had joined them.

He was in his late twenties with short dark hair and a long serious face. His skin was pale, and Ginny suspected he didn't get outside much.

'Sorry, I thought they would enjoy the questions, but I was clearly wrong.'

'Nonsense, it's good for them to expand their thinking,' Heather assured him.

'My friend JM says that it helps develop neural pathways,' Ginny added, and Nathan's worry lines smoothed out.

'That was my hope. Plus, there are so many quizzes in the papers and online, I thought it would be fun to do my own.'

'It was brilliant,' Ginny reassured him. 'You must have spent a lot of time on it.'

His pale cheeks flushed with colour as he busied himself polishing the bar. 'It was nice to use my brain. I finished my PhD six months ago and I didn't realise how much I missed academia. Not that I want to go back there,' he quickly added, as if worried it might offend his new bosses.

Mitch laughed. 'Relax. We know the staff are here for a good time not a long time. Just work hard while you're with us. Speaking of working hard, I'd better do the wages if you lot want to get paid tomorrow. Plus, I need to post some photos of tonight on social media. Creating content is unrelenting.'

'It's also what keeps the pub so busy, so it's a necessary evil,' Heather reminded him before glancing at the large clock on the wall. 'Don't take too long. It's your turn to call last orders.'

Mitch eyed the brass hand bell that sat to the right of the register, then he grinned at Ginny. 'The novelty hasn't got old.'

'It's the same at the library. We take it in turns to remind people we will be closing in fifteen minutes. Though we play bird noises instead of using a bell, and people are getting last-minute books rather than drinks.'

'I thought I recognised you from somewhere,' Nathan said. 'It's an excellent library. Especially the local history section.'

'You have our parish council chairperson to thank for that,' Ginny admitted, thinking of her friend Harold Rowe, who had been an archivist by trade and had volunteered at the small library for many years, carefully building their collection.

'Can't say I've ever seen it,' Mitch said before disappearing into the office. Nearby one of the bar staff discarded a half-pulled pint of bitter and moved to a different tap.

Heather frowned. 'Don't tell me the keg needs changing.'

'At least it means we've been selling lots,' they called out as they pulled a fresh pint. 'Want me to swap it over?'

'That's okay, I'll get Mitch to do it in the morning.'

'It's no bother, I can do it,' Nathan cut in. 'I've got to go down there anyway, to put my quiz notes away.'

Heather frowned. 'Are you sure? We have a second keg, so it isn't urgent, and it's been a long night. Besides—'

'Quizmaster, did you realise it's illegal to not include a Taylor

Swift question?' A woman elbowed her way to the front of the queue and glared at Nathan. She had a black T-shirt with the words *Team Tay-Tay* emblazoned in pink sparkles.

'Not just a question... but a whole category,' a second woman, wearing a matching T-shirt, added.

Nathan swallowed, his Adam's apple bobbing in his throat as he gave Heather a pleading look. It was clear that going to the cellar and changing a beer keg was preferable to discussing the quiz with angry Taylor Swift fans.

'Sorry, he has to slip away. But maybe I can help?' Heather smiled at the women as Nathan gratefully disappeared to the other end of the bar and down the cellar stairs.

Ginny bit back a smile and picked up the tray of drinks. The pub was still full and hopefully if people were going to gripe about the questions, at least they would be buying drinks.

Being careful, she made her way back to the table. 'Poor Nathan. So many people are trying to bribe him to include their favourite categories.'

'You should have heard what they've been saying to Wallace's team.' Hen nodded to a nearby table where the DI was talking to Imogen Smith, the police pathologist, as well as DC Anita Singh and PC Liam Bent. 'I think everyone's forgotten that they're all officers of the law.'

'Let's hope Wallace is equally forgetful come tomorrow morning,' JM retorted as she held up a drink and made a toast. 'Here's to good friends.'

The next half hour was spent discussing the quiz, the upcoming Halloween display in the library and their new plans to start power walking. Personally, Ginny would have preferred to just do regular walking, but JM was insistent that they look after their bone health and their core strength as well as their cardio.

At least she would be doing it with her friends and JM had promised there was no need to wear Lycra if they didn't want to.

They did *not*.

Well, at least Ginny did not.

The crowd had begun to thin out when they were interrupted by the loud peal of a brass bell.

Ginny, who was often in bed by nine, was secretly impressed with her ability to function, even if her eyelids were drooping. She stifled a yawn and reached for her handbag as Mitch gave the bell another loud clang, clang, clang.

'Last orders, folks,' he called out in a strong voice before peering around the expansive wood counter where patrons were starting to line up to get their final drinks of the evening. 'That is if I can find my barman.'

'He went to change the bitter.' Heather joined her husband and frowned. 'But that was over half an hour ago. What could be taking him so long?'

'He's too scared to face us,' a man called out, holding up his empty pint glass. 'Since when do decent pub quizzes have questions about Mesopotamia? It's a mockery. A sham. A farce.'

'That's enough,' Mitch warned and snatched the glass, while Heather walked towards the cellar in search of the missing barman.

'Easy for you to say since you didn't spend a week reading Wikipedia pages on the kings and queens of England. I had all Henry's wives locked in,' the man retorted, but his rant was cut off by a piercing scream.

The whole pub fell silent as Heather reappeared from the cellar, her face drained of colour.

Mitch was immediately by her side. 'It's okay, love. I'm here. What's going on?'

His wife let out a long sob while frantically searching the crowd of faces before pointing her finger in the direction of Wallace's table. 'You need to see this. I-I think Nathan's dead.'

TWO

Wednesday, October 14

The Lost Goat was a quaint whitewashed pub, built sometime in the 1800s, but on Wednesday morning the charming façade was hidden under a sea of flowers, cards and teddy bears. A sharp autumn breeze blew up from the nearby canal and tugged at Ginny's coat.

She shivered and clutched the dahlias and foliage she'd gathered from her garden the previous evening. Nathan might only have lived in Little Shaw for a month, but it was clear by the outpouring of gestures that he had made an impression.

Or was it because so many of the villagers felt the pain of a young light dimmed too soon.

Her throat tightened as she finally found a space to lay the bouquet and card down. It had been almost two years since Eric's death and while it no longer felt like an open wound, the pain was still there in the silence and shadows of her daily life.

Except she wasn't here to mourn Eric.

Today was for the young barman who had spent the last hour of his life being heckled by strangers because of a pub quiz.

Perhaps if that hadn't happened, he wouldn't have felt compelled to escape into the cellar and fallen over a beer keg in the process?

The police had officially put out a statement late yesterday afternoon calling it death by misadventure, and Ginny suspected that was why there were so many flowers and other offerings. As if leaving a tribute might help make sense of something that otherwise seemed too unbelievable.

On instinct, she peered up to the second floor of the pub. It had originally been for the live-in bar staff, but Mitch and Heather also lived there in a separate wing. She hoped they weren't blaming themselves for the accident.

'Are you looking for them?' a voice asked from next to her, and Ginny turned to see Esme Wicks, one of the regular library patrons, shuffling towards her, a large, knitted dinosaur poking out from a tartan shopping trolley. Her steel-grey hair that had once been ruler straight was now a riot of tight curls thanks to a home perm, and her cheeks were bright from the autumn breeze.

'Not really. I just hope they're doing okay. It must be very upsetting for them.'

'Not to mention costing a fortune. I had my own business once. It's tough when the doors are closed. Every day without an income is like a ticking clock.'

'Won't they be opening up today?' Ginny asked with a frown. 'Now the investigation is over, it might be a nice way for people to unite together and share their grief.'

'They're short-staffed—or should I say *no*-staffed—so I doubt they can.'

'What do you mean? What's happened to their staff?' Ginny said before flinching as she remembered Nathan. 'Is it because they're too distraught to keep working there?'

'Distraught? More like terrified.' Esme placed the large dinosaur down next to a bunch of marigolds then seemed to notice Ginny's blank expression. 'They're worried they'll be next on the Quiz Killer's list.'

Ginny's mouth dropped open.

How had a tragic accident suddenly turned into the mass exodus of terrified bar staff trying to escape the murderous (and non-existent) Quiz Killer?

Except she already knew the answer. It was because Little Shaw had become known as the small village with a big murder rate. And it was all her fault.

Well... not the murder part. But, since moving to Little Shaw, Ginny had become tangled up in three murder investigations, which hadn't gone unnoticed by the press. Or the locals, who now thought she was some kind of detective.

Which was nonsense, of course.

She just had too much tenacity and the bad luck of being in the wrong place at the right time. Wallace constantly warned her not to get involved in police business, and now she finally understood why. It wasn't because she was hampering the investigations—though at times she had done just that—it was because she'd normalised it for the villagers to look at everything and see danger and crime.

Oh dear.

'Esme, you don't really believe that, do you?'

'It's not what *I* believe, it's what the staff believe.' Esme flicked away a brittle curl that had fallen across her face. 'You have to admit it's fishy when so many people had a motive to knock him off. I take it that's why you're here, to see what clues you can discover.'

Ginny quickly shook her head and fought back her alarm. 'I promise I'm not. I'm only paying my respects.'

'Of course you are.' Esme winked before making a gesture with her finger and touching her mouth. 'Don't worry, my lips are sealed. If Wallace questions me, I'll deny ever seeing you here.'

'Please don't lie to the police. Not that they have any reason to question you. I swear I'm not looking for clues. It was an accident, remember? Death by misadventure.'

'Good one, Ginny.' Esme gave her another wink and pointed to a large wreath of roses. 'Next you're going to tell me that you haven't noticed… *that.*'

'Noticed what?' Ginny peered at the card attached to the bouquet. *RIP from everyone at Daryl's Mechanics and Tyres.* It didn't give her any clarity, apart from reminding her to get her oil checked next time she got an MOT for her car.

Esme let out a hearty laugh. 'Now I know you're messing with me. Daryl's quiz team was called Spanner in the Works.'

'I'm not sure I follow. What has a quiz team got to do with anything?'

'Ho! What *don't* they have to do with anything?' Esme countered and waggled a finger. 'I happen to know they spent one hundred pounds on that ostentatious display, yet they are such tightwads that they refused to give me a calendar last Christmas. It seems to me like they're overcompensating to throw off any suspicions. Pouring money on a problem and hoping it goes away. It has Quiz Killer written all over it.'

Ginny was pretty sure the mechanic hadn't given Esme a calendar because she didn't have a car and therefore wasn't a customer. As for why they'd spent so much money on a wreath, all she could figure was that business was good… or one of them was related to a florist.

However, she knew from experience that convincing Esme nothing untoward was going on would be difficult, not to mention time-consuming, and Ginny was due at the library in ten minutes.

She didn't like being late at the best of times, and the last two days had been particularly busy, which meant she still had a list of tasks to get through.

She was saved from answering as Esme's twin sister, Elsie, arrived clutching a wreath of plastic bread bags knotted together. She was sporting a matching spiral perm and the two women started comparing notes about the many tributes, leaving Ginny free to say her goodbyes and hurry across the stone bridge towards the library.

It didn't take long to unlock the building and let in her two regular volunteers, Cleo and Andrea. Knowing she wouldn't get much work out of them before they had a cup of tea, Ginny left them gossiping in the staffroom and went to the counter as Slim walked in, puffing to catch his breath.

He was fifty-five with skinny legs and a round belly, but the long greasy hair he once sported had been cut short and was now regularly washed. The other thing he'd changed was that he no longer broke into people's houses and stole from them. Instead, he was turning his life around, and part of that was volunteering at the library several times a week.

Ginny had even managed to convince the parish council to give Slim some paid hours while Connor, her lovely young library assistant, was on holiday in Spain with his grandmother. And she was pleased she had. They had been overrun since Monday, and she suspected that today wouldn't be any different.

'Sorry I'm late, Charlie wanted me to take him to the pub so he could pay his respects to that poor kid. We heard about the verdict. I said I didn't have time to be pushing his wheelchair all over the village now I'm on the payroll. But he was getting antsy so I figured I'd give him one last whirl.'

Ginny nodded, not sure what part of that sentence to reply to. She mentally flipped a coin as Slim dropped his backpack under the desk and fired up the computers. She decided to start at the beginning.

'Did Charlie know Nathan?'

'No better than the next man, but he felt bad about Sunday. You see, he was going to make an official complaint about the misrepresentation of the criminal profession in pub quiz questions. With particular reference to question number fifty-one, involving *It Takes a Thief*. The movie had nothing to do with the business and everything to do with Hollywood trying to minimise the huge amount of planning and skill that is involved. It's a very damaging stereotype.'

'Oh.' Ginny blinked. She had seen Slim and his three team-mates on Sunday but hadn't realised they had all been in a similar line of work. Though she supposed she should have guessed after their name, The Artful Dodgers, was read out. 'Er, is that how you and Charlie met?'

'You bet it is. He was a safe-cracker. Best in the business and smartest guy I've ever met. He was the one who came up with our name—big Dickens fan. Anyway, he's taking the news of Nathan's death badly. He's worried that Nathan somehow felt the malevolent presence of a looming complaint.'

'At least he was in the pub when it happened.' Cleo suddenly descended on them. She was a short woman, in her early sixties, and while her views and manner could be polarising, she was a dedicated volunteer who turned up daily. 'I still can't believe we had to leave early.'

'It's that dratted bus service,' Andrea added. She was several years younger than Cleo and a good foot taller, but in all other aspects she was an echo. 'Next time we'll just have to pay for an Uber. It's too bad that we missed out.'

'You didn't miss anything. Once it happened, Wallace and his team had the pub emptied out quicker than you could say: "the parking warden's down the bottom end of Birch Road." I didn't even finish my drink,' Slim said.

'I still would have liked to be there,' Cleo pronounced. 'At least I would have had an alibi instead of worrying about Wallace turning up on my doorstep and dragging me down to the station.'

'To the station,' Andrea agreed with a shudder.

Ginny sighed. They'd been having a similar conversation for the last two days, no matter how many times she reminded the pair that just because their team had boycotted the second round of the quiz didn't mean the police thought they were involved in Nathan's accident.

'We should never have called ourselves Barrel of Laughs,' Cleo said. 'It's like walking around the village with a large guilty sign above our heads. I can feel people watching me wherever I go.'

'Always watching,' Andrea seconded.

'I must admit it doesn't look good,' Slim said in a cheerful voice as he made his way to the front door to open for the day. Cleo and Andrea trailed after him discussing their possible motives for following Nathan down the stairs and pushing him over, while at the same time admitting that they'd never spoken directly to him.

The rest of the morning didn't get much better when Esme and Elsie arrived and continued to dissect why Cleo and Andrea were seconds away from being arrested. At least Slim was more focused, as he worked at the issues counter, dealing with a steady stream of borrowers, while Ginny made her way through her long to-do list.

A thud of something falling onto the floor made her hurry into the returns room, just behind the counter. She froze at the sight of an overflowing trolley beneath the returns chute. On the floor were several upended books, lying flattened out like butterflies in a Victorian botanical collection.

Just then, another book came flying through the chute, sending a stack of CDs tumbling to the ground, the plastic cases splitting apart as the silver discs winked in the light.

Oh dear. When Connor was with her, they always kept on top of the returns, but without him, things were piling up. Slim hadn't been working yesterday and on Monday she only had one elderly volunteer in to help. But since they preferred to sit out the back and repair the damaged items, Ginny hadn't been able to get to the returns trolley since the weekend.

She could ask Cleo and Andrea to do it, but she suspected they would spend more time discussing Sunday's accident than making the huge piles of books go down. Which meant Ginny would have to ignore her other tasks and do it herself.

Besides, she would need to make sure that no one got overdue fines, since some of the returns would have come in over the weekend and might have been due back on Monday.

She retrieved the books from the ground and swapped the full trolley for an empty one, before sorting everything into piles.

There was something soothing about checking the books for damage before running them across the scanner to take them off the system. She knew that some libraries had software that automatically did this when they went through the return slot, but Ginny suspected it would be a long time before that was in the parish's budget.

She kept her attention on the computer screen to make sure each book had gone through properly, as well as checking for fines.

The steady work was rewarding as the numerous piles went down and she was almost at the end of it when she spied an all too familiar book. It was *The History of Little Shaw*. Harold had advised Ginny to read it when she first moved to the area, but she kept getting distracted by her favourite authors.

Perhaps now was the time to finally finish it?

Turning to the shelf that held all the staff reserves, she checked how many books were waiting for her. There was a new Jill Mansell, and *The House in the Cerulean Sea* by TJ Klune, as well as her towering to-be-read pile at home, not to mention her deep-dive into Eric's favourites.

Hmmm. It would have to wait until next time.

Once it was returned off the system, she flicked through the book, checking for any damage. Everything seemed in order and she was about to close it when her gaze snagged on the tip of something wedged between the pages. It wasn't uncommon for them to find bookmarks and library receipts tucked in as placeholders. Once she'd even discovered an old sock.

With a practised motion, she turned to the correct page and stared down at a faded colour photograph.

It was of a tall woman with thick dark hair that had been neatly tamed, wearing a camel-coloured skirt and jacket. She was staring at the camera with a sad, haunting smile. The style of clothing and the age of the photograph made her think it had been taken some time in the nineteen sixties or early seventies.

Ginny flipped the photo over to see if anything was written on the back, which might help her identify the owner. But there was no name, just a series of numbers: *147-3-2, 89-12-7, 23-8-4, 156-15-3.*

It was written in pencil and was faded with age. Was it phone numbers, a reference? Or—

She cut herself off. Now wasn't the time to get sidetracked. It was more important to discover the owner. Thankfully it was a simple process to look up the borrower.

The library's previous manager had thought that returning bookmarks and other items was a waste of time. However, Ginny couldn't bear to throw away keepsakes of any description and it was an easy thing to give the owner a quick call.

Especially when it concerned such an old photograph.

For all she knew this was a treasured possession. Perhaps the last photograph of a loved one?

She pressed her mouse on the issuing history to bring up the name of the last borrower. Then it would be a matter of calling them, and—

Oh no. All thoughts left her as she stared at the name on the screen.

Nathan Richardson.

THREE

Wednesday, October 14

The wind blew autumn leaves across the footpath as Ginny finally opened her gate and stepped into her small front garden. It had been a long day and she was pleased to be home. Despite the name, Middle Cottage was a semi-detached house with a lovely pink door and a growing number of lavender and rose bushes in the small front garden. Today there was also a discontented black cat sitting on the doormat. His amber eyes were filled with judgement, disappointment and perhaps a little bit of scorn.

'I really need to channel your attitude more often,' she told Edgar and fumbled with the keys. The rescue cat turned away, as if he couldn't bear to look at her. However, as soon as the door was opened, he pushed past and darted through to the kitchen, where his food bowl lived.

He'd been underweight and terrified when Ginny had adopted him... or had he adopted her? Sometimes it was hard to tell. But all shyness was long gone and now he didn't question his right to be waited on hand and foot.

Ginny shed her coat and swapped shoes for slippers before following him into the kitchen. She paused to smile at the bookshelf that still contained her late husband's favourite authors. Her gaze lingered on Eric's old copy of *My Man Jeeves*. Lately she'd started reading his books out loud just in case he wanted to listen in. And after working her way through Arthur Ransome, she had decided that next on the list was PJ Wodehouse.

'Which is perfectly valid and not at all weird,' she told Edgar, who often curled up in her lap while she read. 'I think you'll enjoy it.'

By way of answer, Edgar jumped on the new pink and green trainers Ginny had bought for power walking. Sighing, she turned away from the book and extracted the left shoe from Edgar's claws. He glared and swatted away her fingers as she wrestled it from him. At least one of them seemed to like the shoes.

She put the trainers back in the hall, then settled down with a cup of tea. Next to her was the photograph that once belonged to poor Nathan. There had been no time to think about it at work but now she was free to study it properly.

There was something so melancholy about not being able to return it. Had Nathan even realised it was missing? And why was it there? Had he been using it as a bookmark or was it sentimental to him?

What should she do with it? She could hardly call him, nor could she leave it in the little box of returned items since Nathan would never be able to claim it.

She had walked past The Lost Goat on her way home to ask Mitch and Heather if they could return it to Nathan's next of kin. But even though the deluge of tributes had grown, there had been no sign of the owners, or any sense that they were going to reopen the pub.

Esme must have been right about the staff exodus.

It left Ginny with two options. She could pretend she hadn't found the photograph, or she could go next door and ask Wallace about Nathan's relations. Neither prospect appealed, but only one of them would let her get a good night's sleep, so she finished her cup of tea and stood.

No time like the present.

Five minutes later Ginny was standing outside Wallace's door, holding a bottle of damson gin that she had made last year from the fruit he'd given her. It seemed like a long time since they had argued over the lovely old tree in his garden, but she still felt uncertain whenever she had to speak to him on police business.

She pressed the doorbell but there was no answer.

Frowning, she tried to peer through the frosted glass. His electric vehicle was in the driveway, but now he was dating Imogen Smith, she suddenly worried about interrupting them. Was dating even the correct word to use? He'd never explicitly told her they were, but Ginny wasn't blind and she had seen the lovely pathologist's red Mini Cooper coming and going enough times to know they were doing something together.

She was pleased for them both.

However, she didn't like intruding.

She was just toying with the idea of forgetting about the photograph when the door finally opened and her neighbour stepped out. Usually, he dressed in trousers or jeans and a revolving door of plain jumpers in winter and equally plain T-shirts in summer, but now he was in a pair of blue overalls liberally smeared with white paint.

At least it meant she hadn't interrupted anything worse.

'Ginny, what are you doing here?'

'Is this a bad time? I didn't realise you were doing more work on the place.'

When she first met Wallace, he'd been doing up his house and garden, but she'd quickly discovered that while he was an excellent detective, his DIY skills weren't the best and that the person responsible for the lovely wooden floors and the now overflowing vegetable boxes in the back garden was his father, who visited on a regular basis.

'Only if you don't count spilling four litres of magnolia on the carpet.' He sounded tired.

'Oh dear. It's probably good I brought you this then.' She handed over the gin.

He gave it a cautious look. 'What's it for? Don't tell me it's to celebrate the pub quiz win because I won't believe you.'

She reluctantly laughed. 'No, though I was sorry at how so many of the other teams behaved. You, Imogen, Anita and Liam did ever so well. There were some difficult questions.'

'There were,' he agreed, reluctantly taking the bottle. His fingers were covered in paint and there were flecks of it in his dark hair.

'So, why are you doing DIY?' she said cautiously. 'Don't you usually leave it for Ted? He seems to enjoy this kind of work more than you do.'

'Unfortunately, my father enjoys it a little bit too much. He fell off a ladder two weeks ago and because the antisocial fool never speaks to his neighbours, he had to call his own ambulance.' Wallace's face darkened.

'Is he okay?' Ginny said, not able to hide her alarm. Eric had been a GP and she'd managed his surgery for almost thirty years, so she had seen her fair share of accidents and knew the harm they could cause. Not to mention the damage of being so socially isolated. It was how she had once lived, before meeting her dear, dear friends.

'He's fine. No concussion or broken bones, just some bruising, a sprained ankle and a lecture from me about why he needs to sell his house and move closer.'

'I didn't realise that was on the cards.' Ginny couldn't hide her surprise since both men were very independent.

'It wasn't. But our recent trip to New Zealand proved we could live in each other's pockets without too much collateral damage,' Wallace admitted. 'He seems to agree, since he is going to move in with me until he finds his own place to buy. As for why I'm painting, it's because if I don't, he'll do it himself. You might have noticed he's not good at sitting still.'

Ginny, who had to listen to the incessant whir of power tools every time Ted visited, did know this. She also knew that Wallace's work-life balance was already perilous without adding DIY disasters to the equation.

'I don't think your father will do anything silly... and he certainly won't care what colour the walls are painted,' she said in a diplomatic voice.

'You might have a point,' he said with a rare smile. It didn't last long and his mouth pursed into a tight line. 'But you're not here to talk DIY. How can I help?'

Ginny swallowed. It was the downside of living next to a detective. Not much got past him.

'I was hoping you could give me the details of Nathan Richardson's next of kin.'

His face hardened to granite. 'The coroner has ruled it death by misadventure, which means it's a closed case, and if I have to give you one more speech on interfering, then I swear—'

'It's not like that. I promise.' Ginny slipped the photograph out of her jacket pocket and held it out. 'With Connor away, we are behind at the library and I was returning the books that came through our after-hours slot over the weekend. One had been issued to Nathan and I found this in it.'

Wallace's expression didn't change. 'It could have been there for ages. What makes you think it is his?'

'I can't be sure it is,' Ginny admitted. 'However, it is our policy to check the books each time they are returned to make sure there is no damage... or random photographs left in the pages. That doesn't mean things don't slip through, but I am confident it is his. I'd hate if it were an important photograph and wasn't returned to his family.'

Silence built up between them but was broken by the shrill buzz of his phone. He retrieved it from deep in the overalls.

'Excuse me,' he muttered and studied the screen. Ice crept across his harsh features and the temperature coming off him seemed to change.

'I-is everything okay?' Ginny asked.

'No.' He stared at the screen then dragged his gaze away. 'I need to leave. Sorry.'

'Of course,' Ginny immediately assured him. 'But what about the next of kin? I would like to return this to them. Unless you can.'

He gave her a blank stare as if she were speaking a different language. Then nodded. 'I'll text you the details once I'm back in the office.'

'I won't keep you,' Ginny told him and hurried back down the path into her own garden. By the time she reached the front door, Wallace had discarded the overalls and was shrugging on a jacket as he stalked to his car and climbed in. The electric vehicle silently pulled out onto the street and disappeared into the night, making Ginny think that whatever the message had been about, it was serious.

Still, like he'd reminded her, it was none of her business. With that she stepped back into the house where Edgar was waiting for her, half asleep on her new trainers.

FOUR

Thursday, October 15

'Any news about the next of kin?' JM asked the following morning before thrusting some hand weights in Ginny's direction. They were surprisingly heavy, and her arm muscles ached in protest. She wasn't clear how hand weights were involved in power walking but didn't feel up to asking.

'Nothing,' Ginny admitted. She had told her friends about the photograph and her conversation with Wallace, and they were eager for an update. Unfortunately, Ginny had nothing to tell them.

She hadn't seen Wallace since last night or heard from him. None of which was unusual, she often went days without any sign of him.

What *was* strange was that no one else in the village seemed to know anything about Nathan's family. Did they live close by? Were his parents still alive? Did he have siblings? A partner? Friends?

Ginny had even called Cleo last night, but the gossipy volunteer hadn't been able to help. She'd also tried an online search, but even with her developing internet skills, she had come up blank.

'What if no one's told them about his death?' Hen put her knitting bag into her car before receiving her own set of weights. She studied them dubiously, as if they were a piece of damaged fruit that she didn't care to purchase.

'If that's the case, why did Wallace say he had the next-of-kin information?' Tuppence clutched at her hand weights as she bounced from foot to foot. Ginny wasn't sure if it was to stop the autumn breeze from prickling her skin, or because she was eager to get started on their first official power walk around the park. She looked the part, dressed as she was in bright orange leggings and a thick green jacket. JM appeared equally set for business in a smart navy tracksuit.

Ginny didn't feel quite so prepared in grey tracksuit bottoms and a zip-up jacket. Secretly, she would have preferred to be back in her house with a cup of tea, her cat curled up in her lap and Jeeves in her hand. However, she was far too aware that she needed to improve her fitness.

If only exercise wasn't so *exercise-y*.

'Surely they would have come to see where it happened?' Hen frowned.

'We all deal with our grief differently,' JM reminded her then shut the car door and deposited her keys into a small pack around her waist. 'Right. And we are starting... *now*.'

Without another word she took off at a fast pace around the sodden path that skirted Moorefield Park. A moment later Tuppence followed, leaving Ginny and Hen scampering to catch up.

'I have a terrible feeling we're not going to like this,' Hen said.

'I think you're right.' Ginny sighed.

Thanks to the gloomy weather, the park was practically deserted, which was probably a good thing since no one would have to witness how out-of-shape she was.

As she walked, she kept thinking about Nathan's family and wondering how they were taking the news. It was something she and her friends had all been through, but it had never been for someone so young. Was it different? Did the sense of unfairness go even deeper? Were they currently stuck in the dreadful numbness of disbelief?

'Have you asked Heather and Mitch about it?' Hen said, as if reading her mind.

'I stopped by yesterday but there was no answer,' Ginny replied as the distance between their friends increased. How could anyone walk so quickly?

'I heard they have been taking it ever so badly.' Hen panted, her face already flushed beetroot from trying to keep up the pace.

'I'm not surprised.' Ginny's heart pounded against her ribs with the force of a wrecking ball.

Since moving to Little Shaw, she'd had the misfortune to discover two dead bodies and knew how much it could haunt a person. It was another reason she wanted to check on the lovely couple, just to make sure they were doing okay.

The fact they hadn't opened the pub—let alone the front door —suggested that they weren't.

'Oh dear.' Hen began to wheeze as ahead of them JM and Tuppence lifted their arms up and down, weights in hand, as if they were trying to take flight. 'Are we meant to copy them?'

'I-I'm not sure that's possible.' Ginny tried and failed to raise her arms even a little bit. 'And why are they jumping?'

Hen squinted at their energetic friends, who were now leaping forward on two feet, before swapping into an elegant one-footed position. 'It's like they're playing hopscotch. To think I liked that game once.'

So had Ginny, however she was now too out of breath to reply. Instead, she blinked away the sweat that was beading its way down her brow and tried to ignore the burning sensation in her throat. JM had told them that they had to do three circuits of the park, but at this rate, Ginny wasn't sure she could do one.

Next to her, Hen seemed to have reached the same conclusion as they half walked, half staggered forward, while JM and

Tuppence continued with the kind of training session that would put the SAS to shame.

They finally came to a halt at the colourful playground.

'I told you that would be fun,' JM said, cheeks glowing with good health. 'Now we can do a few burpees and perhaps a plank or two, before continuing.'

'I might just need to sit down for a minute,' Hen admitted, her breath coming out in a steamy column as she collapsed onto a bench.

'I'll keep you company.' Ginny managed to get her rubbery legs to move in the direction of the wooden seat that was slick with morning dew. At this point she didn't care.

'Relax, we're just teasing.' Tuppence grinned, still bouncing on the spot. 'You both did very well and soon you won't even notice the weights.'

'I can't notice them now because my arms are so numb. I thought all that knitting would have given me excellent upper body strength.' Hen dropped the weights that she had still been clutching down to the ground. 'But apparently not.'

'It's all about mixing things up,' JM explained and settled down on a nearby swing, her rich voice carrying over to them. 'So, about Nathan's photograph... what's the next step?'

'I thought I would try Heather and Mitch again after work and see if I can get an address,' Ginny said. 'He must have put it down in his application form. Plus, I could see from the library records that he was living at The Lost Goat, so they must have discussed it with the police.'

'Poor things. I haven't seen them since it happened,' Hen said.

'I'm not sure anyone has,' Tuppence added. 'I hope they're not regretting buying the pub.'

Ginny thought of what Esme had told her, about how costly it was for a business to be closed, even for a day. She had no idea about their financial situation, but she doubted they'd planned for something like this to happen.

'I'm sure they're not. After all, they have both worked there for several years and know what business can be like,' JM said. 'As for their staff leaving, well, good riddance to bad rubbish. There are plenty of other people in this village looking for work. I'm sure they will find the help they need.'

'I suppose you're right,' Hen agreed before wrinkling her nose. 'In the meantime, I would love to know who the woman is in the photograph.'

'And what about the numbers on the back,' Tuppence added. 'Do we have any idea what it means?'

'No. I tried researching it, but nothing came up,' Ginny admitted. It was true that her curiosity had led her to ponder what 147-3-2, 89-12-7, 23-8-4, 156-15-3 meant, but she was stumped. The closest she could come to, was that it might be a date, or an archive reference. She had also tried to match the person in the photograph by using the internet, with no success.

Not that it really mattered since it was hardly her mystery to solve. She was just checking out of habit. Which wasn't exactly the best use of her time, considering the library was extra busy, thanks to Connor's absence.

And that reminded her, she was due to start in an hour and still needed a shower.

She got to her feet and hugged her friends. 'Sorry to love you and leave you, but Slim and I have a full day. We have a class visit and several groups, all before lunchtime.'

'You poor thing. I intend to collapse on the sofa.' Hen stiffly stood.

'Nonsense. That's the worst thing you can do. Your muscles will seize up.' JM made a tutting noise and effortlessly got up from the swing. 'A nice slow lap is what you need. And Ginny, keep us posted on how you get on. If you don't get any answers, I can talk with Wallace.'

'Let's wait and see what I can find out,' Ginny carefully suggested. JM's way of talking was more like a command, and she doubted Wallace would appreciate it.

JM frowned. 'As long as it doesn't take too long. It's important that we return the photograph to Nathan's family. As a memory.'

They were all silent as the soft rustle of leaves fell around them.

JM didn't always show much emotion, but it was clear by the tightness of her jaw that she was thinking of her late wife, Rebecca. Hen's hand snaked up to clasp the locket around her neck, where Ginny knew she kept a photograph of her husband, Adam. Tuppence stopped her bouncing and reached for her wedding ring to Taron, which she still wore. And Ginny thought of Eric's book collection that let her feel like he was still with her every evening.

Being able to remember those who had passed was beyond value.

The four women exchanged a look. They would do whatever it took to ensure the photograph was returned.

FIVE

Thursday, October 15

By the time Ginny stepped out of the library into the dull weather, she felt exhausted. The combination of thirty school children taking part in a library scavenger hunt, combined with the early morning power walk, meant her limbs ached and her brain felt scrambled. The obvious cure was going home for a cup of tea and some peace and quiet, but she forced herself to park her little car outside the pub.

The floral tributes had grown since her last visit, but the sign announcing they were open for business was nowhere in sight. She threaded her way past the offerings and caught a slither of light escaping from under the threshold. Gingerly, she knocked on the sturdy pub door. There was no answer, but inside she could hear the murmur of voices.

As a rule, she didn't like to intrude, but as well as returning the photograph, she hoped she might be able to help Mitch and Heather navigate their grief and guilt. A second knock was rewarded with the thud of footsteps. The curtain in the window twitched, and several seconds later the door cracked open.

'Ginny?' Heather's face appeared in the gap. Her purple hair was tied up and her face was drawn. 'W-we're not opening today.' The last words were accompanied by a sob.

'You poor things,' she said instinctively. 'I'm so sorry to bother you. I shouldn't have come.'

'You might as well let her in,' Mitch's voice called from somewhere deep in the pub. Heather wiped away her tears and inched the door open wide enough for Ginny to step in, before closing it and twisting the lock.

'Are you sure? I don't mean to—' Ginny broke off and took in the upturned chairs, broken glass covering the floor and the sickly stench of spirits and beer. Mitch was standing at the bar, a broom in his hand, a defeated expression in his eyes. Heather crossed back to him and slipped an arm around his waist, as if worried he might fall over.

Neither of them looked like they had slept in a long time.

'Let's sit down.' Heather nodded to one of the few tables that was still upright. Not sure what else to do, Ginny joined them, glass crunching under her shoes as she went.

Everywhere was destruction.

'What on earth has happened? Did someone break in?' Ginny sat down.

'No. That's the worst part of it. There's been so much going on that I forgot to lock the door when we went out this morning,' Heather said, little lines of worry regathering around her brow.

'When we came back, this is what we found,' Mitch added, still clutching the broom.

Ginny's heart broke for them. 'Why would someone do this? Don't tell me it was because of what happened to Nathan? That wasn't your fault.'

'I should have told him to leave the keg until the next day.' Heather shuddered.

'You did. I was there, remember? And I know how seriously you both take your health and safety. Surely no one can blame you?'

'I wouldn't argue if they did.' Mitch's voice was brittle, and

Ginny's heart broke for them both. Despite knowing that logically it made no sense, she suspected she would feel the same way if the positions were reversed. She also realised no good could come from speculation.

'What did the police say?'

The married couple exchanged a troubled glance, but it was Mitch who spoke. 'We haven't called them.'

'Whyever not? I do think they should know, and what about your insurance company? Surely you can't put in a claim without a police report.'

'Well.' Heather gave a sharp laugh. 'Aren't we lucky we don't have insurance then?'

'It was on the list to do, but taking this place over has cost us a fortune and we were waiting until we could afford it.' Mitch wiped his brow. 'I suppose we should be grateful nothing has been taken.'

'No, we've just been left with a bloody big mess, which means we will need to stay shut for longer,' Heather said in a faltering voice.

'Is it true that your staff have left?' Ginny cautiously asked.

Mitch nodded. 'I can't blame them. We only had four... plus Nathan... and they were all new hires. When we were on our bar manager course, we were warned that it's difficult to hold onto staff.'

'But we never expected it to happen to us. I tried so hard to be a good manager,' Heather added.

'It's exceptional circumstances,' Ginny told them both gently. 'If you haven't hired anyone else, how were you planning to open tonight?'

'We figured someone would call about the position. I have it in the window. Maybe it was naïve to expect someone to magically turn up,' Mitch admitted.

'I suppose it doesn't matter now we don't have a bar for them to work in.'

'I know it's a blow, but there must be something that can be done.' Ginny looked around. It still upset her that someone had done this. It was like kicking them while they were down. And the idea that whoever was behind it would just get away with it, caused her blood pressure to spike. 'Even without insurance, I still think you need to call the police. What if something *is* missing?'

'We've checked the CCTV footage, and it doesn't look like anything was taken. They just wanted to make a mess.'

At the mention of footage, Ginny's eyes widened. 'You know who did it?'

'No. The person was wearing a mask and black clothing. We couldn't even tell if it was a man or a woman. All they did was throw things around, as if they were in a rage. It was time-stamped. Can you believe all this happened in under fifteen minutes?' Mitch held out his hands to take in the mess.

'Plus, if we call in the police, they might make us stay shut for even longer. At least this way we can start cleaning up now. And by the time we've finished, we might have found more staff,' Heather added.

Ginny looked around, before catching sight of the dark arch that led down to the cellar. She swallowed. 'I know it must have been a dreadful week for you, considering what happened to Nathan, but maybe it's best if you take a few days to recover? It could be a blessing in disguise.'

'More like a death toll.' Mitch let out a strained sigh. 'The only reason we went out was because we had a meeting with the bank manager. We took a large loan to get this place and we're already falling behind. With all the negative publicity and having to stay shut... things are very tight.'

'This feels like the final nail in the coffin.' Heather shuddered. 'We're stuck in this terrible place, where we can't afford to be shut, but we can't afford to open.'

Unease prickled Ginny's skin.

They had only been running it for a month, and she supposed that any savings they had would have been sunk into the purchase price. Part of her longed to offer comfort but she couldn't think of anything to say that they would believe. Then she blinked and looked around. Her fingers twitched to sweep up the broken glass and restore order to the chaos.

She might not be able to find the words to make them feel better, but she certainly knew her way around a vacuum cleaner and a mop. What's more, she enjoyed cleaning.

And so did her friends.

'Would you think it rude if I offered a suggestion?' she asked cautiously, not wanting to offend them.

'Is it about the police again?' Mitch's brow pushed together.

'No. I can't make you call them if you don't want to. But I could ask JM, Tuppence and Hen to come and help us clean.'

'We couldn't let you do that. What's the point when the universe is trying to stop us from making a go of things?' Heather said, her arms dropping forward, like a puppet with cut strings.

'Let's deal with one crisis at a time.' Ginny reached for her phone. 'Will you let me call them?'

'They must have better things to do than help us,' Mitch protested.

'You should know there is *nothing* they wouldn't do for their friends.'

Heather and Mitch were silent, but their eyes glistened with tears, which Ginny took as assent.

She rang her friends and as expected they were horrified to hear what had happened and all promised to be there within ten minutes. It seemed to create a shift in the two owners and Ginny got to her feet and started righting the fallen tables and stacking the chairs on top of them, so that it would be easier to mop.

It wasn't long before there was a brisk knock at the door, followed by JM's booming voice. 'It's us.'

'What if they don't know who *us* is?' Tuppence demanded from the other side of the door. 'We should have organised a password because I doubt they will open up for just anyone.'

'Do I look like *just anyone?*'

'Maybe I should text Ginny?' came Hen's cautious voice,

which roused Heather, who put down the rubbish bag she'd been holding and hurried over.

As she went, Mitch suddenly turned to Ginny. 'I just realised you never told us why you came here? I gather it wasn't to help us clean up.'

Ginny blinked. She'd been so caught up in the terrible story that she'd forgotten all about the photograph. She slid it out of her sensible black handbag.

'Before Nathan died, he returned some library books through the after-hours slot. I found this in one of them. It looks like it might be important, so I wanted to return it to his relatives. I was hoping to get their address.'

Mitch ran a hand through his unruly hair and flushed. 'We never got a next-of-kin, which was an oversight. I can see that now. But at the time I only thought about references.'

'Oh.' She couldn't quite hide her dismay. 'What happened to his belongings then?'

'We gave them to the police liaison officer who was going to find his family and make sure they were returned. I have no idea if they managed to track anyone down.'

'I see.' Ginny swallowed. Which meant she was right back where she started. And the idea that no one had come to the village to see Nathan's final resting place was saddening.

'Why don't you ask Wallace for it?'

'I did,' she said. 'He seemed... distracted.'

'Tell me about it. That's the other reason I didn't want to report this mess to him. He came in yesterday afternoon and almost bit my head off.'

'What for?' she said, surprised. Despite his abrupt manners, she knew Wallace never acted cruelly to victims. Or people who had been involved in something as traumatic as losing a staff member.

Had it been about Nathan?

Yet why be angry about that, when Wallace was the one who said the case was closed?

Mitch shrugged. 'Can you believe it was because we put his photograph up on social media? His team has won the quiz for three weeks in a row and I thought it would be great publicity, challenge people to defeat the reigning champions. But he thought otherwise and wanted us to take it down.'

'His photograph?' She wrinkled her nose. It was easy enough to imagine the grumpy detective might not like having it taken, but she couldn't understand why he would ask to have it removed. Then again, Mitch shouldn't have posted it without Wallace's permission. 'Did you get him to sign a disclaimer form?'

'No. I didn't even know it was a thing,' Mitch admitted.

'It is. I can give you a copy of what we use in the library. It is a lot safer that way. I gather you *did* take the photograph down.'

Mitch glumly nodded. 'I thought it was better not to rock the boat. Though without the images, it's hard to promote the quiz, which has been our busiest night of the week.'

It explained his reluctance to report the break-in to Wallace. As for the pub quiz, she supposed that was irrelevant until the place was tidied up.

Her thoughts were given another direction as Heather returned, closely followed by JM, Tuppence and Hen, who were all dressed in their cleaning clothes and pulling a small trolley full of brushes, mops and a steam cleaner.

They might not be able to do anything for Nathan, but at least they could help Mitch and Heather get their lives back on track.

SIX

Thursday, October 15

It was almost nine in the evening when Ginny finally collapsed onto one of the comfortable chairs that were clustered around a low coffee table in the far corner of the bar, grateful that they weren't forced to sit on the tall stools, since she doubted her aching muscles would have managed it. Still, it was all worth it. She smiled and peered around. The floors now gleamed, and the brass fixtures had all been polished until they shone. The warm simmering scent of lemon peel filled the space, pushing back the stale alcohol that had first greeted Ginny.

Tuppence had even managed to repair the broken chairs by following a YouTube tutorial. More importantly, with the return to order, Mitch and Heather's haunted expressions had faded.

'Oh, my. The pub has never looked so beautiful.' Heather returned from behind the bar and put down a tray of glasses and a wine bottle.

'We can't thank you enough.' Mitch poured the wine, before handing around the glasses.

'Nonsense,' JM told him in a stern voice. 'It's called reciprocity. Plus, it's an excellent way to get in more steps and some cardio.'

'And so much more fun than my regular post-supper workout.' Tuppence held up a glass.

'Post-supper workout?' Hen's eyes widened in horror as she held up her own glass. 'I didn't know that was a thing. Does knitting count?'

'Or crosswords?' Ginny asked. She wasn't sure she was ready to commit to one workout yet, let alone more. And she suspected Hen had similar thoughts.

'You two are so funny.' Tuppence gave them both a broad smile then turned to Heather and Mitch. 'Here's to you both.'

'I'll second that,' JM announced then looked around. 'Though I still can't believe someone caused all this damage without bothering to steal anything.'

It had been troubling Ginny as well.

She took a sip of her drink, letting the tartness flood through her. While they'd been cleaning, she half expected Heather and Mitch to discover something was missing, or at the very least, a clue as to who was responsible. But nothing seemed to be out of place, except for the obvious mess.

And while she wished the police had been called, now they had tidied up the crime scene, she realised that would only go against them, so decided not to push it.

'Will you be able to open tomorrow?' Hen asked.

'Friday is usually busy so I doubt we could handle it on our own. I was hoping someone would apply to our advertisement, but we've had nothing. Well... nothing from people who are qualified.' Heather put down her glass and despair filled her eyes again.

It was clear that the relief at having the bar restored to its usual state had only been a temporary respite from their financial troubles.

'Qualified?' Hen raised an eyebrow. 'I didn't realise you needed training.'

'Of course you do. Who wants a flat pint? Or the wrong mixer in their gin?' JM demanded in her no-nonsense way. 'I worked in a pub in the eighties and I doubt anything has changed.'

'Except the cash registers,' Tuppence retorted. 'I worked in one as well when I was a student and back then you had to remember the prices and do all the sums in your head. These days it does it all for you.'

Hen laughed. 'And there are more things on the menu than coronation chicken and ploughman's lunch. I did a stint in a pub kitchen one summer and it was so much fun. What about you, Ginny?'

'I'm afraid I'm the odd one out.'

'Too bad,' Tuppence said before sitting up, bolt straight. 'Wait a minute... why don't we help you?'

'What?' Mitch blinked.

'That's an excellent idea.' JM stood up and peered around the numerous tables as if trying to decide how many people would fit in there. 'You said you had four staff members, and there are four of us. Surely that's enough to let you open tomorrow.'

'But you couldn't,' Heather protested.

'Why not?' JM challenged and crossed to the bar in easy strides. Once there she plucked up a pint glass and held it at a forty-five-degree angle and began to pour beer in it. As she went, she slowly straightened the glass until it was full. Then she flicked back the tap and slid the drink onto the bar. 'I haven't lost my touch.'

'Surely you have better things to do than work for us. And the pay isn't wonderful.' Mitch frowned.

'Who said anything about pay?' Tuppence joined JM behind the bar and put a white cloth over her shoulder, eyes gleaming with excitement. 'It will just be for a few days until you're up and running again.'

'It would be an ever so lovely adventure.' Hen clapped her hands.

Mitch and Heather exchanged a baffled look, as if not sure what to make of it.

'None of us would mind. I might not be able to pull a beer, but

I would be happy to help in the kitchen or clear the tables,' Ginny added her own entreaties.

'Oh, do say yes,' Hen urged. 'What better way to honour Nathan than by running another quiz on Sunday? He was so proud of them.'

'Not to mention all the people who want to beat Wallace and his May the Force be With You team,' Tuppence said.

Heather's brows pressed together. 'I forgot about that. Even if we do open the pub, we can't do the quiz without Nathan. He put the questions together and I don't want to get something off the internet. It would be like besmirching his memory.'

'We wouldn't have to. Nathan was already working on the questions for the next three weeks. I am sure we would have enough to do the Sunday session. I could play quizmaster,' Mitch said.

'Are you sure about that, love? I haven't seen any extra questions.'

'That's because you haven't been down to the cellar since it happened.' Mitch squeezed her hand. 'But that's where they are. I told Nathan he could store his research in that old filing cabinet down there.'

'I remember him mentioning that last week,' Ginny admitted.

Heather was silent, as if considering the pros and cons before giving them a grateful smile. 'If you're sure about helping us, it has to be worth a go. That is if we can find the questions.'

'And answers,' Hen chimed in. 'Don't forget how hard the quiz was.'

Mitch got to his feet. 'I'll look now.'

'Be careful.' Heather's face drained of colour, clearly remembering what had happened to Nathan when he'd been down there.

'He won't take any risks.' Hen stretched out and squeezed Heather's hand. 'In the meantime, why don't you tell us about what needs to be done to open up tomorrow?'

The question had a calming effect, and Heather let out her breath. 'If you really mean it about helping, that would be lovely. I will need to go to the wholesalers to stock up the kitchen and then get all the prep done. But we don't usually open up until eleven, if you would like to come in then.'

'Then that is when you will see us,' JM said firmly. Ginny gave them all a grateful smile.

She'd known her friends would want to help Mitch and Heather however they could. Then she mentally adjusted the calendar in her mind. She had arranged for Slim to work in the library tomorrow, so she could have a day off, and while she had planned to do some preserving and housework, she would much rather help the lovely couple.

Her mental planning was cut off by the appearance of Mitch, holding a slim attaché case.

'Nathan kept his notes and research in here.' He sat down and flipped the case open and lifted out a bundle of papers. As he did, a large yellow envelope fluttered out and fell onto the newly polished table.

'I wonder if this is the quiz?' Heather picked it up and slid her hand in. But instead of bringing out a page of questions, she was holding a photograph. 'Okay, so that proves me wrong. What is it? Do you think he was going to include a picture round?'

Ginny leaned forward to study the photograph.

The colour had faded, but it was of a tall young woman with dark hair and large brown eyes. She was standing next to a very old Morris Minor and was laughing at something. There was a brightness to the woman's smile that seemed to reach out through the two-dimensional image.

And she bore a striking resemblance to the woman in Nathan's other photograph.

Was it possible?

Ginny stared at it for several seconds before recalling that she had Nathan's photograph with her. She withdrew it from her handbag and put it on the table so they were sitting side by side. Oh yes, it was definitely the same woman, though in Heather's photograph, the smile was brighter and the sadness that had been clouding her eyes was gone.

It was as if the camera had caught the before and after shot.

There was something melancholy about the two images and everyone was silent as they studied them.

It was JM who spoke first. 'This is proof that the photograph was important to poor Nathan.'

'What are you talking about?' Heather asked.

'I forgot you weren't here,' Mitch said. 'The reason Ginny came to the pub was to ask for Nathan's forwarding address because he returned some library books, not realising that he'd left a photograph in one.'

'That's so sad.' Heather's hand flew to her mouth. 'I wonder if this is his grandmother?'

'Did he mention having one?' Ginny asked.

'Not that I recall, but we've been so busy that I didn't get to know him as well as I should have.' Heather shook her head.

'You can't blame yourself.' JM picked up the photograph to examine it further. Then she turned it over and held it close to her face. 'There's something written on this but it's very faint. Quick, someone give me some light.'

'Here you go.' Tuppence fumbled with the torch app on her phone until a bright light shone out of it. She held it closer to the photograph. 'What does it say?'

'Hold it a bit more to the left. Yes, that's better. Now, let's see...' JM squinted some more. 'It's a name. Sylvie Yates. Never heard of her.'

'Sylvie? Are you sure?' Tuppence put down her phone to examine the photographs again. 'It doesn't look anything like her. This woman is so much taller than Sylvie ever was.'

'You know her?' A prickle of hope ran through Ginny's veins.

'Oh yes. She's lived in Little Shaw for years,' Hen said before taking the photograph from Tuppence. 'But I agree, this doesn't look like her. Sylvie is very petite.'

'It's definitely not her,' Mitch agreed, which caused Heather to wrinkle her nose.

'Who is this Sylvie?' his wife demanded. Like Ginny and JM, she wasn't a native to the village and had moved there from Ireland, by way of London.

'She's a lovely old woman who lived in that blue cottage down past the park. I used to mow her lawns, back when I did odd jobs. She's French, I think, but came to Little Shaw before I was born. A couple of years ago she moved into Ashworth Court.'

'The retirement place?' Tuppence raised an eyebrow.

'It's independent living,' JM corrected. 'I have a friend in there. Dreadful to look at, but it's actually a lovely community. As for whether it's Sylvie in the photograph, the only way to find out is to ask her.'

'I agree,' Ginny said. 'The fact Nathan has these two photographs and one has Sylvie's name on the back means she might be able to help us return them to his family.'

'Or, she might *be* his family,' Tuppence pointed out. 'Mitch, did Nathan say if he had relatives in the area? How did you come to hire him?'

'I can't recall him mentioning it. We have ads up in the bar and in a few windows on the high street, as well as putting up advertisements at Burnley, hoping some of the students might be looking for work. All he told us was that he wanted a break after finishing his PhD, so I suspect that is how he found out about us.'

Ginny nodded. It was the same thing he'd told her as well.

'Seems a strange coincidence, him having these photos then.' Tuppence wrinkled her brow.

'I have no time for coincidences,' JM retorted. 'Let me call my friend at Ashworth, and see if she knows what apartment Sylvie is in. Then I say that Ginny and Hen visit Sylvie tomorrow while Tuppence and I help in the pub.'

They all nodded in agreement and soon made their goodbyes.

Tomorrow was going to be busy.

SEVEN

Friday, October 16

Ashworth Court was a towering purpose-built brick box on the outskirts of Little Shaw with tiny windows that overlooked a treeless stretch of concrete and the carpark beyond. Ginny had driven past it numerous times but never had any desire to stop. It appeared more like an office block than a retirement home. The depressing exterior wasn't helped by the low autumn mist that clung to the ground.

She parked the car and turned off the engine.

'I'm sure it's nicer on the inside. JM's friend seems to enjoy it,' Hen said in a cautious voice, and clutched the knitting bag in her lap. After several failed attempts to get Sylvie's phone number, they had eventually called reception, who passed on their message, and Sylvie had agreed to see them.

'And they do seem to have a lot of facilities,' Ginny added as they walked across the concrete stretch. Out of habit she had gone onto the website to read more about the place. It had listed a nine-hole golf course, a pool, a dining room, an entertainment area and a communal garden.

Perhaps all the greenery was hidden around the back?

'Oh dear.' Hen looked around. 'I know it is dreadful to say, but I am not sure I'd want to end up here.'

Ginny was silent. As much as she wanted to comfort Hen, it was the one aspect of ageing that she struggled to think about since Eric's death.

What will happen as I get older, without you?

'Perhaps they will have a large barn conversion we could all live in together?' Ginny said, trying to push the melancholy thought away and knowing how much Hen loved a cozy environment.

The suggestion worked and her friend brightened. 'Wouldn't that be fun. I never flat-shared when I was younger. I wonder if we would bicker?'

Ginny grinned and put on her best JM voice. 'I have no time for bickering.'

'Nor do I.' Hen laughed. 'And it really is quite a lovely thought. Perhaps Sylvie has found good friends since she has been living here.'

'I hope so. What do you know about her?' Ginny asked as they reached the entrance and stared into the bland reception area.

'She's French, that's a standout feature in these parts, and she always wore the most marvellous outfits. To me she seemed so exotic compared to the other women in the village. She ran the post office but must have retired twenty years ago. She would be in her late eighties by now. I didn't realise she was still in the area. I wonder if she'll remember me?'

Ginny hoped so, since it might make the upcoming interview go better.

They crossed to the reception desk where a sharp-faced woman greeted them. Her name badge read, Carol Trappier. At the mention of Sylvie's name, her face turned into a cool mask.

'I'm not sure Sylvie's up to having visitors.'

'She is expecting us,' Ginny said in a cautious voice, not liking the way Carol was glaring at them both.

'We will make sure we don't wear her out,' Hen added.

The receptionist flinched and then let out a pained sigh, as if she wouldn't be responsible for anything that happened. 'So be it. She's in apartment 44a. Turn left at the community lounge then take the lift at the far end. Don't get in the first one because it's been playing up. Once you're up there, you'll need to walk around the long way because the painters are in. If you go past the coffee machine in the recess, then you have gone too far. But first you need to sign in.'

Carol pushed forward a tablet. Ginny stared at it for several moments before realising she needed to enter her details. She clicked from screen to screen before passing it to Hen.

'Is it okay that I brought scones?' Hen asked once she had completed the sign-in process and handed the tablet back to an uninterested Carol. 'And Ginny made her own raspberry jam. Is there some rule against that? We don't want to cause any problems.'

But instead of answering Carol turned away to gruffly greet someone else.

'Sounds delicious,' a nurse said from nearby. She had dark hair, bright green eyes and a warm smile. Her own nametag read Lizzie Foreman. 'Don't mind Carol—she has a bit going on at home right now. Her father has been ill, but she's usually a sweetheart. And there are no rules about food. Independent living means exactly that.'

'That's good to know,' Ginny admitted, before peering around for the community lounge, which would hopefully lead to the lift. 'I don't suppose you could point us in the right direction. We're here to visit Sylvie Yates.'

At the mention of Sylvie's name, Lizzie broke into a smile. 'Lovely. Poor thing doesn't get many visitors. Here, come with me. This place is a rabbit warren.'

'That's ever so kind of you,' Hen said as they followed the nurse past a small atrium through to an open-plan sitting area. 'How sad she doesn't get many visitors.'

'I'm afraid it's not that uncommon,' Lizzie said as they reached the lift and the metal doors yawned open. 'In Sylvie's case, she has outlived her husband and her son.'

'That's so sad.' Hen's eyes filled with tears and Ginny's own throat tightened.

They both knew what it was like to outlive people you loved.

And now Nathan was dead.

How would Sylvie take the news? And who was Nathan to her? A relation of some kind? It had been teasing Ginny's mind that by asking Sylvie about Nathan, they might be causing her a great deal of pain. And while their intentions were to return his possessions, she couldn't rid herself of the idea it might backfire.

Yet, if someone found a photograph that had once belonged to Eric, I would want it back. No matter how painful it might be.

She turned to Lizzie as they stepped into the lift. 'Does Sylvie have any other relations? A grandson perhaps or great-nephew?'

'I'm afraid not. Just that daughter-in-law of hers.' Lizzie's good humour faded but before she could say anything else, the lift doors opened on the fourth floor. 'I'm going up to five, but if you get out here, just walk to the end and then turn right. You won't have any problems finding the apartment.'

They thanked her and made their way down the hallway, until they found the correct door.

'It's open,' a soft voice called out, with the trace of an accent.

Ginny pushed the door and stepped into a small apartment. The walls might have been plain once, but they were now barely visible underneath a dazzling array of gold-framed paintings, while the floors were covered in handwoven rugs, the rich designs competing for attention. An antique dresser and large bookshelf lined the wall, and every surface was crammed with ceramics, handblown glass bowls and so many other things that Ginny's eyes could hardly take in. Goodness, was that a Faberge egg? Surely the stunning gold and green objet d'art had to be a replica. Then again, considering the lovely brass chess set and porcelain collection, maybe it was real.

'It's like Aladdin's cave,' Hen gasped, before flushing, no doubt worried she was being rude. Ginny couldn't blame her. Aladdin's cave was exactly what it was like.

A soft chuckle came from near a large standing light, the shade obscured by a shawl, and Ginny finally saw a small woman perched in an upright chair. To one side was a walking frame.

Her hair was the colour of snow, but her eyes were dark brown and there was a mischievous smile on her mouth. Her tiny frame was covered in a black crepe jacket with beaded details and thick pearls hung around her neck.

She looked like she had walked straight out of a glorious black and white movie.

'My legs don't work the way they used to so you'll have to excuse me for not getting up,' Sylvie said by way of greeting. Her gaze settled on Hen and she pointed a finger at her. 'You're Meryl's daughter.'

'You *do* remember me.' Hen beamed. 'It's lovely to see you again. I'm so pleased you agreed to our visit.'

'Better than going down to the common room and playing backgammon. I haven't had any competition since Tucker Hodgkinson kicked the bucket.'

'I'm sorry to hear that.' Ginny blinked at the casual approach to death.

'What are you sorry for? That he's dead, or that I'm surrounded by idiots who can't think two moves ahead?' Sylvie retorted then gave them an elfin grin. 'You don't need to answer that. When you get to my age, the gallows humour seems to come naturally. Well, don't just stand there. Take a seat.'

'T-thank you.' Hen dropped down onto a Louis XVI two-seater sofa with pale upholstery. Then she glanced down at the plate of scones still in her hand. 'I wasn't sure if you would like some morning tea. These are freshly made.'

Sylvie's eyes brightened. 'If you bake like your mother, I would love one. There's a kettle in the kitchen, if one of you wanted to make tea.'

'Let me.' Ginny took the plate and walked to the compact

kitchen while Hen and Sylvie chatted about Little Shaw residents they both knew.

Three exquisite bone china teacups had been set out on a tray, along with a matching milk jug and a tiny bowl with three sugar cubes in it. It was clear Sylvie was delighted to have guests, regardless of the reason. It was also clear by the extraordinary décor that she had lived a colourful life. Yet here she was, grateful to be visited by two strangers. Another pang of worry went through Ginny.

Will that be my fate?

Or the fate of my friends?

It was certainly a path Ginny had been walking down after Eric's death… but now she'd learned a new way to connect with people, she hoped that loneliness wouldn't be something in her future.

The kettle boiled and, pleased to push her thoughts away, Ginny made the tea before setting out the scones and jam as well as the butter curls that she'd put in a small container. Once it was laid out, she carried it over and settled it down on an elaborately carved wooden coffee table.

'So, what brings you both here today?' Sylvie asked after finishing her tea and managing to eat half a scone.

'We wanted to ask you some questions about Nathan Richardson,' Ginny said in a cautious voice, hoping that what the nurse had told them was true about Sylvie not having any other relatives besides her daughter-in-law.

'The young man who died last week?' Sylvie's eyes narrowed, though there was curiosity behind her gaze rather than sorrow.

'You heard about what happened?' Hen said.

'Bien sûr. In this place, news travels fast. Much faster than out there.' She waved an arthritic finger at the window. 'I was saddened to hear it. He was a most likeable young man.'

'How did you know him?' Ginny asked, since Sylvie's reaction seemed to confirm he wasn't a relative.

'I didn't. Well… not until a month ago. He came to me with a photograph, full of hope that I was the woman in it. It didn't take him long to realise his mistake. Even when I am sitting, it's hard to disguise the fact I'm five foot nothing. And that was when I was in my prime.'

Ginny and Hen exchanged a worried look.

They had only come here because they thought the photograph might be important to Nathan's family and they wanted to return it. But if Nathan hadn't known who the woman was, did this mean they were chasing a lost cause?

Still, they were here now.

Retrieving the two photographs from her bag, Ginny quickly explained how they had found them and their reason for visiting.

Sylvie listened with interest and then gave them an apologetic smile. 'That I cannot help you with. He told me that his parents had passed, and he had no siblings. After his mother's death last year, he found this photograph in her belongings and my name was on the back of it. There had been talk in the family about his great-aunt, who disappeared when she was twenty. She had been disowned by the family, but he never understood why.'

'Do you know who she is?' Ginny asked, her curiosity roused.

At the question Sylvie's eyes gleamed, as if lit from the inside. 'Oui. We were great friends. Her name was Peggy Barlow. We worked in the post office together, but it has been many years since I have seen her. I didn't know anything about her family, but Nathan immediately recognised the name. He confirmed she was his great-aunt.'

'Poor Nathan. Was he hoping to meet her?' Hen's eyes filled with compassion. 'Is that why he moved to the area?'

'The heart and mind can be mysterious.' Sylvie gave a philo-sophical shrug. 'Maybe he wanted to find his great-aunt, or maybe he wanted to keep himself busy? Who can say? All I know is that it led him to me. That's why I gave him the second photograph.' Sylvie pointed to the one that Ginny had discovered in the library book.

'It belonged to you?' She blinked at the news. Perhaps today wasn't a wasted trip, since if Sylvie originally owned the photograph, at least they could return it to her. 'That was generous of you.'

'Not so much. Memories live in the heart not on a piece of light-sensitive paper.' Then she gave a rueful smile. 'Well... most memories are still in there. Some like to slip away with the years. But oui, he seemed happy. He was intrigued by the number on the back.'

'147-3-2, 89-12-7, 203-8-4, 156-15-3,' Ginny recited from memory. She had also been curious about what it meant. 'Is it a date? Perhaps when the photograph was taken?'

'No. That particular photograph was from 1963 and as for what the numbers mean, I suspect it's some kind of code.'

'Code?' Ginny and Hen both spoke at once.

Giving them a contrite smile Sylvie leaned back in her chair. 'Did I forget to mention that Peggy Barlow was a secret agent who worked for MI5?'

EIGHT

Friday, October 16

A secret agent? MI5?

Ginny blinked, trying to recall everything she knew about the political tensions of the sixties. It had been dubbed the Cold War and included incompatible ideological systems, espionage and covert operations. Earlier on there had been spy rings like the Cambridge Five but surely Peggy Barlow couldn't have been around then. Still, the whole idea was extraordinary. Not because Peggy was a female, but rather that she had been involved in something that seemed to have come directly from a book plot.

Ginny leaned forward. 'What happened to Peggy? Do you know where she went?'

Pain flashed across Sylvie's face. 'No. She left Little Shaw in 1963... the same year the photograph was taken. She promised to stay in touch but, alas, never did.'

'That's dreadful.' Hen's hand flew to her mouth. 'You don't think something bad happened to her, do you?'

'I-I don't know. She never spoke about her work. I only found out by accident. I lent her my raincoat one evening. Poor thing, it only reached her knees, but she still seemed grateful. After she returned it, I discovered a piece of paper in the pocket with a series of numbers written on it, along with a copy of *Pride and Prejudice*.'

Hen frowned. 'I don't follow. How did you work out she was a spy from that? What if she just liked reading? And the numbers could have been a phone number.'

Ginny was also curious, before remembering a documentary she and Eric had seen together about codebreaking during the Second World War.

Gasping, she leaned forward. 'You don't mean it was a book cipher, do you?'

'I do indeed.' Sylvie's eyes twinkled.

Of course.

It made so much sense now that she thought about the long sequence on the back of the photograph. 147-3-2, 89-12-7, 23-8-4, 156-15-3. Page 147, third line, second word. It would lead to a word, and the second sequence would reveal another word, until the entire message was clear.

Why hadn't she thought of it sooner?

More intriguingly, did that mean if she found the right edition of *Pride and Prejudice*, they would be able to decipher the four-word message?

'Do you still have the book?' she asked before she could stop herself.

'I'm afraid not.' Sylvie shook her head, automatically reaching for the photograph to study the code. 'Which makes it so very diffi-cult to get the right message.'

'What message?' Hen blinked at them both.

Ginny flushed. 'Sorry, I got carried away. A book cipher uses a sequence of numbers to denote a chapter, paragraph and word within a certain book.'

'Goodness. I've never heard of them, let alone tried to figure out what it might mean.' Hen turned to Sylvie. 'How did you think to check?'

'I wish I could claim to having any great brilliance, but the truth was that back then codebreaking and spy craft was everywhere. From trench coats and sunglasses through to Ian Fleming and John le Carré, it was a very strange time to live through... though I doubt I would have come to that conclusion if the book hadn't been there as well.'

'Did Peggy admit to it? And what did the message say?' Ginny asked. This wasn't what they had come for, but it was too fascinating to not find out more about it.

'It said: "Find the priest."'

Hen's eyes brightened. 'Oh, was she going to get married?'

Sylvie gave a rueful chuckle. 'That's what she would have me believe. Except we both knew it was a lie. Eventually she admitted the truth and begged me not to betray her. And in all these years I never have... until Nathan came to visit me. Not that I could tell him much. All I really knew about Peggy was that she came to Little Shaw in 1962 and by 1963 she was gone.'

Ginny sucked in her breath.

The past really *was* a foreign country.

It was made more concerning that Peggy seemed to have disappeared into thin air.

'You said that you never heard from her again. Did you try to find her?' Ginny asked.

'Oui, but there was only so much I could do. My wage was a pittance, and no one wanted to listen to someone like me. My accent was stronger back then and there was a lot of mistrust. Then I met Archie and became his wife. After that Louis was born and life took over. Plus—' She broke off and bowed her head.

'Are you okay?' Ginny asked in a gentle voice. 'We didn't mean to stir up old memories.'

'Are there any other kind?' Sylvie retorted in a dry voice and let out a sigh. 'I'm fine. It's painful to remember because at the back of my mind I always worried that something had happened to her. She was scared, you see.'

'Scared of what?' Hen's eyes were wide.

'I'm not sure. I don't know if she was either. She just had the dreadful suspicion that her cover had been blown, and that someone was watching her.'

'Another spy?' Ginny could feel her own eyes widening.

'It probably sounds nonsense now but back then it was a possibility. Or so it seemed to me. Peggy never said anything, but I knew that something had scared her. The last time I saw her, she had that look in her eyes. Fear. As if she was worried that her time was running out.'

'Oh no. You don't mean someone was trying to kill her?' Hen's face drained of colour.

'All I know is that she was scared of something.' Sylvie dropped her gaze, as if overcome with memories.

Ginny shivered at the idea of countries running covert spy operations. It had happened then and she had no doubt it was still happening now.

'What did Nathan say when you told him?' She recalled his detailed quiz questions and love of research. It was hard to imagine that he wouldn't have been curious to find out more about his great-aunt.

'He was shocked, surprised... and completely intrigued. He became determined to move to Little Shaw and find out more about her.'

Ginny sat up straight as something clicked in her mind. 'Wait... when Nathan came to visit you, had he started his job at The Lost Goat?'

Sylvie gave her a sly smile. As if it had been some kind of test. 'Aren't you the clever one? The answer is no. He came to Little Shaw to speak with me, then went to The Lost Goat. You see, back then, the top floor was a boarding house and that's where Peggy lived.'

'I remember my mother telling me that,' Hen gasped. 'Oh, how incredible. So, Nathan went to visit the pub and saw the notice in the window for bar staff.'

'That's correct. At the time I suspected it would be a wild goose chase, but no good ever came from trying to steer a person off the path they want to pursue. So, I didn't stop him. On reflection maybe I should have,' Sylvie admitted, guilt turning her cheeks red.

They were all silent, no doubt thinking about poor Nathan and where his path had led him. Sylvie might be right about how pointless it was to try and steer someone else's life, but when the results ended up so tragically, it didn't make it easier to bear.

'Did he visit you again, or give you an update on what he'd found?' Ginny asked.

'He came back several times. He was fascinated with my collection of trinkets.' She waved an arthritic hand at the crammed shelves. 'And two weeks ago, he told me he had found a person who could give him more information about Peggy Barlow.'

'Oh, my goodness,' Hen squeaked. 'I wonder who it was? Did he mention their name?'

'No. Just that they were keen to help,' Sylvie admitted before her mouth dropped into a serious frown. 'He was going to meet them last Sunday.'

Ginny and Tuppence stared at each other.

Last Sunday was the same day that Nathan was killed.

She thought of the overturned pub. Mitch was so sure nothing had been taken, but was that really true? What if someone had been looking for something Nathan had discovered? Something connected to Peggy Barlow?

Unease prickled her skin and numerous questions flooded through her mind but before she could form them into words, the door swung open dramatically.

'Sylvie, what have I told you about leaving this place unlocked? Anyone could just wander in,' a sharp voice said. It belonged to an elegant woman in her fifties. She was wearing a fitted black skirt suit along with towering black heels, that gave Ginny vertigo just from looking at them. The woman came to a halt, her unfriendly gaze sweeping over them. 'Who are you?'

'These are new friends. Hen and Ginny,' Sylvie announced, her small chin jutting into the air defiantly. 'And this is Veronica. My daughter-in-law.'

Oh. The nurse had mentioned a daughter-in-law when they had been in the lift, and it was clear now why her expression had soured. Veronica didn't seem to be very warm. At least not on the surface.

Though that didn't mean she wasn't perfectly lovely underneath, Ginny tried to remind herself. And if she had been married to Sylvie's son, Louis, that meant she was now his widow. It was a state Ginny couldn't wish on anyone.

'Why have I never heard of them before?' Veronica's icy expression didn't change.

'Who could say? Your mind is a mystery to me,' Sylvie said in a calm voice, though Ginny could almost see the tension zapping between the two women.

'Pot meet kettle,' Veronica retorted before taking in Sylvie's magnificent black outfit. She scowled. 'I thought I told you to wear the pink Chanel jacket today.'

'Wear pink in autumn? That I will not do.' Sylvie gave a firm shake of her head.

Veronica let out a long-suffering sigh. 'Please, Sylvie, they will be here in half an hour. At least put on something a bit less funeral-home.'

'If you choose to refer to Givenchy as funeral-home, far be it from me to correct you,' Sylvie retorted, then slowly rose from her chair, with the help of the walker by her side. She turned to Hen and Ginny and gave them a grateful smile. 'Thank you for visiting me. I do hope you will come again.'

Ginny automatically got to her feet. 'We appreciate your help.'

'It's been so lovely to see you,' Hen added. 'We're ever so sorry if we have kept you too long.'

'Not at all,' Sylvie assured them. 'Your visit will no doubt prove to be the highlight of my day.'

'As ever, Sylvie, your support is touching,' Veronica snapped before turning to Ginny and Hen. 'You will have to excuse my mother-in-law. She delights in taunting me.'

'An old woman needs her hobbies,' Sylvie threw back, then slowly made her way to a door that led further into the apartment.

Once she had left the room, Veronica let out a sigh and turned to Ginny and Hen. 'I'm sorry you had to see that. We have a fractured relationship. I think she blames me for Louis's death. As if I could have stopped him from getting cancer.'

'How terrible.' Hen's whole face softened. 'When did you lose him?'

Veronica gave a little sniff and raised her fingers to her eyes, as if to pat away invisible tears. 'Five years ago, next week. Which is why today is so important.'

'Oh,' Ginny said, not quite sure of the relevance. 'Are you going to the cemetery?'

'Goodness, no. It's because a photographer is coming here for a photoshoot. I'm launching my new business and it's important that my clients understand the full backstory. It's all about tapping into the emotional connection so that people see the "real" me,' she explained.

Hen gave her a blank look. 'A business?'

'Yes. I'm opening my own estate planning consultancy. It's always been a dream of mine and Louis made me promise to do it. I know he's watching me from up above.' Veronica paused to peer at the ceiling. Without meaning to, Ginny and Hen did the same, but all Ginny could see was the ornate chandelier that sent tiny rainbows around the room.

'Oh,' Hen said, uncertainly. 'Well, that sounds lovely.'

'Thank you,' Veronica said with pride as she pressed business cards into both their hands. 'I believe it is a privilege to be allowed into someone's home to help them catalogue the legacy that they wish to pass on, and to ensure that their final wishes are carried out after they are gone.'

The business card was simple with delicate gold font.

Veronica Yates
Yates Estate Consultancy
Walton-on-Marsh

At the sight of Walton-on-Marsh, Ginny stifled a groan. It was a rival village that took itself very seriously, and while hostilities between the two villages had lessened recently, there still wasn't much cross-pollination, which explained why she and Hen had never met Veronica before.

Ginny tucked the card into her purse and was about to walk to the door, when she saw the two photographs of Peggy Barlow still sitting on the coffee table.

Wincing, she exchanged a glance with Hen.

They had both been so distracted by Veronica's entrance that Ginny hadn't thought to ask Sylvie what she wanted to do with the photographs. Did she want hers back? Or should she have them both? It made sense to leave them since Peggy Barlow had been her friend.

And yet, now they knew about Peggy's work as a spy and that Nathan had arranged to meet someone on the day of his death, Ginny was loath to leave them behind. What if there was more to his death than they'd first thought?

She glanced at the door Sylvie had disappeared through, but there was still no sign of the older woman. Indecision gnawed at her, but the issue was solved by Veronica, who suddenly stalked over to the table and snatched the two photographs up.

'I hope she hasn't been boring you with a trip down memory lane,' the woman said in a light voice, but her narrowed eyes and deep frown suggested something else.

Ginny swallowed. 'Of course not. And one of those photographs—'

'Is terrible quality. So blurry,' Veronica cut her off and crossed over to an elaborate lacquered bureau. She twisted a small brass key and put the photographs inside the drawer before locking it again and slipping the key into her jacket pocket. 'Now, if you will excuse me, I need to sort this room out before the photographer arrives. Sylvie has some lovely possessions, but she also has some trash which won't do at all for my image.'

'Of course,' Ginny reluctantly said.

'Please say goodbye to Sylvie for us,' Hen added. 'And good luck with the new business.'

There was no answer so Ginny slipped her handbag over her shoulder and left the apartment, pleased to be away from Veronica's overpowering presence.

'Oh dear,' Hen said as soon as they were back in the carpark. 'I don't think she liked us at all. And why was she so determined to lock the photographs away?'

'I wish I knew,' Ginny said, her mind full of questions. Which was a problem because despite all her promises to Wallace to not get involved in another police case, there was a mystery here that someone needed to look into.

NINE

Friday, October 16

'Bye, JM... and sorry about what happened earlier. My bad.' A burly man with a thick beard and wide arms buried in a leather biker's jacket leaned over the bar as Ginny and Hen arrived at The Lost Goat.

'Mistakes are the best way to learn, Lefty. But make sure I don't hear that kind of language coming out of your mouth again when you are talking about a woman. It's not something I tolerate.' JM appeared from the office and gave him a quick nod of dismissal.

The huge man hung his head and slunk out the door, causing Hen to stifle a giggle.

'Dare we ask what that was about?' Ginny smiled as they reached the bar.

'Nothing much.' JM took the waiter's cloth from over her shoulder and wiped her hands. 'I just needed to have a few words with the silly boy. You know what some people are like once they've had a pint.'

Ginny did, and it was one of the reasons why she had been nervous about volunteering to help out Heather and Mitch. But she hadn't once doubted JM's abilities to manage. Next to her, Hen gave a shudder. Clearly, she had been thinking the same thing.

'How has it been?'

'Excellent fun.' Tuppence appeared from the kitchen balancing two plates of food. 'Just let me deliver these and then Heather said we could be finished for the day. The kitchen is now closed and this is the final order.'

'What about tonight?' Hen's brow wrinkled. 'I thought we would all be working.'

'Turns out they don't need us. Some chap came in earlier to apply for the job. They are giving him a trial and a couple of the women from Heather's wicca coven are coming in to help,' Tuppence explained. 'But I did offer our services for Saturday and Sunday night.'

'Let me make a pot of tea and we can find out how it went with Sylvie.' JM made the hot drinks and put some money in the register before leading them to a table in the corner.

Tuppence joined them several minutes later carrying a tray of Eccles cakes. 'Heather insisted I bring these out. She hasn't lost her touch.'

Ginny, who had only eaten half a scone earlier, let out a happy sigh. The cakes were Heather's speciality and a sure sign she was feeling better, if she had baked a batch.

'Isn't this cosy?' Hen took a sip of tea. 'I'm so pleased you both enjoyed yourself.'

'What is there not to enjoy?' JM said as she picked up her teacup. 'I've always been fascinated by the way people confide to whoever is behind the bar. It's like a confessional.'

'Oh, you lucky thing. Did you hear anything juicy?' Tuppence dragged a pink scrunchy out of her silver curls so that they sprang back around her face.

'I operate under a strict code of confidentiality, and my lips must remain sealed.' JM's stern expression gave way to a rueful smile. 'But in short, no. There weren't any village happenings that we didn't already know about. Enough about the bar, how did you go with Sylvie?'

'She was a delight, and she remembered me.' Hen filled them in on their conversation, with Ginny adding a few extra points.

'A new case.' Tuppence clapped her hands in delight.

The words caused Ginny to flinch.

On the drive over she had been grappling with what to do next. Since moving to Little Shaw, she had been tangled up in enough murders to know that trying to interfere with a police case was a bad idea. But this wasn't a police case. *Well, not yet.*

According to them, Nathan died by misadventure, and even if that wasn't true, she doubted the police would appreciate her suggesting it. Especially without any proof.

Which meant all they were really doing was some gentle digging.

If they found anything untoward, they could immediately hand it to Wallace. And if there was nothing to be discovered, at least they would have learned a bit more about Little Shaw's history during the 1960s.

It was a relief because, like her friends, Ginny couldn't resist the lure of an unanswered question.

'It's definitely fishy. Let's go through this. Nathan visits Sylvie who tells him that his great-aunt was an MI5 spy in the sixties, and that she mysteriously disappeared. Possibly in diabolical circumstances.' JM held up one hand so she could tick off her fingers. 'He gets a live-in job at the same bar where Peggy Barlow once stayed, in order to find out more about her. Someone has information about it, but we have no idea of whether they met, because he died. Did I miss anything?'

'Don't forget the break-in yesterday. What were they looking for?' Ginny held up one of her own fingers.

'That's a good point.' Hen frowned and raised a finger. 'Also, we don't know much about Nathan, which means we should look him up.'

'And we need to find out more about Peggy Barlow.' Tuppence

contributed her own finger. 'Did she really go missing, or did she just move somewhere else?'

'What about Sylvie's daughter-in-law, Veronica? She wasn't happy to see the photographs on the table. She looked like she had seen a ghost,' Hen said, raising another finger.

'What a pity we don't have the code anymore,' Tuppence said.

'I wrote it down and memorised it,' Ginny admitted. It was second nature to her to keep lists and compile details, and she was pleased she had done so, since the temptation to see if she could figure out what the cipher meant was high.

'What a relief.' Tuppence held up her thumb before frowning. 'This is a lot of fingers. We need a murder board.'

'I agree.' Hen hopefully peered around the snug where they were sitting, as if one would suddenly appear.

'I know what we can use.' JM reached for the small handbag she always carried. It had Tardis-like properties and Ginny was no longer surprised by what she carried in it. Her hand emerged from the bag clutching at several dozen cardboard beer mats. She put them on the table and let them scatter. Most of them were either round or square and not much bigger than Ginny's palm.

'Oh, aren't these lovely.' Hen picked one up and examined it.

It had the logo of a beer brand that Ginny had never heard of. She wasn't sure she would want to taste Ned's Brutal Bitter. Another one was an advertisement for car insurance that appeared to be about twenty years old. She squinted closer. Yes, it was from 2001. It explained the air of neglect that clung to the entire collection.

'Why do you have these?' Tuppence picked up one with a giant spider on the front of it.

'Mitch was going to throw them out but that seemed like a pity. I felt they might be useful for something.'

'Useful for putting your beer on,' Tuppence agreed before frowning. 'But how will they help us now?'

Ginny smiled and turned one of the beer mats over to show the flip side was blank. 'I think this is what JM meant. We can write on the back of them.'

'Ooh... and we can move them around like puzzle pieces.' Hen's eyes lit up and she began to turn them all over. 'It's just like sewing a quilt. I always lay out the pieces to make sure the pattern is exactly what I want, and sometimes I need to move things around. You know the old saying: measure twice, cut once.'

'That's brilliant.' Tuppence extracted a large pencil case from her own handbag and unzipped it to display a collection of coloured felt pens. 'Let's get started.'

'Are you sure Mitch won't mind?' Hen asked.

'Mind what?' Mitch appeared by the table, his gaze sweeping over the upturned beer mats. 'Oh, those things. They're all yours. I found boxes of them down in the cellar getting damp and musty. It's the least I can do to thank JM and Tuppence for today. You were both brilliant. Though JM... did I see you asking Razor Hatton to button up his shirt?'

'Of course I did. I have no interest in chest hair at this time of day. Or any time of day if it comes to that. Don't worry, he took it very well.'

Mitch gulped. 'Well... just be careful. Razor and Lefty aren't known for their manners.'

'Nonsense. They just need to be taken in hand. But while we have you here, Mitch, can you give us access to the CCTV footage from last Sunday evening? We believe Nathan was meeting someone to discuss his great-aunt.'

'It's possible that they were speaking in code. On account of being a spy,' Hen added.

'Oh yes. Excellent point.' Tuppence uncapped a bright pink pen and wrote down *Code* on the top of a beer mat, then gave him an encouraging smile.

'Spy? Code?' Mitch gave a dubious look at the teapot. 'Are you all drunk?'

'Of course not,' JM said. 'I never drink on the job. We've decided to investigate Nathan's death.'

Mitch opened his mouth and then shut it again before sitting down. 'Now I'm the one who needs a stiff drink. You had better tell me what this is about. Because you lot aren't the only ones that Wallace has a short temper with. I don't want him thinking that I'm meddling in police business.'

'Why would he?' JM demanded, ignoring the numerous times they had done just that. Plus, Ginny could understand Mitch's hesitance. Before he had met Heather, he had gone through a bad time and Wallace had arrested him on more than one occasion. It was one of the reasons the brewery had been reluctant for Mitch to take over the pub.

'This is what we know so far.' Ginny gave him a brief rundown of what they had discovered. 'It might be nothing, but we want to see what we can find out. However, we'd never do anything to put you or Heather at risk.'

The panicked look faded. 'Sorry, I should have known you wouldn't. But I swear I never heard Nathan speaking in code or having any clandestine meetings.'

'What about *Pride and Prejudice?*' Hen suddenly asked. 'That's the book that Peggy Barlow used to decipher her codes. I don't suppose you happened to notice if he had a copy?'

It was an excellent question and Ginny leaned forward.

If they had the correct copy they could decipher the code on the back of the photograph.

Mitch shook his head. 'He had a stack of books in his room, but we just boxed them up and gave them to the police. I didn't read the titles.'

'Rookie mistake.' JM sighed, trying to make the best of a bad situation.

'Wait, let me get that down. *No Austen.*' Tuppence wrote on the beer mat. Then she capped the felt pen and reached for an orange one, which she used to underline it three times. 'Okay, you may now continue.'

Mitch frowned. 'I don't have anything else to add. If Nathan met with anyone, I didn't know about it.'

'That's disappointing.' Tuppence put down the pen.

'Don't take it personally,' Hen assured him. 'This is just how we work a case.'

'Hen's right,' JM agreed and snatched up one of the spare beer mats. On one side was a sleepy-looking garden gnome wearing a dressing gown and the words *Esme's Handcrafted Gnomes* underneath it. On the other side was a photograph of a much younger Esme sitting in a pottery studio with a wide smile on her face.

Ginny's eyes widened. Esme had mentioned she'd once run her own business, but Ginny hadn't given much thought to what it might be. Though, as she studied Esme's beaming face, she had to admit that it did seem very on brand for her.

Her friends didn't seem surprised at the beer mat and JM simply poised it on her thumb knuckle, prepared to flip it. 'We need to decide who is going to search Nathan's bedroom and who will search the cellar. I suggest we go in pairs.'

'Oh yes. Safety in numbers. That's always best when a killer is involved,' Tuppence confirmed.

'Killer?' Mitch's face went pale.

'Yes, of course. It's important to keep an open mind when it comes to things like this. Now, who wants Esme and who wants the gnome?'

TEN

Friday, October 16

The cellar of The Lost Goat was just as damp and depressing as Ginny had envisioned. A wooden staircase had been cut into the floor behind the bar, making it necessary for them to duck their heads on the way down. The concrete seeped with moisture and the blackened beams of the overhead floorboards above spoke to a bygone era.

Perhaps that explained the goose bumps travelling up and down Ginny's arms?

'Over that side are all the kegs.' Mitch waved them forward and flicked on an overhead light. It didn't reach into all of the shadowy corners and while Ginny had brought a torch, she wasn't looking forward to using it. 'The small office Nathan worked from is to your right.'

'And… this is where I found him.' Heather pointed to a spot on the floor.

Ginny's hands went clammy as she studied the space.

There were no blood stains or police chalk, but nor was there any of the dust that coated the rest of the floor. She knew from the police statement that it had been death by misadventure, caused when Nathan fell over a beer keg and hit his head. As to the exact position of the keg, it was hard to say. Yet, Ginny imagined it must have been nearby for Imogen, the pathologist, to arrive at that verdict.

Despite her puckered flesh she moved forward to examine the area better. She had no real idea of what she was looking for, but they had to start somewhere. She glanced towards the line of kegs that were hooked up with tubes leading up to the bar. She tried to picture Nathan changing one over and then turning around, not noticing the empty keg behind him.

But it was just as easy to imagine someone following him down the stairs and pushing him over. If he had been taken unaware, it would be simple to make it appear like an accident.

She shivered and wrapped her arms around her torso.

The longer they were down here, the less she liked it. Next to her JM gave a little shudder, which was the closest Ginny had ever seen her friend come to showing fear.

'I'm starting to think Hen and Tuppence got the better end of the bargain,' JM murmured and peered around, as if trying to decide where to start. 'It's hard to imagine the police missed anything.'

Ginny had been thinking the same thing as she leaned forward to inspect the dark spaces behind the kegs. But there was nothing and she and JM both moved into the small office. There was a filing cabinet that was empty apart from yet more beer mats. An ancient laptop sat on the desk, but when JM tried to turn it on, the screen remained blank.

'The police have already searched it, but it came back as corrupted. In other words, it doesn't work,' Heather said.

'Nor does the printer,' Mitch added. 'It's become a dumping ground down here, and I'm still trying to get it all in order.'

Even Ginny, who usually loved tidying up, didn't relish the task ahead of him.

She peered behind the broken computer tower, in the hope a stray piece of information might have been wedged there. But there was nothing and after another fifteen minutes they called it quits and returned to the bar just as Hen and Tuppence descended the stairs that hugged the far wall of the pub.

'Any luck?' Tuppence asked in a hopeful voice.

'No, though I'm pleased I didn't need to change any kegs today,' JM admitted. 'I can't say I'm a fan of the place.'

'I agree,' Heather said. 'Next week I am going to get my coven to come and cleanse it. There is a lot of negative energy down there. In the meantime, Mitch and I have decided that he's the only one who will go down there.'

'Certainly a better way to retain staff,' JM agreed before settling at the table they had deserted. 'How did you two go?'

'Go on, Hen. Tell them what you found,' Tuppence said in an encouraging voice.

'It might not mean anything.' Hen coloured as she retrieved a piece of paper that was covered in pencil shading.

'What might be nothing?' JM demanded, eyes fixing on the paper. Ginny did the same thing and was able to make out the letter W. There were more letters, but it was difficult to decipher them from the distance.

'I found an empty notepad down the back of the wardrobe,' Hen admitted, her cheeks now bright red from being the centre of attention. 'But when I looked at it closely, I could see the imprint of writing on it.'

'And... don't forget the best part,' Tuppence cut in, holding up a blank notepad. 'It's from the same university where Nathan studied, which means it's clearly his.'

'Excellent work,' JM informed them, still trying to see what was written on the page Hen was clutching. 'But please put us out of our misery. What does it say?'

'Windscale,' Hen admitted.

'Windscale?' Heather wrinkled her nose. 'What's that when it's at home?'

'It was a nuclear power plant over in Cumbria,' Hen told her. 'There was a dreadful fire there in the late fifties. It was before my time, but I remember helping Alyson with a school assignment.'

'And it was right in the middle of the tensions after World War Two,' Tuppence added, reaching for a beer mat and writing down the name of the power plant. Then she turned to Mitch and Heather. 'I noticed there was wallpaper in the bedrooms. How would you feel if we ripped it off?'

'Ripped it off?' Heather said in a faint voice, looking very much like someone who had accidentally stepped into quicksand and was uncertain what their next move should be.

'I saw a movie once where they ripped up the wallpaper and there was a secret message written behind it.'

'The only thing I've ever seen under wallpaper is more wallpaper,' Mitch retorted. 'Why would anyone write a message there?'

'Not anyone... Peggy Barlow. We know she lived here so who is to say she didn't write something?'

'Because most people don't deface the walls... spy or no.' Mitch folded his arms together and looked mulish.

'If you ask me, it's a wasted opportunity, but it's your call.' Tuppence patted his arm.

'Tuppence is right... not about ripping off the wallpaper, which I don't hold with, but about us needing to figure out what the connection is,' JM said.

'It's something we can research,' Ginny said.

'I'll add it to the list.' Tuppence scribbled the words down then peered around. 'Though that reminds me that we also need to look at the CCTV footage.'

'I only have two cameras.' Mitch pointed to a shelf behind the bar and another by the front door. 'The police have already asked about it and I've sent them a copy. I am sure if anything untoward was happening, they would have found it.'

'Oh, you're sure, are you?' JM gave him a stern look. 'Do you think they are searching for secret codes? Or spies? Or mysterious strangers? Not that I'm questioning their methods, but it's hard for them to investigate fully when they are not in the possession of the facts.'

Mitch ran a hand through his dark hair. Then shrugged. 'Okay, fine. You can look at the footage, but please don't get in Wallace's way.'

'Wallace won't even know we're here. We'll be as discreet as, er... whatever something really discreet can be.' Tuppence bounced to her feet, with her usual inexhaustible energy. 'Now, where is it?'

'Wait... you can't look at it now.' Mitch's eyes widened and Heather looked equally alarmed. 'We're still in service and I've already let you go through the place. I'll get it for you once I've finished for the night.'

'Oh.' Tuppence sat back down. 'You mean we should come back after closing time? Because while I appreciate the dramatics and adventure... that is a bit late for me.'

His jaw flickered and he shook his head. 'Not tonight. Come back tomorrow. In the afternoon,' he added quickly. 'It's always quiet after Saturday lunch so I'll shut the pub for a couple of hours. Let's say two o'clock.'

'Jolly good. I am much more energetic during the day.' Tuppence beamed in approval. 'And we need to get a list together of everyone who came to last Sunday's quiz night.'

'I can do that,' he promised then headed back to the bar where a customer was waiting. Once he was out of earshot they turned back to the beer mats, where Tuppence was busily writing a title on each one.

Break-in. Mysterious meeting. MI5. Nathan Richardson. Peggy Barlow. Suspects. No Austen. Windscale.

She added the one that said *Code* to the pile.

Beneath each was a blank space just waiting for the details to be filled in.

'So, what's the plan?' Hen asked.

'The most important thing is finding out who Nathan was meeting and what they discussed,' Ginny said, her mind sifting through the little they did know.

It all centred around Nathan's death. Was it really an accident, or was it tied to his decision to look into Peggy Barlow? And if it was connected, it led to the bigger question of why it still mattered more than sixty years later. Sylvie's words came back to her.

All I know is that she was scared of something.

'It sounds like we need to do some research,' JM said in a firm voice. 'Ginny, are you working tomorrow?'

'Yes. I'm on until two, so I can come straight to the pub after my shift. And while I'm there I will get some reference books and see what newspapers we have in the stacks. Sylvie told us that Peggy moved to Little Shaw in 1962 and left in '63, so those are the dates I'll focus on.'

'I hope they survived the fire,' Tuppence said.

Ginny shuddered. She hated thinking of the fire that had almost destroyed the storage area at the back of the library, known as the stacks. It had since been rebuilt and while some of the books and newspapers had survived, part of the collection had been destroyed.

'We can cross that bridge when we come to it. In the meantime, may I suggest that we each take a beer mat home and see what we can find out. Then we can meet up tomorrow at the library and go over everything.' JM picked up the beer mats and shuffled them despite their uneven sizes, then she dealt them one each, like a poker game.

Obediently Ginny picked up the closest beer mat. On one side was a very large drawing of a fish, and underneath were the words: *Red Herring Ale… so good you could drink it all day.*

Ginny hoped that it wasn't an omen. Still, there was no point being superstitious so she flipped it over and studied it.

No Austen.

Despite the sad circumstances, she couldn't help but smile. She had three different editions of *Pride and Prejudice* and while Eric had often teased her over her addiction to buying pretty copies of the same book, she was pleased she had.

As soon as she got home, she would see if any of them held the answer to the cipher on the back of the photograph. And with that she tucked it into her purse and helped the others clean the table before heading out to the late afternoon gloom.

ELEVEN

Saturday, October 17

Ginny gently picked Edgar up from off the top of *My Man Jeeves* and resettled him on a kitchen chair. 'I thought you had left this destructive book behaviour behind.'

Edgar yawned in response.

'Are you protesting that I've finished reading the book out loud, or that you didn't like it?' She retrieved the book from the floor and slipped it onto the shelf before turning back to the pile of Eric's history books that she'd left on the kitchen table. Now, if Edgar wanted to knock one of them onto the ground so that it conveniently opened on a useful page, she wouldn't be mad about it.

Last night she had spent several hours searching for any mention of Little Shaw and MI5, but she hadn't been able to find anything.

Next to the pile were the three copies of *Pride and Prejudice*. They were all published before 1962, but none of them had borne fruit. She stared at the three messages that had resulted from her deciphering attempts.

Jane. Ball. Mr Collins. No.

Carriage. Regiment. Sister. Cough.
Musical. Mud. Tolerable. Fortune.

Sighing, Ginny slipped the books back onto the shelf. There were more copies at the library she could try, but she didn't even know if *Pride and Prejudice* was the correct book... let alone what edition had been used when the cipher was created.

For the first time in her life, she wished her favourite author was a little *less* popular.

Sighing, she checked the clock. It was time to leave.

'I'm afraid ciphers and Jane Austen will have to wait until I've opened the library and finished my tasks,' she told Edgar.

Edgar blinked and went back to sleep. Ginny gave him an affectionate pat and stepped outside. She tried to leave the car at home whenever possible, but after agreeing to go power walking tomorrow she decided to drive. Plus, it would let her take out more history books to continue researching tonight.

Feeling justified, she climbed in and made the short trip to her job.

Despite the dull sky, the park next door to the library was full and high-pitched squeals rang out as children made the most of the weather before it got too cold to play outside. The library had been built as a Victorian parish school with high windows, rough stone walls, and narrow flower beds outside it. Parts of it had been modernised including a wide cement path and a large after-hours returns slot cut into the side wall.

Parked in front of the slot was a wheelchair with red ribbons wrapped around the spokes. And the owner of the wheelchair was leaning perilously forward, trying to push a book through the slot, while a pile of books sat in his lap. It was Slim's friend, Charlie, and she hurried up to him.

'Oh dear, I didn't realise you couldn't get close enough. Here, let me.' Ginny held out her hands for the remaining books and Charlie flushed.

'Don't blame yourself, it's this chair. I'm on a waiting list for a better one,' he told her in a deep baritone voice. He had a wide stomach and long dark hair that hung down his back in a wave. It was remarkably shiny and thick considering he must be around her own age.

'If there is a problem with our accessibility, please let me know,' Ginny said, her hands still out. 'But I'm happy to take the books for you.'

'You're a gem. Thank you.' He passed over a pile of non-fiction books. Her arms protested at the weight and she readjusted them, noticing the top title. *The Greatest Great Train Robbery*. 'I have been poorly of late, but it has meant I've had loads more time to read.'

'A silver lining.' Ginny smiled. She never got tired of hearing about people rediscovering their love of books. 'Slim will be here in half an hour, when we officially open. But if you would like to wait inside until he arrives, you are more than welcome.'

Charlie shook his head, long hair dancing around his shoulders. 'That's very kind of you, but my daughter and the grandkids are at the park and we're heading to Blackpool in a minute. Not often she gets the day off work and she wanted to take her old man out. But Slim has the list of the new books I'm after and he'll bring them along to the quiz tomorrow night. Speaking of which, I heard the Merry Widows had to pull out so you can work.'

'I'm afraid so,' Ginny agreed, not really surprised that the news had already spread around the village. There wasn't much that stayed a secret in Little Shaw.

'That's what I call a win/win. You're helping Mitch and Heather, and helping us out by not competing,' he chortled, then without another word he unlocked the brakes on his wheelchair and rolled away in the direction of the park. As soon as he was out of sight, she lowered the heavy pile of books down and searched for her swipe card and keys. The rest of the titles had a similar theme, except they involved a diamond heist, a pearl heist and, of all things, a feather heist.

It seemed that these days you could heist just about anything.

Ginny bit her lip, remembering what Charlie's occupation had been. A safe-cracker. She hoped these were for leisure reading, and that his criminal days were behind him.

Once the door was unlocked, she carried in the books and went through the morning opening ritual before it was time to let in the public. Slim arrived not long after, followed by Cleo and Andrea who were still talking about the Quiz Killer.

'It's like I can feel their eyes on me *all* the time,' Cleo complained in a loud voice. 'I swear I haven't slept since it happened.'

'All the time,' Andrea echoed.

Oh dear. Ginny wanted to remind them there was no proof that Nathan had been murdered. Yet, what she and her friends were doing was no different from all of Cleo and Andrea's speculations. She winced. Probably best not to examine that particular thought too deeply.

She waited until the volunteers had settled into their morning routine of shelving books before telling Slim she was going out to the stacks. He was happy to man the desk so she made her way out of the library and down the lane that led to the new storage area. The advantage of having to rescue the items that survived the fire was that everything was exactly where it was meant to be, and she quickly located the copies of the local newspaper and let out a small sigh of relief as she checked the dates.

Back then it had come out weekly, and there, in pristine condition were fifty copies from 1962, as well as a bumper Christmas edition. It was the same for the following year, and Ginny piled them all onto her trolley and returned to the main library, where Slim was busy issuing a large stack of books, though there was no customer standing in front of him.

The smile that had been on her lips faded as she caught sight of the words *The Dastardly Black Truffle Heist*.

'You okay, Mrs Cole? You look like someone just nicked your last fiver.'

'Who are these books for?' Ginny tried to school her features—after all, it wasn't her place to judge, but it was hard not to worry about Slim, who had been doing so well lately.

'They're for Charlie. I hope that's okay. I have his card. It's on account of his disability, he doesn't get much time in here.'

'It's not that,' Ginny protested, though overall she didn't like people letting others use their library cards, but at least Charlie had a legitimate reason. 'It's just I noticed he returned a lot of... er... books on criminal activity this morning, and I don't mean to judge, but I would hate for you to get tangled up in anything, if he was still trying to—'

'Return to a life of crime? Don't worry about that.' Slim finished scanning the books and grinned. At least she hadn't offended him, but the niggle remained.

'Are you sure?'

'One hundred and fifty percent.' Slim picked up the next book that had a cruise ship on the cover and a photograph of a man dangling over the side, and the title *High Sea Heist* running along the top. 'Truth is that Charlie's got the writing bug. Just like me. So, he's studying his comparative titles before starting his own heist books. It's going to be for his grandkids. I think he feels guilty about not being around much for his own family. To think it's all because of me and my new leaf.'

Ginny blinked at the pride in Slim's voice.

And it was very well deserved. Slim had started writing his own story not long after he joined them at the library but lately, he hadn't mentioned it, and she had assumed he had lost interest. She heard that was a thing with some first-time authors.

'I'm pleased to hear it and sorry if I over-stepped.' She bit back her guilt.

'Nah. Don't worry about it. Seems weird to me as well, especially the part where I'm considered a good influence.'

'How is the writing going?'

He gave her a rueful look and scanned the last of the books. 'Not as fast as I would like. I didn't realise it would take so much research. I swear that if a copper ever looked at my internet search history, I'd be back in jail before I knew what was happening. Last night I was trying to find the best way to build a bomb. There are some amazing websites, not to mention YouTube. Your Tuppence would love it.'

Ginny wasn't sure it was a good idea for Tuppence to go looking for a way to build her own bomb and was just about to say so when Slim's words fully hit.

Search history.

She peered around at the returns room, where she had first found the books that Nathan had returned before his death. Oh, she was a fool not to have thought of it sooner.

The photograph had been in a book, yet it hadn't occurred to her for a minute that the same book might be what she needed to decode the numbers. The sequence crashed into her mind. It was the clue she hadn't been able to unlock.

147-3-2, 89-12-7, 203-8-4, 156-15-3.

But now it was so obvious. Excitement darted up her spine as she hurried to the computer and tapped at the keyboard. Nathan had returned three books before he died. But why had he borrowed them? Was it because he suspected one of them was the cipher Peggy Barlow had used to leave her message on the back of that photograph? Ginny certainly hoped so.

TWELVE

Ginny stared at the screen.

The History of Little Shaw, Little Shaw Architecture Through the Ages and *Little Shaw from the Industrial Revolution to Now,* had been returned last week, and all of them had been immediately issued to the one person. Callum Lovelace.

She frowned and clicked through to the next screen so she could check the time of issue.

They had gone back out the same day that she had processed them. It wasn't uncommon for the recently returned books to be issued again quickly, since they were shelved in a separate area, but it was the new releases that usually went first, not heavy books on local history that were over sixty years old.

She didn't recognise the name and couldn't recall seeing him in the library before. Then again, she hadn't seen Nathan either. She supposed it was the downside of the self-issue machines that had finally become popular with some of their patrons.

Trying not to let it get to her, Ginny checked the catalogue in the hope that they had multiple copies of the three books that Nathan had returned. They did not. Part of her longed to call

Callum Lovelace and ask him to return the books immediately so she could decipher the code, but she didn't dare abuse her powers. And she knew how outlandish it would sound to ring someone up and ask them to help decipher a secret code that might be part of a murder investigation.

It was just a pity that Harold was away in Provence doing a cookery course with his husband, Myles. Though she suspected Myles would be doing the cooking while Harold explored the countryside. Still, she could have used Harold's expertise, not to mention his book collection, which was sure to have a copy of each of the books.

Short of breaking into his lovely house, there wasn't much she could do.

Biting back her frustration, she cleared the screen just as her friends trailed into the library and made their way to one of the long reading tables.

'Don't even think about it.' JM's loud voice was directed at the magazine rack. Ginny followed her gaze to where Esme and Elsie were both lurking behind a collection of *Lovely Lancashire Gardens,* as if hoping to overhear something.

Oh dear. She hurried over to the two elderly sisters and told them about the new books that she had finished cataloguing yesterday. 'They're still behind the counter, but if you ask Slim to bring the trolley out, you are welcome to look at them before anyone else does.'

'Hear that, Elsie? Ginny has new books we can look at. It's nice to know that at least *someone* cares about us,' Esme huffed, shooting JM a dark glance before they both ambled away.

'Poor things, they probably only wanted to help,' Hen said.

'They can help me by staying on the other side of the room,' JM retorted as she brought out the beer mats and spread them on the table. 'The last thing we need is the pair of them telling tales to Wallace.'

Ginny opened her mouth to protest but quickly shut it again.

That was exactly the sort of thing that the two sisters *would* do, not out of malice but rather out of an overactive sense of... something.

'How did we all go with our assignments?' Tuppence lowered her voice and pushed a sketch book onto the table. 'I thought I would paint pictures instead of writing notes. In case I was intercepted. All this talk of spy craft seemed like a reminder to be careful.'

'Oh, that's a good idea.' Hen smoothed out her own piece of paper and gave it a doubtful look. 'I suppose I could swallow mine if push came to shove.'

'It's amazing what people are capable of when forced into a high-pressure situation. I for one have memorised all my information. I find it's safest not to leave a paper trail.' JM tapped her scalp to indicate her excellent memory.

Ginny wrinkled her nose and showed them her three attempts at deciphering the code. 'I'm sorry I didn't think to conceal it. Mind you, considering I was using the wrong books, I suppose it doesn't matter. In better news, I think I've discovered what book we *should* be using.'

'You found it? How wonderful.' Hen clapped before putting her hand over her mouth and sinking back down so that her chin was resting on the table. For some reason JM and Tuppence followed suit, leaving Ginny with no other choice but to do the same. She couldn't help but think of the Hungry Hippo game.

'Yes and no.' Ginny tried not to feel awkward in the new position as she explained what had happened, and the fact that until the books were returned, or Harold came back from his break, there wasn't much they could do.

'Another holiday?' JM scowled. 'It seems excessive.'

'He has had a busy year now he is on the parish council. And in his defence, he didn't know we would need him.'

'I've been working on my lockpicking, if you *do* change your mind about breaking in,' Tuppence said in a hopeful voice.

'Sorry, I think we will just have to wait.'

'Nonsense, why can't we visit the man and ask for the books?' JM demanded in a stage whisper. 'What do we know about him?'

'Callum Lovelace? He's very nice,' Hen assured them.

'Yes, everyone knows Dr Lovelace. At one time he was our only GP before that new surgery opened by the supermarket. He retired a couple of years ago and lives in Acton Manor. It's a gorgeous old building on the way to the hospital, been in the family for generations. The one with all the roses,' Tuppence explained.

'Oh, I know the chap. We did a garden tour there,' JM said, voice rising enough to attract Esme and Elsie's attention. At the desk, Slim seemed to notice and waved a book at them, clearly trying to throw them off the scent.

'How old is he?' Ginny asked, her mind trying to think of why a retired doctor might be interested in Nathan's library books. 'Was he somehow involved with what happened to Peggy Barlow all those years ago?'

'He must be seventy-five. Which means, oh—' Hen wrinkled her nose, as if concentrating. 'He was only a boy when Peggy was in Little Shaw.'

'Doesn't mean he can't be involved. What if he's trying to protect a mysterious secret?' JM suggested.

'Go on... What kind of mysterious secret?' Tuppence's eyes glowed with excitement.

'That I couldn't tell you,' JM admitted.

'Is there another reason he might want to borrow the same local history books that Nathan had?' Ginny wondered, almost to herself.

'Actually, I did hear that he's trying to write his own book.' Tuppence raised an eyebrow. 'He was talking about it last Saturday afternoon when he was having a cup of tea with some of the Historical Society members. They were in that new tearoom that's just opened up. Actually, he's the history expert for the Archivists quiz team.'

'History expert?' JM raised an eyebrow. 'And you didn't think to mention that sooner?'

'I only just remembered it,' Tuppence admitted before sitting up and rolling her shoulders. 'All this slouching is stopping my mind from functioning at its optimal levels.'

The rest of them straightened up too and Ginny could feel the circulation returning to her shoulders as she considered what Tuppence had said. Not only was Callum Lovelace in one of the quiz teams, but he was an expert on history... and writing a book.

Maybe JM was right about the mysterious secret?

'Did he say what the book is about?'

'Not in words I could understand,' Tuppence admitted. 'But it sounded dry and boring. Which reminds me, if he does publish it, you might want to put him off from doing an author visit at the library. He'd send everyone to sleep.'

Ginny wrinkled her nose. She was always keen to showcase local authors, even when they weren't quite so engaging in their day-to-day lives. After all, wasn't that why they preferred to write in the first place?

But she would dearly love to know more about this book. Could it have something to do with Peggy Barlow?

Perhaps he saw Nathan as competition? After all, a biography of an MI5 spy written by a great-nephew, who held a PhD, might be better received than something written by a retired local doctor.

'Let's add him to a beer mat.' Tuppence reached for her pencil case and picked up a beer mat with a black sheep on one side. She flipped it over and wrote his name down. 'Our first suspect. Now, would you like to hear what I found out?'

'Oh, yes please.' Hen picked up her knitting and once again the soft click of her needles filled the space.

'My mission... which I chose to accept was researching the Windscale disaster.' Tuppence flicked open the pad to show a pencil sketch of a nuclear power plant, with huge plumes of smoke rising up.

Ginny's eyes widened. She hadn't been alive in 1957, but she had heard about the dreadful fire that had happened in the Cumbrian plant.

Next to her, Hen shivered. 'It was the worst nuclear accident in the United Kingdom. Radioactive material was released into the atmosphere and was considered responsible for several hundred cancer-related deaths. But how is it tied to international relations?'

Tuppence turned the page and showed a gaggle of people wearing dark suits all running towards a finish line. 'It's believed that it was part of the arms race that developed during that period. It's possible the government cut corners, but I really couldn't say. Not with so many eyes and ears on us.'

Eyes and ears? Ginny swivelled around but Esme and Elsie were engrossed with the new books and currently had them spread out across the carpet, blocking anyone from using the self-issue machines. And the only other person nearby was one of their legally deaf patrons.

JM tapped her chin. 'As the oldest, I have the best memory of it, and while it was a terrible tragedy I'm not sure how it fits with Peggy Barlow. It happened five years before she moved to Little Shaw, and Cumbria is over one hundred miles away.'

Tuppence wrinkled her nose. 'Well, yes, there is that. But it must be important if Nathan wrote it down.'

'What if it was for the quiz?' Hen asked.

'Good point,' JM agreed. 'Though it's useful for us to know some backstory. Unfortunately, it doesn't leave us with much to go on. My own mission was to research Nathan, but apart from finding information about his thesis—on Victorian burial rituals— he lived a very analogue life with barely any digital footprint. Thank goodness for my genealogy software. After a little digging I discovered that his parents are both dead and there are no other living relatives.'

'What about Peggy Barlow?' Ginny asked. 'Did she come up in the family tree?'

JM nodded. 'Yes, she was definitely his maternal great-aunt. I will tell you what I did find strange, was that there was no death certificate. However, if she was still alive, she would be eighty-nine years old.'

'The fact Nathan did his doctoral thesis on the Victorians suggests he was attached to the history department, which explains his interest in finding out about Peggy,' Ginny pointed out and Tuppence obediently jotted everything down before turning to Hen and giving her an encouraging smile to go next.

'My assignment was about the break-in, so I called Heather to see if she remembered anything else, but she just reiterated that nothing was taken. She is convinced it was just someone trying to cause trouble. I can't help wondering if they were looking for something though.'

'It's like in a painting where we focus on the negative space,' Tuppence agreed, then she wrinkled her nose. 'Not that I'm sure how to do that when it comes to break-ins.'

'I think we've spent enough time reporting in,' JM announced, suddenly sitting back up. 'Let's start researching. Ginny, how did you go with the newspapers?'

'Very well.' She stood and retrieved her trolley, which she had left in her office, to ensure that none of the regular customers helped themselves. She returned several minutes later. 'Here is every edition published over the two-year period that Peggy Barlow lived in Little Shaw.'

'Oh, well done.' Hen put down her knitting to clap her hands. 'Talk about a stroke of good luck.'

'If you call it good luck to have to read through one hundred-odd newspapers with a dubious grasp of the English language, then far be it from me to argue the point,' JM said, clearly still remembering some of their other research sessions that involved later editions of the paper, which were little more than puff pieces.

'It might not be so bad.' Tuppence reached for one. 'And the sooner we start, the sooner we will know what they contain.'

With that, Ginny took her library trolley and brought over a collection of local history books and all the copies of *Pride and Prejudice* that they had on the shelf. Then she excused herself to join Slim at the counter while her friends huddled around the long table, trying to ignore Elsie and Esme, who had resumed their hovering.

'Those two are asking for trouble. If I was a betting man, I'd say JM would be about to pick a fight,' Slim commented, glancing over at them, as he put a pile of books on the counter. Ginny grimaced, but before she was forced to intervene, the two sisters disappeared back into the 600s. At least that was one crisis averted.

The rest of the morning passed in peace, and Ginny managed to slip over to the table several times to see how they were faring. After JM's initial fears about the quality of the articles were waylaid, they had worked out a system to skim over each page quickly before moving on. And it meant that by the time her friends packed up to leave for lunch they had gone through a third of the papers.

'Not a sausage.' Tuppence stood and rolled her shoulders to shake out the knots. 'Though someone has graffitied the society page section, giving all the women horns and tails. Makes me realise that not a lot has changed.'

'Not a lot has changed?' JM's eyebrow shot up. 'The ones I read were full of advertisements for telegrams, typewriters and tobacco.'

'It's so funny looking back on it all,' Hen agreed before holding up one newspaper. 'I didn't find anything either, and Ginny, I hate to tell you that this one has a page missing.'

'See, I told you nothing's changed. It's just like when I go to the doctor's office and no matter how early I am, someone has already cut out the crossword or the best recipes,' Tuppence complained. 'People always steal the good stuff.'

'It is a nuisance,' Ginny agreed, taking the paper, even though there wasn't much she could do. 'How about you put the ones you have checked on the bottom of the trolley and we can go through the others on Monday. I'll keep them locked up in my office so they are safe.'

'Very wise,' agreed JM. 'In the meantime, I suggest we visit Callum Lovelace before we have to meet Mitch at the pub.'

However, Ginny—who had visions of them tearing the books from his possession and accusing him of murder—managed to convince them to wait, at least until they had looked at the CCTV footage.

'That way we will have a better idea of who Nathan spoke to.'

Her logic seemed to work and her friends promised not to visit the retired doctor just yet. Ginny blew out her breath and pushed the trolley of newspapers into her office before locking it.

They hadn't been as helpful as she had hoped, which meant it would be up to the CCTV to give them the answers they needed.

THIRTEEN

Saturday, October 17

Slim insisted that he was happy to close the library, allowing Ginny to leave a few minutes before two o'clock to make the short drive to the pub. In the carpark were three small silver cars almost identical to her own, which meant her friends had already arrived. She pulled up next to them and made her way to the kitchen door at the back, which was where Mitch had told them to enter.

The heavenly smell of onions and garlic enveloped her as she peered in.

'Ginny. Good to see you.' Heather appeared from a large walk-in fridge holding a container. 'Mitch is through in the office, and everyone else is here. I've made a pot of tea and as soon as the prep is done, I'll send in some pastries.'

'Please don't go to any trouble. We're here to help... not cause more work. And you must be tired after your lunch shift.'

'Nonsense. It's nice to be back to business as usual. Plus, I have three of my coven sisters in the kitchen. As soon as they heard how short-staffed we were, they insisted. It's amazing how generous people can be.'

'I'm so pleased,' Ginny said. 'I'll go through and see them now, and I promise we won't do anything to cause trouble.'

'Of course you won't,' Heather said hotly. 'Mitch told me he had been worried, which is such nonsense. If something did happen to poor Nathan, it's our duty to get to the bottom of it. My coven believes that: "An' ye harm none, do what ye will." It means we always consider our actions before we go ahead. I know that you, Hen, Tuppence and JM operate the same way. You help people and leave them better than you found them.'

'Thank you. We certainly try to.' Her throat tightened at the unexpected compliment.

Heather smiled and headed over to the workbench, leaving Ginny to make her way into the main bar. The office was off to one side of it, and she followed the voices.

'We're just looking at the CCTV footage now,' Hen said by way of greeting and pointed to the computer screen. It was all in black and white and some of the figures were blurred as they moved around the pub, holding onto drinks.

'Nathan worked the lunch and evening shift, so we've started at the beginning,' Tuppence added and reached for another beer mat. 'I've been making a list of everyone in the pub. It seems like most of the village was here at one point or another. Ohhh... is that the new hairdresser who has a mobile van?'

'Yes, that's her,' JM confirmed and leaned forward to get closer to the screen. 'We'd only just started the lunch shift here. At this rate it will take all day.'

'I have sped it up but can make it go even faster,' Mitch said hopefully as he glanced at the clock on the wall.

'Not too fast or it will make everyone blurry.' Hen shook her head.

'What if you show us how to operate it, then we can go through it ourselves,' Ginny tactfully suggested, aware that he must have other things to do, even with Heather's coven helping in the kitchen.

He looked relieved as he showed them how to operate the

computer then reached for a piece of paper. 'I've made a list of all the quiz teams who took part last Sunday, too.'

'Excellent. I will add them to our murder board.' Tuppence took it, her eyes still glued to the computer screen. She let out a little gasp. 'Look, there's Eric from The Quizard of Oz with a plate of sausage and mash. That is very suspicious.'

'Is it?' Mitch frowned. 'He often comes with his family for Sunday lunch. Said he loves Heather's gravy almost as much as he loves quiz nights.'

'It is jolly good gravy,' Tuppence conceded before uncapping a green pen. 'But we still need to make a note of it.'

'Has anyone spoken to Nathan? Other than just when he is pouring them drinks? Or does he disappear for a period of time?' Ginny studied the screen and the growing list of names on the beer mats. Maybe they needed one called Needle and Haystack?

'This footage is from twelve-thirty, but Nathan's shift didn't start until one pm,' Mitch said then pointed. 'Look, there he is. I don't mean to cast a damper over this, but don't forget there are only two cameras, which means we have blind spots.'

Ginny had been worried about that and as she studied the screen, it was easy to see that if someone knew where the cameras were, they could avoid them. Still, beggars couldn't be choosers and this was all they had.

'We'll bear that in mind,' she told him.

'Okay, well, I have some prep to do for tomorrow, including going over all the quiz questions. I'm a little bit nervous about how it will go.' Mitch got to his feet.

'You will do a wonderful job and it's a lovely way to honour Nathan,' Ginny assured him, and after he left, she was the one who kept her finger hovering over the buttons as they continued to study the footage.

It was slow going as they watched Nathan serve drinks and take lunch orders. He could be seen chatting to customers across the bar, but never for very long. It went on and on, and Ginny started to appreciate just how much time went into this kind of research.

Her respect for the police increased even more.

Finally, his lunch shift was over and the quiz teams began to come into the pub.

The film dragged and Ginny could feel her limbs getting restless. She was usually good at sitting still, but there was something unnerving about watching what they now knew was Nathan's last shift. Sighing, she tried to focus on him as he carried a tray of Guiness to a round table where three people were deep in conversation.

She turned to JM. 'Is it usual for him to do table service? We always go to the bar to order our drinks.'

'Yes, but Guinness takes a long time to pour so it's not uncommon to deliver it. But... look, he's stopping to talk with them.'

They were all silent as they watched Nathan hover around the table for several minutes, attempting what appeared to be a one-way conversation.

'I wonder what he's asking them?' Hen said.

'Whatever it is, they don't like it. Look how sour-faced they are,' Tuppence pointed out.

'Who are they?' JM asked. 'I don't remember seeing them last week.'

'The Archivists. They are serious quizzers and always wipe the floor when it comes to history questions,' Hen said. 'Though it doesn't seem like Callum Lovelace is there. There are only three of them.'

'But they ordered four drinks.' Ginny studied the screen. 'Did that mean they were expecting him to show up?'

'More than likely. We all know how hard the quiz is without having a history expert there.' Tuppence shuddered. 'And when I heard him speaking last Saturday, I'm sure he mentioned he would be there.'

'So, where was he? Busy setting up a trap for Nathan in the

cellar?' JM made a clicking noise with her tongue. 'It's one of the many questions I have for them.'

'That's if they talk to us. They're very fussy, but Ginny's so smart I think they will make an exception,' Tuppence said.

Ginny could feel warmth hit her cheeks. 'I'm really not. Eric was much better at history than I ever was. I seem to have the knack of remembering things, that is all.'

'You're too modest,' JM said in a stern voice. 'You should accept the compliment.'

'JM's right. It's time we owned our talents,' Tuppence agreed, but Ginny managed to avoid answering. She didn't think anything she did *could* be described as a talent. At the most, she was efficient, punctual and didn't like to see anyone upset. But she doubted those skills could be called anything more than ordinary.

She turned back to the footage and stopped several times to make a note of people that Nathan spoke to. Tuppence added it to a separate beer mat as Mitch popped his head into the office to say he and Heather needed to go out.

'We open at six pm, and will be back before then,' he said. 'Are you still okay to all work tonight? We have Heather's coven for the kitchen, but it's only me doing front of house.'

'Of course,' JM assured him.

Ginny inwardly winced. They hadn't even finished going through the footage. Once Mitch left she turned to her friends. 'I suggest we move it along so we can get to the end.'

They all concurred and after a bit of fiddling, Ginny managed to increase the speed, and they were soon watching Nathan, Mitch and Heather zoom back and forth behind the bar as if they were on skateboards.

'Wait... what's that?' Hen yelped and pointed to the screen as an almost blurry Nathan appeared from the cellar door holding a crate of wine bottles. He was followed by a large man with an angry scowl on his face.

Her breath caught, and she rewound the footage and made a note of the time stamp. It was from seven in the evening... almost four hours before Nathan's death. She pressed play and this time the man's features were clearly visible. He had a round face, a bald head and the shoulders of an aging rugby player. She had seen him around the village but had no idea who he was.

Hen let out a soft gasp. 'It's Ned Warner. He was the ex-editor of the local newspaper and never let anyone look at his archives.'

Ginny's skin prickled. Had Nathan been talking to him about Peggy Barlow? After all, judging by his age, Ned Warner could well have been working as a young reporter in the sixties. She paused the footage as her friends all spoke at once.

'Oh dear. I wonder what they were talking about?'

'Damn. I knew I should have been practising my lipreading.'

'I have no time for secretive conversations.'

Ginny's mind churned with her own set of questions. Why had Ned been with Nathan in the cellar? Was it to do with his aunt? Or could it be plain old-fashioned bribery? After all, she had seen enough of it going on last week. Maybe his team, Hold the Front Page, had nominated him to deliver the bribe? Either way, they couldn't avoid confronting him now.

She opened her mouth but before any words came out, footsteps sounded from out in the bar.

That was strange.

Mitch and Heather weren't due back yet. Unless they were early. She quickly got to her feet just as an all too familiar face appeared in the office door.

Detective Inspector James Wallace.

FOURTEEN

Saturday, October 17

'I hope I'm not interrupting anything,' Wallace said in a cool voice, his sharp eyes seeming to take in everything about the small office.

Ginny swallowed and fiddled with the computer mouse so she could minimise the screen while JM smoothly stepped in front of her, blocking Wallace from the CCTV footage. At the same time Hen gave him a wide smile and threw the long scarf she had been knitting over the coloured marker pens and scattered beer mats, while Tuppence, who had been in the process of reading the list of teams who had attended last week's quiz, quickly began to fold it up until it resembled a sailor's hat. She put it on her curls.

'That's better. William dared me to dress like a pirate today. Now, we will see who has the last laugh,' Tuppence announced and bustled Wallace out of the office. 'Speaking of laughing... we had better leave. It's bad luck to stay in here too long.'

'Is that a pirate superstition?' Wallace arched an eyebrow but allowed himself to be led back around the bar. Ginny gave Tuppence a grateful nod for thinking so quickly on her feet. It was the exact thing that William, one of the older library regulars, *would* dare someone to do.

'Exactly so. Everyone knows pirates don't like confined spaces,' Tuppence assured him.

'It comes from ye olde times,' Hen added, almost pushing him around to the other side of the bar, while JM donned one of the large white aprons they were required to wear.

'How could I forget? Dare I ask why the four of you are here?'

'We're helping out until they get more staff.' Tuppence used her hand to dust away an imaginary spot on the bar. Something flickered across Wallace's face as he ground his jaw together. Oh dear. Maybe they were trying too hard to cover their tracks?

Ginny glanced over to the main entrance, which was still locked. 'How did you get in? It's thirty minutes until opening time.'

'I came through the kitchen.'

'I'm afraid we can't serve you until six o'clock,' JM said in a stern voice.

'When is Mitch back?' Wallace said, ignoring the statement.

'We can't possibly say. It's a privacy issue, as I'm sure you will understand. On account of being a detective and all,' Tuppence informed him.

'Can we help with something?' Ginny quickly added as a small vein in the side of his temple began to throb. Her own panic increased. Was this about Nathan?

He was silent for several seconds, as if trying to decide, then handed over a folded-up piece of paper. 'I want to know if this person came into the bar yesterday.'

Yesterday?

Ginny's relief was overwhelming. This was clearly about a separate case.

'Well, you're in luck. Tuppence and I worked the lunch shift.' JM reached for the paper and unfolded it.

'Not that Ginny and Hen were doing anything they shouldn't have been doing. Obviously,' Tuppence added with a bright smile, but Wallace didn't seem to notice as he waited intently for JM to inspect the photograph printed on the sheet of paper. It further confirmed Ginny's suspicion it was connected to a separate case.

She leaned closer.

It was of a man in his mid-thirties with a trimmed beard. JM and Tuppence both studied the photograph before shaking their heads in unison.

'Sorry, if he was in here, I didn't see him,' Tuppence said.

'Nor I.' JM's answer was definitive.

Wallace gritted his teeth. 'It could have been in the evening. Please show it to Mitch and Heather and ask them to call me if they saw him.'

'Why? What's it about?' JM wanted to know.

'Just give them the message,' Wallace said, ignoring the challenging look that was being thrown at him.

'Of course,' Ginny assured him quickly. 'Though if you want to wait, he won't be long.'

'I don't have time.'

'Or you can give it to him yourself at tomorrow's quiz,' Hen added.

'I won't be going,' he simply said and turned back towards the kitchen.

'Won't be there? Oh, let me guess... date night with the lovely pathologist?' Tuppence teased.

'Don't forget.' Wallace met the question with a blank stare.

'We won't.' Ginny had given up trying to read the detective's stony gaze, but part of her couldn't help but worry that he was deeply bothered about something that had nothing to do with Nathan's death.

Was it the imminent arrival of his father, or had something happened with his relationship with Imogen? Either way, she hoped not. He'd been very closed off and prickly when they first met but lately, she had seen him softening as he let people into his life. She would hate if he regressed. Still, there wasn't much she could do about it right now.

She waited until he was gone before putting the picture into Mitch's office on top of his keyboard where he could see it. Then she returned to her friends, who were discussing the news that May the Force be With You wouldn't be defending their three-week winning streak.

'I expect there will be a few complaints. Victory isn't as sweet if the title holders aren't there to contest it,' Tuppence explained sagely.

'I have no time for that kind of nonsense,' JM said. 'Besides, Wallace's team won't be the only no-shows. We won't be able to compete either.'

How many other teams would stay away? If none of them came, it would make the job of looking for answers more difficult. Though their absence might in turn suggest something. She grimaced. *Oh dear.* Now she was sounding like Esme and Elsie, turning everything into a mysterious knot, instead of just accepting it at face value.

Sighing, she returned to the office. They hadn't finished going through the footage, but she reluctantly shut down the computer just as the others followed her.

'We'd better get this place tidied up.' Hen packed away her discarded knitting while Tuppence rounded up the beer mats she had been using to make notes.

'More importantly, we need a plan. Someone needs to speak with Callum Lovelace, and then there is Ned Warner.' JM plucked the beer mats from Tuppence and flicked through them. 'I for one don't think we should wait until tomorrow night's quiz.'

'Ned usually comes into the pub on a Saturday night. We could question him while we're working,' Hen suggested before frowning. 'But I've only ever seen Callum come in for the quiz, so I doubt we'll have him in here tonight.'

'In that case we'd better go to him,' Tuppence said.

'Except we promised Mitch we would work,' Hen reminded them.

'That's easily solved,' JM announced. 'Heather has her coven helping in the kitchen, and I'm sure three of us could manage the bar, leaving one of us free to go. I would offer to do it myself but as the most experienced bartender, I feel duty bound to stay here.'

'I could go.' Tuppence's eyes flashed with excitement before dimming. 'Though I had better get a good disguise.'

'A disguise? But you've known Callum as long as I have.' Hen's nose wrinkled. 'I hope you're not thinking of wearing the horse costume from last year's pantomime.'

'You don't think it would work?' Tuppence's shoulders sagged.

'Sorry, I don't like to dampen the mood, but I can't see it helping,' Hen admitted, guilt filling her large eyes.

'What's this about disguises? I thought he was a lovely chap,' JM said.

'He is. Very lovely,' Hen quickly defended before sighing. 'Though in the last few years he has become a trifle—'

'Eccentric,' Tuppence finished off. 'Which is why I thought the horse costume might work. But Hen's right. I doubt it would get me across the threshold.'

'What kind of eccentric?' Ginny asked in a cautious voice, thinking of the lovely library books he currently had in his possession. Even without them being the key to unlock the coded message, she would hate for something to happen to them.

'Oh, nothing to be alarmed about.' Tuppence shook her head so violently that the paper hat flew off, releasing her curls. 'Just a bit grumpy.'

'But I'm sure he wouldn't be grumpy with you,' Hen added. 'On account of being a doctor's wife.'

'Good point.' Tuppence brightened. 'You wouldn't even need a costume then.'

Ginny wasn't sure her marriage to Eric would help get any information out of a grumpy ex-doctor.

'Excellent, so is it decided that Ginny will go?' JM asked.

She swallowed. She hadn't been looking forward to working in the pub all night, preferring the quieter environment of the library to a noisy taproom. But she wasn't sure interviewing someone who might have been involved in Nathan Richardson's death was much better.

Still, there was only one way to get to the truth so she forced a smile. 'Of course I'll do it.'

FIFTEEN

Saturday, October 17

The clocks hadn't gone back yet, which meant it was technically daylight, but Ginny wasn't sure the bullet grey skyline could really count. She tried to console herself that bad things seldom happened in the late afternoon, no matter the weather.

After leaving her friends, she made the short drive and pulled up outside a classic Georgian two-storey manor house, whose matchbox-redbrick symmetry was thrown off by a side wing that was covered in large scaffolding, no doubt there to rescue the crumbling wall and missing roof shingles.

Still, the house was delightful with the long windows to let in the light, and smaller windows peeking up from the exposed basement. Large beds of roses flanked the pathway, and she tried to be cheered by the velvet petals and heady perfume that trailed her as she made her way up the stone stairs to the door. Despite the glorious view, there were so many things she would rather be doing. Drinking tea. Pretending not to talk to her dead husband. Even visiting the police station.

Nonsense. She chided herself. She needed to stop being silly and get on with it. So, taking a deep breath, she clasped the heavy iron knocker and let it fall.

Too late she remembered that the last time she knocked on someone's door to ask questions, she had inadvertently discovered a killer. Her fingers tightened around her handbag. Maybe she should have listened to her many excuses? Or taken Tuppence up on the horse costume?

Before she could change her mind, there was a shuffling noise and the door opened to reveal a tall man wearing dark denim jeans that looked as stiff as cardboard, teamed with a crisp shirt. His lean face was shaved and he was holding a cup of tea.

Callum Lovelace.

'Yes? What do you want?' One grizzly eyebrow raised at the sight of her and her confidence wavered. This sort of thing always seemed so much easier in theory.

'Er, hello, my name is Ginny Cole.' She plastered on her brightest fake-it-until-you-make-it smile. 'I do hate to trouble you, but I was hoping I could ask you a few questions.'

The eyebrow dropped but his mouth was tight with suspicion. 'If you want to show me a rash, let me inform you that I'm retired.'

Despite her nerves, Ginny burst out laughing, suddenly understanding the alarmed expression. It was the same one Eric had sported when someone came up to him at a social event, trying to get a two-minute diagnosis on everything from infected cuts through to dark purple love bites.

'Goodness, no. It's nothing like that. You might know I work in the library, and I wanted to ask you about some of the books you recently borrowed.'

'Books?' he repeated, dark eyes studying her, as if trying to discover a deeper meaning. However, he inched the door open. 'Are you interested in local history?'

'In a manner of speaking,' she said cautiously. 'I wouldn't ask if it wasn't important.'

His expression soured again. 'That's what they all say. You

wouldn't believe how many people turn up on my doorstep looking for free medical advice. They don't like taking no for an answer.'

'It's difficult when something happens to a loved one, especially in the evening. People don't always think properly because of the worry.' She gave him a sympathetic nod. Once again, he quirked an eyebrow, and she quickly added: 'My husband was also a GP. Before he died.'

Familiar pain caught in her throat, but she dug her nails into the soft flesh on her arm, to stop herself from getting lost in Eric's memory. Something must have shown on her face because Callum's expression softened.

'Sorry to hear that.' He finally stepped back and ushered her inside. 'Please, come in.'

'Thank you.' She followed him down a wide hallway filled with paintings, past several closed doors through to a huge kitchen that looked onto a well-kept lawn. An Aga was nestled in what had once been the fireplace and the long wooden table was covered in looming towers of reference books that dotted every available space. It seemed to reinforce the rumour that he was writing a book.

And suggest that despite the size of the house, he spent most of his time in the kitchen.

Then again, considering how expensive it must be to keep the entire place warm, maybe he did it as an economy?

'Would you like a cup of tea? The kettle is still warm,' he offered but she shook her head, nerves once more appearing. However, she did sit down across the table from him as he moved away several folders of notes.

'I can't stay long but thank you for seeing me. I must say you have a lovely house.'

He peered around as if noticing it for the first time. 'Yes, I suppose it is. I was born here, you see, so I am used to it. And of course, I never married, which means I tend to treat it like an office. I probably shouldn't be telling you that.'

Ginny's lips twitched. 'Your secret is safe with me.'

'You said this is about library books? I'm not sure an after-hours visit by a librarian is much better than having patients banging on my door.'

'I appreciate that it's a little... unorthodox. The reason I'm interested in the books is because they had only recently been returned by Nathan Richardson.'

As she spoke, she studied his face to see how he reacted. But the guarded expression from earlier was gone, replaced by one of genuine sadness as his eyes clouded over. It helped ease some of her own nerves. Was it usual for a killer to react like that? In her limited experience it wasn't, but then she had only interacted with three killers before so her sample group wasn't large.

'Such a tragedy. It's funny that in my line of business I should still find it shocking but there we go.' He leaned back in his chair and cradled his teacup.

'It sounds like you knew him,' she said, cautiously, not wanting to overstep, but not wanting to beat around the bush. 'Were you close?'

'I wouldn't say that. I only met him a handful of times.'

Ginny closed her eyes and tried to decide what it all meant. 'Were you aware that he had been the previous borrower of the three books on Little Shaw history?'

'Well, yes. I assumed he had because I was the one to recommend them to him,' he admitted.

Her spine straightened. 'Why would you do that?'

Callum put down his cup and ran a hand through his silver hair. 'Nathan wanted some help researching local history.'

'Was it about his great-aunt, Peggy Barlow?'

Callum's posture straightened. 'You know about Peggy?'

'I know Nathan was eager to find out what happened to her,' Ginny admitted.

He sighed. 'That's right. I always thought it was a pity that Peggy Barlow's name has been forgotten in history. But it's often the way with spies from that era. Their whole persona depends on them keeping deep cover.'

So, it was true.

Ginny caught her breath. Up until now the only account of Peggy had come from Sylvie. And while there was no reason not to trust her, the fact they couldn't find any information about the MI5 spy had been concerning. But what Callum said made sense.

For Peggy to be successful she obviously couldn't go around talking about it.

Her life would have to be constantly in the shadows.

'How do *you* know about her?' Ginny asked. They had already established that Callum couldn't have been much older than a schoolboy when Peggy had been in Little Shaw.

'My father was also a doctor and she was his patient.' Callum put down his teacup and lifted a shoebox that had been resting on a nearby chair. 'He patched her up several times for knife wounds and broken bones—not the kind of injuries that most postal workers received. It led him to developing a fascination with her.'

'Yes, but it's hardly enough to assume someone is a spy.' Ginny tried not to shudder at the other reasons why women could end up in a doctor's surgery with unexplained wounds.

He flushed. 'You're correct. However, according to my father, there were a lot of rumours swirling around about her.'

'What kind of rumours?'

'About her and Mikhail Volkov,' Callum said. At Ginny's blank expression he continued, 'He was a nuclear specialist who defected to Britain. There was a huge kick up about it when he walked into the embassy and asked for asylum. Ater that, it was presumed he was involved in the Windscale Advanced Gas-cooled Reactor, which was a second-generation fission reactor built in 1962.'

Windscale.

Ginny's skin prickled as she remembered the black and white sketch Tuppence had done of the burning facility. Was this why they had found the name in Nathan's bedroom? 'I thought it burned down in 1957.'

'The fire was in Unit One,' Callum clarified. 'But they continued to work on the other project, which was focused on supplying electricity, rather than any kind of military advantage. Though Volkov's involvement was kept very hush-hush.'

Ginny wasn't surprised. Still, it was a lot to take in and she closed her eyes, trying to piece it all together. But even if Volkov was involved in the second project at Windscale, it was hard to see where Peggy fitted in, since Windscale was one hundred miles away. Not really commuter friendly.

Her confusion must have shown on her face and Callum sighed. 'You're trying to figure out how Volkov and Peggy met, aren't you?'

She really *did* have the worst poker face. 'If Peggy was meant to be his contact, it doesn't make much sense.'

'I agree, though it's not clear if she was ever his contact, or involved in another part of the war effort. All I have managed to discover is that before Peggy Barlow moved to Little Shaw, she was based in Cumbria for several years.'

Ginny sucked in a breath. That made more sense. Sort of. 'You think that Volkov followed her to Little Shaw? It seems risky if the government was wanting to keep his involvement a secret.'

At this Callum's mouth began to twitch. 'It seems that not even all the intrigue from the Cold War period could compete with local gossip,' he said and lifted out a handful of carefully clipped newspaper articles. 'It was never confirmed, but there were numerous sightings—of him on his own, and of him talking to Peggy. It was just local gossip, but it didn't stop stories like this being printed.' Without another word, he handed Ginny one of the clippings.

The Scientist and the Spy Who Loved Him

It is believed that Dr Mikhail Volkov, famous for defecting from the East three years ago, has been living in Little Shaw for an undisclosed period of time. Several locals have seen a man matching Volkov's description walking down the high street. And while it has yet to be confirmed, another source, who wishes to remain nameless, is convinced that he's not alone.

'I saw him with that woman from the post office. And let me tell you... they weren't talking about the price of stamps.'

Postal worker, Peggy Barlow, denies ever meeting the man. Yet only days after this interview, both Barlow and Volkov disappeared into seemingly thin air. Which leaves us to wonder who Peggy Barlow really is? Was she just caught in the crossfires of international tensions, or was she part of it?

Ginny read it a second time and tried to imagine how Nathan reacted to the news that his great-aunt might have been involved with a famous defector? Especially for a historian. It was the stuff that movies were made of, but she suspected the reality wasn't quite as glamorous.

If it was true, they would have been in constant danger.

'Do you believe it?'

'That's like asking if I believe whatever garbage the gutter press print. However, my father kept all the clippings, and my research suggests that someone was definitely after them. Though it's impossible to say if it was the Russians or the British.'

'But why would the British be after her, if that's who she worked for?' Ginny gasped, too late remembering the plot of the numerous thrillers she and Eric had read over the years.

At the question Callum's face became more guarded and he put back the newspaper article. 'This is one of the theories I am exploring as part of my book. However, at this point... I do need to be protective of my work. I'm sorry I can't help you more.' As if to demonstrate he put the shoebox under his chair, his eyes not leaving hers.

She opened her mouth to protest but then closed it again. She supposed if he had been researching Peggy for years, with the aim to write a book, it wasn't fair to expect him to tell her everything she wanted to know.

All the same there was only one reason that she could imagine both countries trying to find Peggy: so they could reclaim Mikhail Volkov. Ice skittered along her veins as she recalled Sylvie's words.

Peggy had that look in her eyes. Fear. As if she was worried that her time was running out.

Was that what happened? Had someone found Peggy and Mikhail? Then what? But Ginny could only think of one outcome. That they had been killed.

It was a dreadful thought but one that wouldn't go away. Especially now that Peggy's great-nephew had investigated it and also ended up dead. Did that mean someone was still out there, trying to hold onto secrets? But who? And how? Surely anyone who had been around at the time was now dead, or too infirm to do anything.

Unless it was a would-be author protecting their life's work.

SIXTEEN

Saturday, October 17

Tension crept back through her veins as Ginny stared at Callum Lovelace. There was nothing threatening about his appearance, but that didn't mean he wasn't capable of doing something to a rival author. Especially if that person was a blood connection to the unknown spy and was an academic into the bargain.

'Were you worried about Nathan's interest in Peggy Barlow?' she asked in a cautious voice, reminding herself that her friends knew where she was.

But instead of refusing to answer her, the guarded expression on Callum's face lifted. 'It's hard to hide everything in this village, so it's true that some people are aware of my research. Someone needs to bring Peggy Barlow back into the light. I suppose someone on one of the quiz teams told him about me. All I know is that he asked for information and I told him the same thing I've told you. It's all things that are readily available, if you know where to look.'

Ginny frowned. Despite his body language relaxing, it still didn't make sense. She could understand him speaking with her, since she probably didn't appear a threat. But why would he have so easily passed on the information to Nathan?

'Yes, it must have been strange for you to suddenly be approached by someone who isn't from Little Shaw. Weren't you worried about what he might do... or find?'

A ripple of irritation flashed in his eyes and then he let out a reluctant sigh. 'If you must know, he promised to show me a photograph of Peggy Barlow.'

It was said with such seriousness, that Ginny wondered if she had missed something? Then she peered around at the stacks of research that covered the room and recalled him saying how difficult it was to find out much about her.

'You hadn't seen what she looked like before?'

'I suppose it's a bit like meeting your idol. For so long I've been researching her, but she was just a name. For Nathan to bring out that yellow envelope and show me the photograph of her...'

Was there a reason Callum had only used the singular, even though Nathan had two photographs of his great-aunt?

'What did it look like?' she asked

'She was standing next to a car. And she looked so happy. I was quite overcome.'

Ginny could well imagine. Peggy's face flashed into her mind. That photograph had been full of light and happiness. Laughing at something a person off camera had said. Was that person Mikhail?

Then she thought of the first photograph. The one she had found in the library book. In it, Peggy had looked solemn and possibly scared. It was also the one with the book cipher on the back. Her thoughts returned to Nathan. Why had he only shown Callum one of the photographs, and why had he placed the other one in the library book that he returned through the after-hours slot?

Was it an accident, or had he done it on purpose?

If so, that would imply he knew that someone might want to harm him?

She shivered as she thought of the overturned pub, where nothing had been taken. Not even the second photograph in the yellow envelope. Her head began to whirl with so many unanswered questions and loose threads that didn't make sense.

'Did Nathan seem upset when he showed you the photograph? Or mention if he had any other ones?'

His mouth twitched. 'He told me there was another one and that if I helped him, I could see it. I was hoping to talk to him about it at the quiz night last Sunday, but I ended up stuck here thanks to my nephew. He's going through a tough divorce and turned up unexpectedly; as much as I hate letting down my fellow Archivists, I had to make my apologies and stay at home.'

'So you weren't at the pub last Sunday?' Ginny asked, feeling foolish for not establishing that at the beginning. Especially when she had seen Nathan deliver four drinks to the table, even though Callum hadn't arrived. Of course, it didn't mean he couldn't have sneaked in during the quiz and made his way to the cellar. But if the rest of his team were there, it would have been difficult to do, especially given his height.

'No.' He shook his head. 'In retrospect I was pleased to avoid such an inauspicious ending. Poor Nathan.'

Pinching her brow, she wondered if she should just leave since clearly Callum didn't kill Nathan and while he had shared some information about Peggy and Mikhail, he seemed reticent to tell her anything else about the spy and the scientist. Which meant the only suspect left was Ned Warner.

She squared her shoulders and took in a deep breath. 'Did he mention if he had spoken to anyone else?' Ginny dared ask, thinking of Ned Warner's dark expression as he had followed Nathan out of the cellar.

The retired doctor's frown increased, and he used his foot to hook the shoebox even closer to him. 'What's this really about? Why do you want to know?'

Ginny swallowed. She had clearly gone too far. Shifting in her chair, she got ready to leave, but then she sat back down. There was no point stopping now. 'I happened to have noticed Nathan speaking to Ned Warner on the night he died—he was the editor of the local paper before he retired. It makes sense if Nathan approached him as well.'

At the mention of Ned Warner's name, Callum's expression darkened. 'Don't talk to me about *that* man.'

'You don't like him?'

'There is no love lost between us.' Callum's eyes blazed, transforming him from a mild-mannered ex-doctor with a passion for British spies... into something else. 'That man has no idea what the fourth estate even means. If he had any sense of public interest, he would have made his archives available to everyone instead of guarding them like Cerberus. And then once he retired, he had the cheek to take the archives with him.'

Ginny shivered. 'Why would he do that? Do you think he was hiding something, or just wanted copies of his articles?'

'Ho.' Callum let out a bitter bark of laughter. 'I'll tell you why. It's because he was also trying to write a biography about Peggy and is a narrow-minded bitter man who was scared of some healthy competition. If it wasn't for the Little Shaw library and my father's own collection of newspaper clippings, I would have been lost.'

So there were two people in Little Shaw trying to write a biography on Peggy Barlow. It seemed extreme considering how little information was available about her.

But was it also the motive?

This wasn't the first rivalry she had been involved with, and she knew how far the villagers of Little Shaw could go when it came to their nemeses.

She glanced at the towers of books, remembering the code that Peggy had written on the back of the photograph. She peered around, searching for the library books, before locating them on a wooden stool. Part of her longed to take them with her, but she could hardly do that when Callum was a library patron who had borrowed them in good faith.

But *why* had he borrowed them? If he was the one to recommend them to Nathan, then surely he had already read them? Unless they were the cipher.

'Did Nathan tell you about the code he found on the back of Peggy's photograph?' Ginny asked, her gaze still fixed on the library books.

At the mention of it, Callum's face reddened, making him look more like a guilty child than a retired doctor. She took that as a yes. And it also explained why he had taken the books out of the library himself.

He had wanted to solve the puzzle as much as she did.

'Yes.' Callum gave her a rueful sigh and reached over for a piece of paper, where three nonsensical sentences were scrawled. 'He showed me the code and mentioned he was looking for the book that Peggy used as a cipher. We discussed possible books and used some from my own collection. But none provided the answer, and so I mentioned several titles in the Little Shaw library's local history section. I presumed that if he managed to decipher the message, he would come back to me, but of course he died before that could happen. Then when I saw the same titles on the recently returned shelf, I guessed that Nathan had been the last borrower, and I decided to see what I could find out.'

'And what did you discover?' Ginny stared at the three rambling sentences.

Harness. Rain. Old. North.
Thatch. Cotton. Worm. Blue.
Waltz. Onion. Mary. Bucket.

'The only thing I discovered was that none of the books were connected to the cipher.' Callum held up his hands. 'There's nothing more frustrating than an unsolved riddle.'

Ginny thought of her years of solving crosswords and nodded her head in agreement. It was certainly very unsatisfying. And that was only a crossword. This involved the death of a lovely young man. She got to her feet. 'Thank you for talking to me. I suppose I will see you tomorrow night at the quiz?'

'Yes. The Archivists are not happy about last week so I

promised to be there.' He nodded and walked her to the door. Then he paused, his hand poised over the handle. 'Mrs Cole... Ginny... if you do happen to find that other photograph of Peggy Barlow, or any other information about her, you will let me see it, won't you?'

His voice sounded nervous. Like a young child worried about being denied a treat. Ginny could almost feel sorry for him. He had spent his life researching an invisible woman who had done her best to hide from the world.

'If I do get them, I will happily pass them over,' she promised, thinking of the two photographs Veronica Yates had locked in Sylvie's dresser.

'Thank you.' For the first time since she had arrived, he seemed genuinely happy and she took her leave.

Her mind was still spinning as she climbed into her car and started the engine.

Callum might no longer be a suspect, but she still had numerous questions for Ned Warner, the ex-editor of the local newspaper. Was he the reason that Nathan had purposely removed the photograph from the pub and hidden it away in a library book? Because he was worried what would happen if Ned Warner discovered it?

SEVENTEEN

Sunday, October 18

It was official. Ginny was not a fan of power walking. Her breath came out in a column of misty plumes that did nothing to increase her enjoyment as sweat beaded her forehead. Next to her Hen continued to wheeze as she leaned heavily against a set of swings the following morning.

'Isn't that a great way to get rid of the cobwebs?' Tuppence laid the beer mats out along the bottom of the slide in the children's playground, which was currently empty apart from four panting widows.

Well, make that two panting widows, and two much fitter ones.

'It most certainly is,' JM agreed, doing a couple of extra stretches, as if to prove which kind of widow *she* was.

Ginny swallowed, finally managing to straighten up as her vision came back into focus, letting her see the early morning. Despite her pounding heart, it had the makings of a beautiful autumn day, once the low fog lifted. She took in a deep breath and started to feel more like herself.

'Have a mug of hot chocolate.' Hen, who had recovered her breath, reached for the large thermos that she had been carrying in a backpack. She poured the contents out into four enamel mugs and passed them around, along with a tub of homemade ginger biscuits.

It was possible that hot chocolate and ginger biscuits would undo all the benefits of the power walking, but Ginny was too achy to care. She gratefully took a mug and curled her fingers around it, breathing in the sugary warmth. She took a sip and finally felt ready to turn her attention to the makeshift murder board.

'Right, Ginny, I think you should go first. Tell us what Callum Lovelace said. Did he let you through the door?'

Ginny nodded. Last night her plan had been to visit her friends at The Lost Goat and fill them in, but JM had texted to say Mitch was trialling two new bar staff and had sent them home. They'd exchanged several more texts and decided to have a proper catch-up over an early power-walking session. Personally, Ginny would have preferred a nice warm living room session with plates of cake but hadn't wanted to appear lazy.

In the end, she had gone home and done as much research as she could on Mikhail Volkov. There hadn't been any mention of Peggy Barlow that she could find, but there were plenty of articles on the scientist who had defected to the West.

Unfortunately, what Callum told her was true. There were no more mentions of him since 1963, apart from every few years when someone would raise the discussion online about the missing scientist. The general consensus was that he had been killed by a shadowy figure whose identity would probably never be known.

It had made Ginny shiver all over again. Had that been Peggy's fate as well?

And Nathan's?

No wonder she hadn't slept well. Rubbing her arms, she pushed away the unnerving thought and told her friends every-thing she had learned from Callum, including the fact he hadn't been at the pub last Sunday night.

After she finished, JM frowned and picked up the beer mat with his name on it. 'How do you know he was telling you the truth? Did you check the books for yourself? Maybe he had deciphered the message and was trying to throw you off the scent?

'It seemed rude to ask to look at the books when he didn't offer them to me,' she admitted. 'But he did already have his attempts at deciphering on a piece of paper. They made as much sense as my ones did. Plus, if he was trying to hide something then why tell me about Volkov.'

'That's a valid point,' JM conceded.

'So, you *really* don't think he's guilty?' Tuppence double checked and when Ginny shook her head, the other woman let out a long sigh. 'Oh well. So much for our first suspect.'

'Try not to take it personally, we now have more information about Peggy and Mikhail. And don't forget there's Ned Warner.' Hen patted Tuppence's arm in support.

'That's true.' Tuppence reached for a blank beer mat and scrawled his name along the top and then added two inverted Vs next to it. 'To be fair, he fits more nicely as a villain.'

'It's the eyebrows,' Hen explained, almost apologetically. 'They are very peaked.'

'Definitely a case of nominative determinism,' JM agreed.

Ginny wrinkled her nose; she well knew the theory of how a particular name could influence the career someone might do. So that someone whose last name was Baker, might in fact become a baker. But she'd never heard of it applying to eyebrows before. At least it now explained the two inverted Vs next to his name.

'I know he was the editor for the local newspaper, which would give him access to all kinds of information, and that he took a lot of the archives with him when he left. He appears to be in his seventies, but do we know his real age? Is it possible he knew Peggy?' Ginny asked.

'Hard to say. He has one of those faces that could make him seventy or one hundred and ten,' Hen admitted. 'I remember him working there when I was in my teens because I tried to put a classified ad in the paper and he yelled at me for having a spelling mistake.'

'He's seventy-four,' JM announced as she held up her phone. 'I've just looked him up on my genealogy software. Which means he might have met Peggy, though he would have been very young at the time.'

'Excellent.' Tuppence wrote it down on the beer mat. 'So, we know his age, that he was also writing a book on Peggy Barlow and that he refused to share information on it. Which means he could have seen Nathan as a rival.'

'It says here he has a daughter called Lena and that his wife is dead,' JM added.

'That's right. Lena is a sweetheart though last I heard she was estranged from him. Proof of his nasty temper.' Hen shuddered.

'We also know that he had some kind of argument with Nathan before he died,' Ginny said. 'And that he appears large enough to easily push someone over a beer keg.'

'Oh dear.' Hen's face paled. 'That is means, motive and opportunity. Yet, it seems so far-fetched.'

'This whole case is far-fetched,' Ginny agreed, unable to get Ned Warner's angry face out of her mind. 'We have a nuclear scientist who publicly defected, before disappearing into thin air at the same time as Peggy Barlow. According to Callum both British and Russian agents might have been after them. And then when Peggy's great-nephew starts investigating, he is killed.'

'Which means we have three people we need to focus on.' Tuppence gathered up the two beer mats with Peggy and Mikhail's names on them and drew a stick figure arm on the right side of one, and on the left side of the other, then joined them together, as if they were holding hands. Next to them she added Nathan's own beer mat.

'We have lots of random pieces of information.' JM took the remaining beer mats and put them in a large circle around the three names, so that it made a halo.

'And one ex-newspaper editor.' Hen moved Ned Warner's card into the centre of the circle and set it on top of Peggy, Mikhail and Nathan. They were silent as they all stared at it.

'We need to pay Ned Warner a visit. Let's go before our shift,' JM said and glanced at her watch.

Hen shivered. 'Is that wise? If he is behind Nathan's death, we could be walking into a trap.'

'And if we don't go, he might come after us,' JM retorted, her mouth setting into a mulish frown. 'You saw what he looked like on the CCTV footage. I prefer to keep my enemies in front of me and not let them sneak around in the cellar while I'm working the bar.'

'How about we all go?' Tuppence suggested.

JM shook her head. 'Ginny's cover has been compromised. If Ned knows she went to visit his arch-rival last night, he might clam up. Or, worse, go underground.'

'Underground?' Hen blinked. 'Like a secret bunker?'

'No, not like a secret bunker,' JM said then tilted her head sideways in acknowledgement. 'Well, maybe they do have one.'

'I don't like to rub it in, but this wouldn't have happened if we'd used the horse costume,' Tuppence said. 'Still, Ginny could go visit Lena. See if she will dish the dirt on her father.'

'I'm not sure about this. Maybe we should pass it all onto Wallace?' Ginny suggested, trying not to think of all the things that could go wrong if Ned Warner was the person behind it all.

'Good luck with that. I have hardly seen him all week. Usually when we're working on a case, we're forever falling over him. But this time we've only seen him once and that's when he came into the pub to ask about something completely unrelated. He didn't even seem to care that we might be involved in something,' JM said, almost sounding offended.

Ginny couldn't help but agree.

Despite being unnerved by the police, she had to admit there had also previously been a level of comfort in knowing the grumpy detective was looking over her shoulder. It had been like an anchor ensuring that none of them did anything too rash, like going to visit a potential killer.

'Do we know where Warner lives?' Ginny asked, swallowing back her reservations.

'He's in that fancy housing estate past JM's place,' Tuppence said. 'I can't remember the number, but I know the house. And Lena lives in the end terrace on Elgin Street. It has a yellow door.'

Elgin Street wasn't far from the library, and Ginny knew it well, so she reluctantly nodded. 'Okay, but please be careful, we don't know what he's capable of.'

'He's the one who should be worried about us.' JM's eyes gleamed. 'My hands are lethal weapons.'

'And I have my knitting needles,' Hen seconded.

'I'm not a fan of violence, but I don't mind disabling vehicles. I could let down his tyres before we go inside.'

Ginny wasn't sure that letting down someone's tyres before discovering if they were guilty was the best idea, but short of locking her friends up, there wasn't much she could do. She swallowed. 'Okay. I will talk to Lena and we can meet up later on today.'

'Excellent. Between interrogating Ned Warner and talking to the quiz teams tonight, I think we'll have this case wrapped up before anyone can sneeze,' JM announced then did several star jumps. 'I suggest we start walking back to our cars. We don't want our muscles to seize up by standing still for too long.'

Ginny drained her hot chocolate before handing the mug back to Hen.

Her muscles had seized up half an hour ago and had progressed onto the quietly rocking in the corner while sobbing stage. But, if they moved, it might help them come up with a good excuse for asking if Lena thought her estranged father was a killer.

EIGHTEEN

Sunday, October 18

Elgin Street was one of the narrow sloping streets that ran off Denstone, and while they were lovely to look at, Ginny knew from when she had been house hunting that they had terrible parking, so she left her car outside the library and made the short walk. Her muscles still ached, and she longed for a bath.

Finally, she reached the house with the yellow door, and she cautiously rapped on it. There was no answer, so she tried it again. But after several more minutes she decided Lena wasn't at home.

Ginny didn't know whether to be pleased or disappointed. Scrap that, she was pleased and selfishly hoped her friends discovered Ned Warner to be equally absent. Because while she was determined to get to the bottom of the mystery, she wasn't keen on them stepping into any more dangerous situations.

She checked her watch. It was almost twelve, and they were due to meet at the pub at four, which meant she might have time to soak her muscles in a bath after all. The sun had managed to peek out from between the grey clouds and cries of children playing at the park by the library greeted her as Ginny reached her car. A hopeful ice-cream van was parked nearby, and several families lined up for 99s. Smiling, she searched in her handbag for her keys when a flash of something red caught her eye.

It came from the side of the library, and before Ginny knew it, adrenaline was roaring in her ears as time seemed to slow down.

She could still recall the plumes of smoke that ran down the lane. Oh dear. She took several deep breaths and when she looked again, she realised it wasn't a fire but simply the sun bouncing off the metallic red paint of a car, parked down there.

'That will teach you to overreact,' she scolded herself and stepped forward. Despite it being a no-parking zone, cars did occasionally use it when the library was closed. And while there was a good chance it was just a tired mother wanting to take her children to the playground, Ginny had to make sure it wasn't another attempt at breaking into the lovely new stacks.

Her nerves jangled as she cautiously walked down the lane, gripping her car keys in lieu of a weapon. Not that she would need it. After all, it was broad daylight, and the park was full of families and children.

As she got closer, a familiar red Mini Cooper came into view. It was one she had seen enough times parked outside Wallace's house. Imogen Smith. Except there was no sign of the lovely pathologist, so Ginny approached.

That's odd.

The car was wedged so close to the wall that it was as if a giant hand had lifted it up and planted it there. Not being the best parallel parker, it seemed incredible that someone could manoeuvre their car like that. More importantly, why would Imogen want to? It was like she was trying to hide it from view.

A phone rang from the other side of the fence and a moment later a man began to speak. 'If they think I'm going to listen to them, they have another think coming. No one tells Ned Warner what he can do. Now, I have some *business* I need to attend to.'

There was real anger in the voice as he said the word 'business'; Ginny's throat tightened with nerves.

Ned Warner?

Despite her panic, she glanced towards the fence and immediately recognised the bald head and thick shoulders from the CCTV footage she had seen at The Lost Goat. He was facing the other way, and Ginny sucked in her breath, praying he wouldn't turn. However, eventually the sound of his retreating footsteps told her that he'd gone.

Where was he going in such a bad temper? Was it to see Lena?

Ginny wasn't sure that was a good idea, especially if they were estranged. Should Ginny warn her? But what would she say? That she might have heard Ned Warner ranting from the other side of a fence?

It would be difficult considering she'd never met either of them. All she would be doing was inserting herself into someone's private business.

She let out a breath and was about to turn when something moved from inside the red car and Imogen appeared from the backseat.

Ginny's mouth dropped open.

Imogen flushed. 'I am sorry if I frightened you.'

'I feel like I'm the one who frightened you,' Ginny said, taking a step closer. 'I didn't mean to, but ever since the fire down here, I tend to check if I see anything untoward.'

'Like a grown woman hiding in their car?' Imogen gave her a rueful smile.

'Not to mention the parking. I'm not even sure how you managed it.'

This drew a smile from her. 'My father drove trucks in the Army. He taught me a thing or two. But again, I'm sorry to be parking on library property.'

'Don't mind that. Is everything okay?' Ginny scanned her face. Her mouth was tight but there were no obvious signs of distress.

'Yes, I'm fine. Well, fine-ish. I'm in the middle of a case and it was... necessary for me to stay out of sight.'

Why would Imogen have to stay out of sight of Ned Warner?

Was it something to do with Nathan Richardson? It seemed strange to think, since even if Ned had been behind it, Imogen was the pathologist, which meant she was involved in the death by misadventure verdict.

Unless she had more evidence to prove it wasn't. Was that the case she was in the middle of? Ginny swallowed. Part of her longed to ask but knew Imogen wouldn't be able to answer.

'Of course. Well, I hope the case goes well.'

'Thank you, and it's good to see you again, Ginny.' Imogen retrieved her car keys from her pocket and climbed back in the passenger's side and shuffled over to the driver's seat, which was too close to the wall to open.

Ginny watched in awe as Imogen manoeuvred the small car out of the tight space and drove back down the lane, no doubt towards the police station and Wallace. Once she was gone, Ginny retrieved her phone and sent her friends a text message.

> Meet me at the park next to the library. I have news.

'Tell me exactly what he said.' Tuppence took the cap off her pen half an hour later as they all sat on one of the park benches. The sun had shifted back behind the clouds and most of the families had gone home, leaving only a few bored teenagers sitting at the swings.

'He said: "*If they think I'm going to listen to them, they have another think coming. No one tells Ned Warner what he can do,*"' Ginny dutifully repeated.

'And it was definitely him?' JM double checked.

'Yes, I looked as soon as I heard his name. At first, I thought he was referring to Lena but then when Imogen got out the car, I wondered if he had been talking about her.'

'I don't blame her. He has a nasty temper.' Hen clutched at her knitting needles. 'When we were looking for his house, you should have heard the terrible things his neighbours said about him.'

'He wasn't popular,' Tuppence agreed. 'Which is probably why they were all so happy that he moved out last year.'

'When we asked where he was now one person said, "hell," and a second said, "probably in prison."' Hen cast on.

'Those were the more PG comments,' JM added.

Her friends had already explained that they couldn't find Ned Warner and that none of his neighbours had a forwarding address. Now she had heard him venting his spleen, she was relieved they hadn't found him.

'I wonder if he's living with Lena?' JM tapped her chin. 'It explains why he's over this way.'

'For Lena's sake, I hope he isn't,' Hen said as her needles clinked together. Then she frowned. 'And why would he be looking for Imogen?'

'Sounds to me like he's trying to intimidate a witness... or in this case a pathologist. Clearly it means that Imogen and Wallace are both working on this case together. It's just like them to not tell us.' JM glowered.

'I knew something fishy was going on with him,' Tuppence added.

Ginny didn't feel up to reminding them that Wallace never told them about the cases he was working on. Then she let out a soft groan as she realised what this now meant.

She turned to her friends. 'If Wallace is working the case we'll need to make sure we don't get in his way.'

'That won't be hard since he isn't going to the quiz tonight,' Tuppence said. 'Which means we can ask as many questions as we want. And Ned should be there because the Archivists have registered.'

'Excellent because I am looking forward to having a conversation with Mr Warner. And if he thinks he can scare me, he will soon learn how wrong he is.'

Ginny swallowed. 'Yes, but remember we should still be discreet.'

'But of course.' JM gave her a broad smile. 'Discretion is my middle name.'

NINETEEN

Sunday, October 18

'Are you sure you didn't speak to Nathan Richardson last Sunday?' JM pressed a small woman clutching two glasses of port and lemonade. 'And word of warning, I have a built-in sensor so will know if you are lying. Are we clear?'

Ginny looked up from the dishwasher that she was in the process of emptying. The steam fogged her vision but as it cleared, she could see that the woman was in her mid-fifties and only came up to JM's shoulder.

Oh dear. So much for being discreet.

'I-I don't know anything.' The woman let out a small squeak and darted back to the table, next to the snug where Slim's team was sitting, with Charlie's wheelchair taking up the helm.

On a busy night, Charlie might have been knocked and bustled, but the prediction that not all teams would turn up had been correct and the pub was only half full, with none of the banter that had been part of last week's competition.

Maybe it had been a mistake to run the quiz so soon after Nathan's death?

Then she thought of Heather and Mitch's precarious financial position and she pushed the thought aside. At least if they were open, they would be earning money.

'Please don't tell me you're still scaring the customers. At this rate we won't have anyone left by the time I start the quiz.' Mitch returned to the bar, his eyes narrowing as the tiny woman gathered up her handbag and headed for the exit.

'Of course I didn't scare her. But there was something beady about her eyes that I don't trust.'

'You don't trust Sister Bernadette? Her team, Bad Habits, is one of our longest running participants. They have been quizzing before I even started working here.'

'All the more reason to suspect them. And I don't care what she says, I didn't offer her physical violence.'

'I should hope not,' Mitch retorted, still looking harassed.

'How did your new bar staff go last night?' Ginny asked, hoping that it would calm him down.

'One was a flake who only wanted free booze. I sent them home after an hour. But the other was great and was meant to come in to work the lunch shift but never turned up. I'm starting to think we're cursed.'

'We can help out as long as you need us,' Hen assured him and they all chimed in with agreement.

'Thank you. I don't know what Heather and I would do without you all,' he said as a timer went off on his phone. 'I need to start the quiz questions, and while I appreciate you wanting to find out what happened to Nathan, remember that you can't scare the punters. Or threaten them. It's already a slow night... I don't want to make it worse.'

'Easy for him to say,' JM muttered as Mitch disappeared towards the stage. 'It's been challenging to get these quizsters to speak. They are strangely tight-lipped. It took all my skill to even get that woman in the Know-it-Alls to so much as look at me.'

Ginny hadn't fared much better. She had spoken to several

people but none of them admitted to having exchanged more than a few words with Nathan last weekend.

'It was the same with the Archivists. All I did was ask them where Callum was and they swore at me in Middle English, which seems a little bit unreasonable,' Hen said. 'What even is a curdogge?'

'Whatever it is, they shouldn't have said it.' Tuppence bristled then dropped her shoulders. 'And Callum isn't the only one missing. There is no sign of Ned Warner either. I tried to ask his team members from Hold the Front Page, but they just glared at me and said "no comment" as if I was a journalist.'

Ginny frowned. She had hoped to ask Callum a few more questions about Peggy. But perhaps he had been busy researching and lost track of time. As for Ned Warner. The longer he was absent, the more suspicious he became.

'Surely they won't compete without a full contingent.' JM peered over to the Hold the Front Page table, where two women were huddled, talking in low voices and only occasionally glancing towards the pub entrance, as if expecting their missing team member to walk in.

'It's risky,' Tuppence agreed. 'Not to mention annoying that they're so tight-lipped. They're the ones who know Ned Warner the best. I wonder if JM should try to break them?'

'There is no try, only do.' JM cracked her knuckles, eyes gleaming.

Hen looked alarmed and stepped forward. 'I don't mind talking to them. I know them both, though we're not exactly friends.'

'I don't blame you. I was in a book group with them once, but when they started saying rude things about people who read romance, I decided to leave.' Tuppence frowned.

Ginny had seen them both around the village but had never spoken to them. Though, now she knew their thoughts on genre fiction, she wasn't in a hurry to do so. She gave Hen an encouraging smile.

'Are you sure you don't mind?'

'Of course not,' Hen said in a brave voice. 'It's about time I put myself on the line. Plus, I can always spill a drink on their heads if they get too rude.'

'Now that's a jolly good idea.' Tuppence beamed.

From the stage the hiss and crackle of the microphone broke up the noise and the whole pub went silent as Mitch requested they take a minute to remember Nathan. After it was finished, he coughed into the microphone.

'Okay, folks. Let's get our thinking caps on. First question is: In Celsius, what is the melting point of gold?'

'Who cares when these questions are so *dreadful?*' someone yelled out.

'Dear me, that wasn't very nice.' Hen picked up an empty tray and walked around the bar. 'I'm going in.'

'While you do that, I'll have another go at the Village Idiots,' Tuppence said and Ginny glanced at the table where three towers of shot glasses swayed each time anyone moved. She hoped the team weren't as drunk as they appeared.

After Hen and Tuppence disappeared onto the floor, Ginny wished she had a bit more of their bravery. Unfortunately, striking up random conversations with people in the middle of a pub wasn't one of her skills. She tried to imagine how Peggy Barlow might've handled the situation. Would she have put on her red lipstick and got to work?

Or had Ginny just watched too many movies?

Either way, she doubted she would have made a very good spy.

At the other end of the bar JM was having a heated discussion with a customer while Tuppence and Hen were both deep in conversation with the quiz teams. Everyone was settled with drinks so she looked around for some work to do. Her eyes snagged on the tiny camera hidden in the shelving unit that housed the spirits.

That reminded her that they never finished looking through the CCTV footage from last Sunday. At least that was something she could do with confidence. The thought of a few minutes of peace and quiet were appealing so she slipped away to the office.

It was pretty much as they'd left it, but several crates of tonic water were now piled up on the far end of the desk, as if Mitch had put them down and got distracted mid-task. She'd have to move them before the end of the night. Ignoring them for now, she settled down at the computer and brought up the footage.

By speeding through it, she managed to get up to where they had left off after Wallace had interrupted them. As the footage continued, Nathan was off camera for a good part of it, but she knew that was because he had been on the makeshift stage reading out the quiz questions. A few punters wandered up to the bar, and Heather served them, before it quietened down. Once the quiz was over, Nathan reappeared into the shot and Ginny grimaced as she watched herself walk up to the bar.

It was quite surreal to observe herself like this. And oh dear, why were her shoulders so slumped? She really must remember to stand up straight.

Sighing, she returned her attention to the screen, just as Nathan looked across the bar to where a short woman with a cross around her neck was standing. Sister Bernadette? Nathan raised an eyebrow in recognition and moved towards her, but before he could, the bar person next to him held up the half-full pint of bitter.

Ginny stared at the screen, her stomach twisting as Nathan made his way towards the cellar.

No. Don't go down there.

As pointless as it was, the words caught in her throat. It was dreadful knowing he would never come out again.

Taking a steady breath, she forced herself to keep watching the cellar entrance. Sister Bernadette was soon served by Heather and a trickle of other customers made their way to the bar.

But no one ventured down into the cellar until after Mitch called last orders and Heather went to find Nathan before reappearing, face drained of colour.

After that, the tape was a blur and she watched as Wallace and Imogen made their way down to Nathan while PC Bent and DC

Singh helped keep everyone calm. Ginny pressed stop on the tape and leaned back in her chair.

There were definitely blind spots that the camera couldn't pick up, so she wasn't really surprised that the killer wasn't caught on tape. She rewound it back. Perhaps she should go through it again in case she had missed something. But just as she pressed play Hen rushed into the office.

'There you are. We couldn't find you anywhere.'

'We even tried the cellar. No wonder you didn't like it, it is straight out of a horror movie. All it needed was a Victorian doll to float through the air and attack us, to really set the scene,' Tuppence added with a shiver.

'Tuppence, you're going to give me nightmares for a month,' Hen complained.

'Sorry, I didn't mean to scare you.' Tuppence patted her arm. 'But it is a scary place, so I was relieved that Ginny wasn't down there.'

'I didn't mean for you to worry about me. I thought I would go through the rest of the CCTV footage,' Ginny said as a loud scream echoed from somewhere in the pub.

'What was that?' Tuppence demanded, already turning to head back out to the bar. They all followed her in time to see a woman from the Archivists sobbing hysterically into another man's shoulder.

JM turned to one of the customers leaning against the bar. 'What's wrong with her?'

'Beats me. Last question was on Patagonia. Maybe it hit a nerve?' the man guessed as several people went up to comfort the wailing woman.

Whispers made their way around the pub as phones started to buzz and ring.

Hen's own phone went and she fumbled for it. 'Oh. No.' Her hand flew to her mouth as she looked up at Ginny, JM and Tuppence. 'My neighbour is friends with someone who just let them know there's been a murder.'

'Another one?' the man at the bar said. 'Do they think it's the Quiz Killer?'

'There is no Quiz Killer,' JM growled before turning back to Hen, who had gone quite pale. 'Who is it?'

'It's Callum. Callum Lovelace is dead.'

TWENTY

Monday, October 19

The following morning Ginny stared at her office door, longing to close it and block out the chatter coming from the main floor of the library. As a rule, she wasn't fond of a shut door policy, but she also wasn't fond of pressing the wrong button on the newest batch of books that she was ordering.

Trying to order.

'As you know, my dreams always come true,' Cleo's voice rang out. 'I come from a long line of psychics and when Callum Lovelace came to me last night... he was dripping with water... which tells me that he drowned.' There was a slight pause before Cleo spoke again. 'Though it is possible that happened in a past life... but still, it's clear he was trying to give me a message.'

'It's how he met his brutal ends at the hands of the Quiz Killer,' Andrea elaborated. 'Why don't you tell them about the vision you had last week, Cleo?'

'Oh yes, please do,' several voices chimed up. 'If anyone can solve Callum's death, it's you.'

Ginny stood and pushed her chair back.

The ordering would have to wait. She hurried out to the floor to where Cleo was holding court, surrounded by a group of women who were meant to be discussing their latest book club read. She sent out a silent apology to Gillian McAllister, the brilliant author of the neglected books that were sitting in a pile on the table.

Ginny's appearance seemed to break up the group and Cleo and Andrea drifted to the returns room, leaving the group to continue discussing *Wrong Place, Wrong Time*.

She appreciated they all needed to process and talk about what had happened to Callum but after a full morning where every library regular provided updates, she had developed a headache, and she suspected she wasn't the only one. More importantly, the police had yet to release any information, which meant so far everything was conjecture.

Except even without knowing anything about the murder, it was hard not to connect it to Nathan's death. It was also hard not to blame herself and a ripple of guilt went through her.

Had her visit somehow put him in danger? Would the police want to speak to her? Did they know she had seen him, or should she tell them?

Question after question crowded her mind. When did he even die? Had it been on Saturday night after her visit, or was it sometime on the Sunday?

She thought of her run-in with Imogen yesterday. It seemed unlikely the pathologist would have been there if Callum's body had been discovered, which meant it must have happened sometime between twelve pm and nine pm on Sunday when the news had filtered into the pub.

It was difficult to think that thirty-six hours ago Callum had been alive and sitting across the table from her. The throb between her brows increased and another stab of guilt went through her. This was probably the real reason for her headache, which meant it was unfair to blame Cleo and Andrea for it. Feeling terrible, she walked into the returns room to apologise to them.

They were both discussing a banana bread recipe in a magazine when Ginny joined them.

'Sorry if I was a bit short before. I should never have broken up your conversation.'

'It's okay,' Cleo assured her with surprising understanding. 'We all deal with death differently and the Quiz Killer has us all on edge.'

'I daren't go out on my own.' Andrea shuddered. 'To think it could have been us, if we hadn't been at the pub.'

Ginny couldn't quite follow the logic but didn't feel up to asking. However, it did occur to her that the two volunteers might have known Callum. 'Were you friends with him?'

'Oh yes. He went to school with my husband and was my doctor for many years. Lovely man,' Cleo said with a sigh, making her more human than she usually appeared. 'I can't quite believe he's dead. And we don't even know how it happened.'

'Yes, we do,' Tuppence suddenly called from the issues counter. They all turned around.

'What have you found out?' Cleo elbowed her way past Ginny to where Tuppence was holding multiple copies of the local newspaper. Andrea followed her.

'No need to snatch,' Tuppence protested as Cleo lunged for the paper. 'We bought enough copies to keep you all happy. Here you go.'

'That was very kind of you,' Ginny said as Cleo took the newspaper and hurried back to the book club so they could go over the news together.

'It's going to be all over the village soon enough,' Hen said. 'And the police are going to hold a press conference this afternoon.'

'What do they say? Have they released a statement?' Ginny asked as Tuppence passed her the newspaper.

'No statement but lots of speculation. But if you read between the lines, it appears he was attacked from behind and died from a blow to the head,' JM said.

'They haven't ruled out a burglary gone wrong. You were at Callum's place, Ginny. What do you think?' Hen asked.

'I only went through the hallway into the kitchen. He had

some lovely paintings on the walls. But there were also piles and piles of research everywhere.' She closed her eyes and felt another wave of guilt go through her. 'I've been worried that my visit might have made things worse.'

'Nonsense.' JM's voice was stern. 'Furthermore, I don't think it has anything to do with a burglary. We know there is a connection between Nathan and Callum. They were both interested in Peggy Barlow. It seems to me that they got too close to something.'

'Like the truth of how Peggy and Mikhail disappeared.' Hen shuddered then patted Ginny's arm. 'JM's right. You can't blame yourself. We all decided you should be the one to visit.'

'Exactly,' JM agreed. 'Now, we need to focus on what to do next. Ginny, have you heard from the police? Do they know about your visit?'

She shook her head. 'No and I'm not sure if I should wait to hear from them or contact them.'

'Don't go borrowing trouble,' Tuppence advised. 'What if they have already arrested someone and don't need your statement?'

JM lifted a brow. 'Like Ned Warner. It's no secret he has been making himself unpleasant to lots of people. And he wasn't at the pub last night.'

It was a good point, but Ginny wasn't sure. 'I think we would have heard if he had been arrested.'

Tuppence sighed. 'True, though we need to update Callum Lovelace's card.'

'I'm on it.' Tuppence reached into her bag for a pen. It didn't take them long to put Peggy Barlow and Mikhail Volkov in the middle, along with Nathan and Callum.

'Right. What do we know?' JM asked.

'We know that Nathan was researching what happened to his great-aunt and that he visited Callum Lovelace about it. That's how he found out about Mikhail and Peggy's disappearance.' Tuppence pointed to the MI5 beer mat.

'And we know that Nathan argued with Ned Warner the

Sunday night he was killed,' Hen added. 'But we have no idea what it was about.'

'We can guess that it was over Peggy Barlow.' JM tapped her chin in a thoughtful gesture. 'It also makes Ned Warner the most likely suspect for both murders. I wonder if any of Callum's research was taken?'

Ginny nodded. 'It's certainly a motive even if it seems an extreme thing to do. Plus, if he killed Nathan for the same reason, that might explain why I found Peggy's photograph in the library book. Maybe he wanted to stop Ned from getting it?'

'Especially because that was the photograph that had the book cipher on the back,' Tuppence added then wrinkled her nose. 'Not that we've cracked it.'

'Cracked what?' Slim asked as he appeared at Ginny's shoulder holding an envelope.

'Nothing.' Tuppence got to her feet and stepped in front of the beer mats as Hen hastily pushed them into her knitting bag. 'What do you want?'

'I want to win the lotto. What about you?' Slim bounced back and Ginny quickly got to her feet before Tuppence could answer.

'Sorry, Slim, do you need me at the counter? I won't be a moment.'

'No sweat. Things have quietened down since the newspaper article came out. Most of them have headed over to the station. They want to get front row seats at the press conference. It's not until this afternoon but you know what they are like.'

She did indeed and looking around, Ginny realised the library had all but emptied out.

'All the same, I didn't mean to desert you.'

'Nothing I couldn't handle.' Slim waved the envelope at her. 'I just wanted to give you this. It came through the returns slot.'

Ginny stared at the white envelope. Her name had been typed on the front and it was sealed shut. There could be no mistake it was for her. Her friends let out a collective gasp as Ginny tentatively took it.

'T-thank you, Slim. I won't be long.'

'No worries. I'll message Connor that the detective club is hard at work,' he said, then disappeared back to the counter before she could remind him that they weren't called that. Instead, she took the envelope and sat back down.

'Should you be touching it without gloves?' Hen wanted to know. 'It could be poisonous.'

'Or the killer's fingerprints could be on it,' Tuppence added.

'Or it could be a customer wanting Ginny to order them in a special book,' JM reminded them all and gave her a stern look. 'Are you going to open it?'

Ginny carefully lifted out a single sheet of paper. Then she frowned. On it was typed:

Hamlet 3:1

'*Hamlet*?' JM scrunched her brows together. 'Is someone trying to tell us that Nathan was murdered by his uncle?'

'Or someone called Claudius?' Tuppence added.

'Though what does the 3:1 mean?' Hen said.

It was the same thing Ginny was trying to work out. Eric had been the Shakespeare expert, but Ginny was relatively familiar with most of the plays. She closed her eyes as she went over the story in her mind, then she stiffened as she thought of the book ciphers. Except 3:1 couldn't be a cipher because there wasn't enough information.

Unless it was for the act and scene.

She stood up to see if the library copy was on the shelf, when she suddenly remembered the CCTV images she had been looking at the previous night. Sister Bernadette had been at the far end of the bar, trying to catch Nathan's attention. And he had responded to her, before getting distracted by the bitter that needed to be changed over.

Sister Bernadette.

Hamlet act three, scene one. Of course. She let out a small gasp as she turned to her friends.

'I-I think it's referring to a passage in the play.'

'What passage?'

'Get thee to a nunnery,' she quoted and then filled her friends in on the CCTV footage that she'd seen. 'Sister Bernadette wants to talk to us.'

'Oh, aren't you clever?' Hen clapped her hands. Then wrinkled her nose. 'But why all the secrecy?'

'Probably because two men have been killed in the space of a week. If it was me, I wouldn't want to draw attention to myself,' JM said and leaned forward. 'I told you she had beady eyes.'

Ginny swallowed and got back to her feet. 'Let's wait and see what she says. We can go there after work, if you don't mind waiting.'

'Of course not. She sent the note to you, which means you're our best chance of getting her to talk,' JM agreed and cracked her knuckles, making Ginny very pleased they were all going together. It was hard to imagine what the diminutive Sister Bernadette could possibly have to say to them, but she hoped it would help fill in the missing pieces of the puzzle.

TWENTY-ONE

Tuesday, October 20

The Sisters of Compassion was a single level yellow brick building sprawled out across a green lawn, half hidden beneath autumn leaves. A church in matching bricks with a dramatic roof line and modern stained-glass windows stood to one side, dull in the morning light. Further along was a large garage door with the words *Thou Shall Not Park Here* painted across the front.

They had driven up yesterday, after the library closed, only to discover a conference was taking place, so they had agreed to try again in the morning. At least it was a good excuse to not go power walking.

'I had no idea this place existed.' Ginny climbed out of her car and peered around. Several nuns, complete in their habits, glided past, deep in conversation. Gardeners were hard at work in the large flower beds while a group of women sat in one corner of the garden, near a marble statue of a mother and child.

It was like its own little microcosm.

'I've been here a few times. They often have events and meetings in the larger rooms.' JM pointed to a long wing that looked out onto the surrounding trees. 'And a rather excellent art collection.'

'The sisters run a soup kitchen, which is very popular, especially this time of year when it's getting cold,' Hen added with a shiver as they crossed the gravel carpark and followed the signs to the office.

A serious-looking young man sat at the reception. Ginny's friends stopped to study him before pushing her forward, as if deciding she would be best to make their request. Not sure whether to be bolstered by their confidence or concerned, she crossed the floor alone.

Her footsteps rang in her ear, and she tried to erase the image of Sister Bernadette looking towards the cellar as Nathan disappeared to his fate. Except, if she was involved, then why would she have sent Ginny the note? Unless they had deciphered it incorrectly, and by speaking with the sister, they might be getting in over their heads.

Again.

She reached the counter and forced a smile. 'My name is Ginny Cole and I would like to speak with Sister Bernadette.'

'Sorry, she isn't available until next week. Would you like me to make an appointment for you?'

'An appointment?' JM growled from somewhere behind her.

'Tell him about *Hamlet*,' Tuppence encouraged.

'Maybe we should have brought him some cake as a way to sweeten the deal?' Hen wondered.

'I hate be a nuisance but it's very important I speak with her today,' Ginny quickly broke in before things escalated. 'I would really appreciate your help.'

His face softened, but colour flooded up his neck. 'I'm sorry, I wish I could, but—'

'It's okay, Peter. I am happy to speak with them,' a voice said from behind a wooden door and moments later the diminutive figure of Sister Bernadette appeared.

She was wearing black trousers, an oversized purple cardigan and a gold cross around her neck. Her coppery hair was cut short, and the dispersed light from the office window seemed to form a halo around her small person.

Ginny blinked.

'Are you sure?' Peter frowned.

'I am.' The sister gave a wave of her tiny hand, at the same time revealing navy nail polish. 'Please, won't you all come into my office?'

'Thank you,' Ginny murmured to the young man as she passed into a light-filled office. Like the building, it had a modern feel, with a white desk and black office chair. Four leather chairs faced the desk.

Suddenly Ginny felt very much like she was back at school.

She exchanged a glance with her friends. The sister wasn't acting like she had done anything sinister. Then again, if she *had* done something untoward, surely she would try to hide it.

Sister Bernadette settled herself behind the desk and steepled her fingers. 'Thank you for coming in to see me.'

'We're only here because Ginny's so good with her Shakespeare,' Hen confessed, as she clutched at her knitting bag.

'She didn't even need to look up the play.' Tuppence beamed with pride.

'Of course, this all could have been avoided if you had just answered my questions on Sunday night.' JM's tone was frosty. 'I knew you were hiding something.'

Sister Bernadette bowed her head and let out a small sigh. 'I'm sorry that I ran off, but your questions caught me by surprise... and then when I heard what happened to Callum Lovelace, I realised I needed to find out *why* you want to know who Nathan Richardson was talking to last Sunday.'

Even without the halo-style light surrounding her, the small woman had a confessional air radiating off her. Ginny didn't consider herself religious, but nor did she like lying, especially when she couldn't think of a good reason *not* to tell the truth.

'I'm not sure what we're hoping to find,' she admitted. 'We know that Nathan was looking into his great-aunt, Peggy Barlow, who might have been a spy. He had arranged to meet someone about it, last Sunday night, however, several people spoke with him that night, so we're trying to find them all. Including you.'

Silence stretched between them, causing Ginny to regret ever opening her mouth. She was usually so much better at keeping her thoughts to herself. Would they be judged as nosey women with too much time on their hands? Or worse… meddlers?

Instead, Sister Bernadette exhaled. 'You're right. We did arrange to meet last Sunday night.'

'What?' Hen choked and then put her hand over her mouth. 'Goodness, I'm sorry, that was so rude. I just hadn't expected someone like you to be involved in this.'

'It's a bit like four widows getting tangled up in numerous murder investigations?' Sister Bernadette said but there was no anger in her words, just gentle amusement.

Ginny could feel heat rising in her cheeks, while her friends squirmed in their seats. They all knew how easily women became invisible as they got older, yet here they were, falling into the same trap.

'Please accept our apology,' JM said in a formal voice and then leaned forward. 'And perhaps I was a *little* overzealous at the bar.'

'You were committed, and there's no need to apologise,' Bernadette assured them and lowered her hands to her lap. 'I should have spoken to you then, but I must admit your questions threw me.'

'Why?' Hen asked. 'What did Nathan want to talk to you about?'

'About Peggy Barlow. He had heard about my research. I'm writing a book on her.'

Hen and Tuppence exchanged a glance and Ginny rubbed her brow.

It was JM who spoke first. 'At this point I would be more surprised to meet someone who *isn't* writing a book. By my count that makes three people. And all about a woman that most of us have never heard of.'

'Which is exactly why I'm writing this. Peggy's story deserves to be brought into the light,' Sister Bernadette said, echoing Callum's own words.

'Did you know about Ned and Callum's research?' Ginny asked.

Sister Bernadette's face tightened. 'Yes. I did try to discuss it with them but they both felt very strongly that they should be the ones to write it. Far be it for a woman to tell a woman's story.'

While Ginny did agree with her about the irony that two men thought they had more right to tell Peggy's story, where did Nathan fit in? After all, he was related to her. Again, she wondered if this was more about a race to tell the MI5 spy's story, or to stop someone else from doing it.

Still, it did explain why Nathan had spoken to Ned, Callum and Sister Bernadette.

'What did you tell Nathan?' she asked.

'I told him everything I had discovered about her. We met up twice, and then he came back to see me with this.' Sister Bernadette reached into a desk drawer and retrieved a folded newspaper page. There was a jagged edge down one side, where someone had ripped it away from the rest of the paper. The date read *April 1962*.

'The missing page from our collection.' Ginny couldn't hide her shock.

Did that mean Nathan had requested the newspapers from the stacks? Why had she never thought to check? More importantly, since she knew she hadn't been the one to retrieve them for him, it must have been Slim, Cleo or Andrea, so why didn't they mention it? After all, the three of them had examined every aspect of Nathan's death and were not known for keeping quiet with their thoughts.

Unless Nathan had come in earlier in the month, before Connor had gone on his break.

That made more sense.

It was also beside the point, and Ginny's brow pushed together as she studied the page in question, which was full of advertisements and nonsense articles. What had Nathan possibly seen in it, that could have been of interest?

Sister Bernadette seemed to note her confusion and turned the paper over to reveal a half-page article.

Hiding in Plain Sight: Lancashire's Secret Past

Little Shaw town hall was packed to the rafters as visiting scholar, Dr Ewan Cranfield, shared his years of research on the plight of the recusant Catholic priests who refused to abandon their faith and instead escaped persecution by hiding away in those claustrophobic spaces known as priest holes. Examples of these can be found from Speke Hall through to Samlesbury Hall... and perhaps in Little Shaw.

Yes, that's correct. Our very own Little Shaw might soon be added to the map of places that made up an elaborate network. Dr Cranfield, a professor from Liverpool, has dedicated his life to discovering these spaces that nod back to a bygone era in our turbulent history. When asked about what has happened to them since, Cranfield explained that while some of the more significant houses proudly display the priest holes to the public, we also know that priest holes were used to store valuable heirlooms through to stolen goods and contraband items. He explained the purpose of his visit to Little Shaw was to look more closely into the claims that our valiant village was once part of the network that offered refuge to the fleeing priests.

The evening, which was a huge success, was sponsored by Little Shaw Historical Society, and chairman, Trevor Millman, is quoted as saying: 'It's quite the coup to have Dr Cranfield spend an evening with us and talk about the historical importance of Little Shaw.' Unlike our neighbours in Walton-on-Marsh, of whom the much-admired professor could not be enticed to comment on. Don't forget to join us next month when our speaker will be talking about the lost art of dowsing.'

There was a photograph of Dr Cranfield and Trevor Millman, looking very pleased with themselves, as well as several sweeping images of the audience. Ginny's gaze settled onto the now familiar face of Peggy Barlow.

Her hand flew to her mouth as she remembered the message Sylvie had discovered in the raincoat she had lent to Peggy.

Find the priest.

Was a priest hole what Peggy had been referring to?

More importantly, was that what Nathan had believed?

She searched her mind for what little she knew about priest holes. Though it wasn't much more than what she'd learned in history class. They had been specially designed cupboards and hiding places used during the reformation period to save Catholic priests from persecution. So why was Peggy there?

Then she let out a groan and re-read the article.

Priest holes were used to store everything from valuable heirlooms through to stolen goods and contraband items.

She met Sister Bernadette's gaze. 'Nathan believed that Peggy Barlow hid something important in a priest hole and he wanted to find out where it was.'

'That's correct,' the sister agreed.

'Do you think he showed it to Ned and Callum as well?'

'I do not. I was the only person he spoke to about it.' Sister Bernadette shook her head, making her look even tinier in the large cardigan. 'After all, what better way to learn about the local history of the Catholic church than here? As soon as he gave it to me, I started going through our archives.'

'Wait? You didn't know about there being a priest hole in Little Shaw?' Tuppence jumped to her feet and prowled the room, energy rolling off her.

'Yes, of course I had heard the rumours about it and about Dr Cranfield's theory. Unfortunately, he is no longer alive, but we had several articles on him and I discovered there was a local craftsman, Alfred Meeks, who was rumoured to have built at least two in the area. He wasn't nearly as famous as Nicholas Owen, although his work is respected. His signature was a tiny rose carved into either the bricks or the wood, but getting access to buildings isn't easy. Plus, some of our more recent buildings are built around the shell of older constructions, making it almost impossible to know what lies below. However, I based my research on what buildings a post-mistress in 1962 would have access to, and if there could be a priest hole there.'

Ginny's heart pounded.

The sister had to be talking about The Lost Goat.

Not only was it the place where Nathan had died, but it was also where Peggy Barlow had been a boarder for almost two years. Was it possible? Then she frowned. As far as she knew, the pub hadn't been built until well after the seventeenth century.

Sister Bernadette gave her a soft smile. 'I can see you have done the maths. It's true that the pub wasn't built at the height of the Reformation, but as I said it's not uncommon for new buildings to be built on top of old ones.'

'So there really could be a priest hole somewhere in the cellar?' JM asked.

A flash of pain crossed Sister Bernadette's face. 'I wish I hadn't said anything—I was a victim of my own hubris. I was so eager to find the truth about Peggy Barlow before Ned Warner and Callum Lovelace, that I didn't consider the consequences of my words. I did try to warn Nathan that he might not like what he found, but I never expected him to be killed. Or for anything to happen to Callum.'

'That's why you sent a cryptic note. Because you were worried someone might target you next,' Tuppence declared.

A flush ran up Sister Bernadette's neck. 'Maybe it's what I deserve?'

'None of this is your fault,' Ginny quietly said, thinking of the footage she had viewed. Sister Bernadette had tried to speak with him but hadn't succeeded. 'Nathan was going down to the cellar regardless of whether there was a priest hole. A keg needed to be changed and he offered to do it.'

Sister Bernadette swallowed and nodded her head. 'Thank you for letting me know. All week I've been praying on it, wondering if I should have gone to the police but then when I heard the verdict, I tried to convince myself it really *was* just a terrible accident.'

Ginny couldn't blame her since she had been doing the same thing.

And maybe it had been.

Yet, there were still too many unanswered questions.

Nathan had been looking for a priest hole that Peggy Barlow had allegedly used to hide something important. And now he was dead. Did that mean he'd found it? Or had someone gone down there after him, to stop that from happening?

Oh dear.

Then she thought of Ned Warner. He was unaccounted for in the half hour before Nathan was found by Heather and hadn't been at The Lost Goat on Sunday night when everyone had heard about Callum's murder. Three men, all interested in Peggy Barlow... and now two of them were dead.

Had Ned known about the priest hole and assumed that it was Callum Lovelace who had told Nathan about it, rather than Sister Bernadette?

'Do you think he will try and come after you?' Hen said in a horrified voice.

Sister Bernadette swallowed but instead of answering, she just crossed herself and a calm expression came over her. Clearly, she was concerned but also willing to trust she would be safe.

It seemed that all roads kept leading back to Ned Warner. Ginny shivered as she thought of his angry rant that she had accidently overheard. Had it been directed at the nun?

'One last question. Did Nathan have any idea what Peggy Barlow had hidden in the priest hole?' Ginny asked.

'If he did, he never confided in me about it.'

They all thanked the sister and slowly made their way back outside to the car. It seemed the only way to find out if Nathan had discovered the priest hole was to go back to the place where he died.

Down to the cellar.

TWENTY-TWO

Tuesday, October 20

'It's not there.' JM clambered back up the cellar stairs. It had been a fruitless search, and after tapping all the walls and floorboards to see if they could find any hidden cupboards or tunnel doors, Ginny had retreated upstairs to study the floor plans that Mitch had retrieved for them. It was to see if there were any inconsistencies with the layout, but as far as they could tell, there weren't.

Sister Bernadette had given them a photograph of a rose carved into a wooden door panel and explained it was the maker's mark that the local builder, Alfred Meeks, had used to mark his work. She had also begged them to be careful.

However, there had been no sign of any roses.

'I admit I'm relieved.' Heather brushed away the dust from her jeans. 'I've read of people finding old priest holes and discovering skeletons in there.'

Ginny thought of the warning Sister Bernadette had given Nathan. That he might not like what he found. She swallowed and glanced at her watch. It was eleven-thirty, and she was due at the library in half an hour. There would be no time for a shower.

'What happens now?' Mitch asked from over by the bar. The

pub had opened half an hour ago but there were only a couple of tourists drinking shandies at the far end.

'Our only real suspect now is Ned Warner, so I suggest we regroup at the library and continue researching him.' JM got to her feet.

'Do you know where he is living now?' Ginny asked. 'We can't seem to get his current address.'

'Sorry, he never mentioned it, but I can ask around,' Heather said.

They made their goodbyes and left.

The library, usually quiet before lunch, was full of people talking in low voices. Feeling guilty for leaving Slim and the volunteers on their own, Ginny hurried to the counter.

'How is it going?'

Slim grinned. 'Everything is under control. The new volunteer is shelving the non-fiction and there was no infighting with the scrabble players, which I call a success.'

'Thank you, Slim, I never doubted your ability.'

'I do seem to have a knack,' he agreed. 'Plus, with yesterday's press conference, everyone is pre-occupied.'

Of course. How could she have forgotten about it?

'What happened? Did the police release more information?'

'Nope. Just spoke around in circles and mentioned things like "early days" and "follow all leads." The only thing they did say was that nothing was stolen and that the place was ransacked. Whoever is behind it, clearly isn't a professional.'

'What makes you say that?'

'It's simple. If they were professional hitmen, they wouldn't have created such a mess... and if they were a burglar they wouldn't have left so much valuable loot behind. It's almost offensive. Word on the street is that Lovelace had a large jewellery collection that he'd inherited from his mother. What's more, in a house that old, I bet there were all kinds of collectibles.'

Ginny's lips pressed together. Slim was right. Why *would* someone create such a mess if they were just there to kill Callum? Then she thought of all the stacks of books and the shoebox with the newspaper clippings that Callum's father had collected. What if the person had been looking for something else?

And could the police really know if anything had been taken?

Especially if they weren't looking for it?

'I see... well, hopefully they will give us more information soon. Why don't you take your lunch break now?'

He agreed and sauntered off to the staffroom, whistling as he went. Ginny spent the next half hour at the issues counter, while her friends settled themselves in the reading corner over by the children's section going through the rest of the old newspapers.

When Slim returned, Ginny slipped away to see how they were getting on. The newspapers were pushed to one side and Tuppence was frowning at two beer mats sitting on the coffee table.

Ned Warner and *Sister Bernadette*.

Her stomach tightened and it was clear where their thoughts had been going. That if Ned Warner's motive was to stop anyone jumping him to publish a biography on Peggy Warner, then Sister Bernadette could be in danger.

'As loath as I am to say this, we only have two options,' JM said. 'We either find Ned and get him to confess before he can hurt anyone else. Or... we hand the whole thing over to Wallace. It's clear they have no idea what's going on, because otherwise they would have called Ginny in for questioning.'

JM's words only tightened the growing knot in Ginny's stomach. It had been building as her fear of the police and her need for justice competed. It was true; she had seen Callum within thirty-six hours of his death, yet she hadn't been contacted for a statement. Should she have called them straight away to tell the police what they had talked about?

Her worry had been that she would be seen as interfering... but what if they thought she had purposely been withholding information? Or what if, as JM suggested, Wallace didn't know anything about Peggy Barlow? It was clear he was working on a separate case at the same time, and while she now understood how common this was, it didn't mean she and her friends should solve it on their own.

'I think we should talk to them,' she finally admitted. 'What if we go to the station after work?'

But before they could answer, JM's phone rang. 'It's Mitch. Hang on while I take it.'

JM untangled her long legs and moved across to a shelf of picture books.

Tuppence's eyes were wide. 'Do you think he's found something? Maybe he went down to the cellar again after we left?'

'He didn't,' JM replied as she rejoined them. 'The dratted barman never turned up. He only did two shifts and now isn't answering his phone. Mitch asked if we could go in.'

'Of course.' Tuppence was immediately on her feet, gathering up the beer mats. 'We can pump people to find out where Ned Warner lives.'

'Excellent idea. I have to deliver some knitting to the hospital for the neonatal ward, but I can come along as soon as I'm done,' Hen promised before turning to Ginny. 'Unless you want me to go to the police station with you. I don't mind.'

Ginny gave her a grateful smile. 'Thank you. But it's probably best if I go on my own. I'll give them a statement about my conversation with Callum Lovelace... and then talk them through what we know.'

JM nodded. 'Good. But don't let them bully you. And if you need me to come down... I am sure the pub can do without me for half an hour.'

'I promise,' Ginny said then made her way back to the issues counter, where the rest of the afternoon was filled with patrons wanting to issue books, complaining about the free wi-fi speed and asking about the blue book that they had once seen on the shelves and now couldn't locate. The nerves in her stomach had spread so that it was hard to stay focused. And never did time move so quickly.

Funny how that happened when something dreadful was looming on the horizon.

Then she thought of Sister Bernadette, tiny in stature and trusting that her faith would keep her safe. It very well might... but Ginny wouldn't be able to live with herself if she didn't do everything in her power to make sure it wasn't put to the test.

Finally, it was closing time and she was just walking to the front door to lock it before they went through the final shut down, when Charlie rolled in, a wide grin on his face.

'Eh, what do you think about my new wheels?' He patted the arms of a very smart-looking electric wheelchair that seemed almost as big as Ginny's car. 'The funding finally came through. She's a beauty, ain't she? And powered, which means Slim doesn't need to push me everywhere.'

'About time.' Slim appeared and clapped his friend on the shoulder. 'She is indeed a good specimen. You'd better name her.'

'Slow down, I need to know her better first,' Charlie retorted as he pressed a button and sped across the floor, managing to hit the table where Ginny's workbag was propped up. 'Damn, sorry about that, Ginny. I guess I'm still on my L plates with this thing.'

'Don't worry about it.' Ginny rushed over and gathered up her lunchbox, thermos and spare book she always carried, along with several of the beer mats.

Charlie peered over with interest then whistled. 'Oh... boy. Don't tell me you have anything to do with Ned Warner. Now he's a nasty piece of work.'

Ginny, who was still on her knees, straightened her spine and stared up at Charlie. 'You know him?'

'Know him?' Charlie let out a bark of laughter. 'You could say that. I once tried to get my hands on that old Milners safe of his. Such a classic that it would have been a real honour to...' He paused and coughed. 'To open it. You should have seen the way he carried on. Anyone would think I was trying to take his life savings.'

'You were,' Slim retorted with a chortle.

Charlie raised an eyebrow, appearing much struck. Then he shrugged. 'Yes, well, I suppose that's true. But there was no need for him to be so rude. He started swearing up a storm. It put an end to our friendship, I can tell you.'

Friendship?

She took a steadying breath and got to her feet, still clutching at the beer mat. A safe-cracker and a newspaper editor seemed an unlikely friendship. 'I didn't realise you knew him.'

'Oh, aye.' Charlie nodded. 'You could say we were associates.'

She must have looked bewildered because Slim coughed. 'Ned Warner wasn't above going about getting his information in a variety of ways. And while he never did any of that phone tapping stuff... he was quite happy to request the occasional break-in.'

'You both worked for him?'

'In our line of business it's often feast or famine. And we never stole anything, just took photographs. And let me tell you that takes some restraint to ignore piles of cash and jewels crammed into safes and focus on the documents. But that's what being a professional is all about.'

'I-I see, and do you know where Ned Warner lives? I would really like to talk to him.'

'You're the only one,' Charlie retorted. 'But if you must know, he is at Ashworth Court.'

'Ashworth Court?' Ginny croaked, thinking of Sylvie. Ice filled her veins. She had been so worried that Ned might try to harm Sister Bernadette, but what if he considered Sylvie a threat as well? After all, she was the one who had given Nathan the second photograph of Peggy Barlow and knew more about her than anyone.

'That's the place,' Charlie agreed. 'Wouldn't catch me moving there. I've heard some zingers about it. Why—'

'Can't see a fancy place like that letting the likes of us in it,' Slim cut him off before turning to Ginny. 'I don't want to pry, but would you like me to help in any way? We make quite the team, and Ned isn't exactly a nice character. There were rumours that we weren't the only associates he worked with...'

Ginny shivered. Was he implying that Ned Warner had hired thugs to do his dirty work? 'There's nothing to help with,' Ginny quickly assured him. While she was touched by the offer, the last thing she wanted to do was lead him into any trouble. Besides, her next step was to take everything to the police and they could deal with Ned Warner and his vicious temper.

'Well then, I'll be off. I need to make sure Charlie doesn't take out half the population of Little Shaw with his bad driving.'

'I'll have you know I once drove for the Mulligans and they said I had all the makings of a first rate stoppo man. But I decided that my talents lay elsewhere.'

'Probably for the best, since the Mulligans are now all behind bars,' Slim retorted.

'Well, they had the wrong stoppo man, didn't they?' Charlie fired back with a grin, and the pair of them disappeared outside. Ginny locked the door and called her friends. There was no answer, so she left a message, telling them what she had discovered, and that she was going to tell the police about it.

Then she checked the time.

With that she climbed into her car and drove directly to the police station.

TWENTY-THREE

Little Shaw Police Station had been built in the sixties in a time when function was more important than decorative design. Several crisp packets were caught against the concrete ramp along with a pile of burnished leaves, as the autumn wind swirled around the building. Ginny bent to retrieve the litter, her body still protesting after Sunday's power walk.

There were no recycling bins in the station so she popped them into her bag and with more bravado than she felt, pushed open the utilitarian doors and stepped inside.

The reception area was empty and there was no one behind the counter. She stepped forward just as a harassed-looking woman appeared on the other side. Ginny didn't recognise her but smiled all the same.

'My name is Ginny Cole. I need to speak with DI Wallace.'

'Sorry, love, he's not here.'

'Are you sure? It's quite important,' she pushed but the woman just shook her head. 'Or DC Singh.'

'She's not here either,' the woman said with a dull finality. 'I'll let them know you came by. Do they have your number?'

Ginny nodded then peered around the empty reception area in the hopes that Anita or Wallace would suddenly walk in.

They didn't.

Sighing, she thanked the woman and walked back outside. The wind had picked up, and it whipped against her coat. Soon it would be time to swap into something warmer. She pulled it closer and hurried to the car. Indecision clawed at her. Should she just go home and wait to hear from Wallace? Or should she call him?

After all, he was the one always telling her not to meddle in police business, and she had an uneasy feeling that's exactly what this was. She made the call, but it went straight to voicemail. Knowing he probably wouldn't bother to listen to it, she constructed a text message.

> Hello James, I am very sorry to disturb you, but I have some important information. Please call me back at your earliest convenience. Best wishes from your neighbour, Ginny (Cole).

Pausing to study the message, she finally pressed send. To think that a year ago she hardly ever remembered to carry her phone with her, yet now she was casually texting. She was almost surprised when a message pinged straight back. But her excitement didn't last long.

> busy

Ginny stared at it. One word. And not even a capital letter or full stop. She chewed her lip. Was it bad manners for her to text him back? Then again, he was the one who had forgone the rules of grammar. Feeling justified, she typed out a second message.

> Hello James, I know how much work you do, but this is quite urgent and if you could please call me as soon as you are able to, I would appreciate it. Yours truly, Ginny.

She hit send and then studied the screen, but whatever compelled him to reply to the first text, had obviously deserted him and her phone didn't ping again. Should she try Anita? But what if they were on a job together and it just made Wallace grumpier to know she was going behind his back?

Ginny pinched her brow.

The decision of what to do would have been easier if she didn't have Ned Warner's address racing through her mind.

What would Wallace say if she went there on her own? It was a rhetorical question since she knew full well what his feelings would be.

Then she stiffened. Just because she couldn't risk confronting Ned, didn't mean she couldn't speak to Sylvie Yates about him, since they were practically neighbours now.

Besides, visiting an eighty-nine-year-old woman could hardly be considered dangerous.

Decision made, she drove to the retirement home.

Ashworth Court appeared even more depressing than the police station against the dull late afternoon sky and as she stepped into the reception area a swirl of autumn leaves followed. The same receptionist, Carol, was at the desk and Ginny smiled at her.

Carol stared back blankly. 'Who are you here to see?'

'Sylvie Yates,' Ginny said, trying not to mind being forgotten.

At the mention of Sylvie's name, the receptionist's expression tightened. 'She's not here. That daughter-in-law took her out over an hour ago.'

'Aren't they back yet?' Lizzie, the same nurse that had helped them last time, appeared, her mouth set in a frown.

'Nope. But what do you expect?' Carol retorted. 'That woman is more interested in using Sylvie as a calling card, than as someone who needs their routine. Look at the weather out there. It's miserable.'

'Poor Sylvie deserves better,' Lizzie agreed with a sigh.

Ginny studied them both then frowned. 'I'm not sure I understand. Was Veronica not meant to take Sylvie out?'

'Technically it's none of our business, but it's clear that Veronica Yates is only using the poor old duck to get new clients. Sylvie has lived in the area for so long and everyone loves her, so what better way to get someone to open the door to you? Especially when they're rich,' Carol said.

She tried not to think of how frail Sylvie was and how windy it was outside. It hardly seemed good weather to take out an elderly woman. Especially if what they were saying was true. And while there was nothing technically wrong with it, she could understand why the Ashworth staff weren't happy.

It also meant it was a wasted trip.

She was about to turn away when she remembered Ned Warner. Would it be such a silly thing to talk to him? After all, what could really happen to her while she was here?

'Actually.' She coughed and tried to appear confident. 'While I am here, I should visit Ned Warner, too.'

'Why do you want to visit him?' Carol's face darkened. The question caught Ginny off-guard and before she could answer, Lizzie gave the receptionist a questioning look, as if she, too, had been surprised by the response.

'It's personal,' Ginny finally answered.

'You're a braver person than I am, then,' Lizzie said when it was clear Carol wasn't going to answer. 'Carol, hand over the signing-in tablet.'

'Far be it from me to stop you from getting your head snapped off.' Carol passed over the tablet, her face still tight with tension. 'He's only lived here a year and has managed to piss off just about everyone he comes across.'

That tracked with everything Ginny had heard about him. Yet right now he was their only suspect.

Lizzie must have read her expression and gave her a smile. 'Listen to us, we shouldn't be talking about him. It's not our place to judge. He's up on the seventh floor. 77c. Use the same lift that you took up to Sylvie's and he's second on the right.'

'And brace yourself,' Carol added before Lizzie gave her a

warning look. Carol shrugged. 'Better you than me is all I am saying.'

'Thank you.' Ginny once again filled her details into the tablet and said goodbye to the staff before making her way up to the seventh floor.

Ned Warner's door was shut but there was the low hum of the radio coming from it. That was promising and Ginny knocked. There was no answer and she tried again. Perhaps he was deaf? She tried once more, her knuckles stinging with the effort.

Frustration flooded her as she shifted from foot to foot, trying to decide what her next step should be. She checked her phone but there were no messages from Wallace. There were, however, numerous text messages from her friends, who were still at The Lost Goat. She let them know what she was doing, and Tuppence immediately pinged her back with the offer to come and pick the locks.

Ginny decided that probably wouldn't help matters.

She tried one last time and was about to leave when the door inched open and a head peered out. But it wasn't Ned Warner. It was a woman in her forties with thick hair that was pulled back from her face, and a smudge of dirt on her forehead.

'Sorry, I was cleaning the bathroom and didn't hear the door go. Can I help you?'

'I-I'm not sure,' Ginny said cautiously, wondering if she had the wrong apartment. 'I was hoping to talk to Ned Warner. Does he live here?'

'Yes... though he's asleep right now. He's had a rather long night.'

'I hope everything is okay.'

'Not really.' The woman's eyes filled with tears, but she brushed them away. 'We thought he had early-stage dementia but... it turns out it's not so early.'

'I'm sorry to hear that. And to disturb you.' Ginny's heart filled with sympathy. This was something she had seen affect so many of their patients and their families over the years and she knew how cruel it could be. Part of her wondered how long Ned would be able to continue with independent living.

'That's okay.' The door opened further. She was wearing jeans and an oversized shirt that was rolled at the sleeves. 'I'm Lena. What was it you wanted to see him about?'

Lena? At the realisation the woman was Ned's daughter, so many things fell into place. Did that explain his angry outbursts and why she had seen him wandering around the park? Was that why Lena hadn't been at home the other day, because she had been looking for her father?

'It's not important,' Ginny said, feeling terrible for turning up unannounced when the family was going through such an upheaval. 'Though I really am sorry to hear about his condition.'

Lena sighed. 'That's very sweet of you. Look, I'm just about to boil the kettle for a cup of tea. Would you like to come inside?'

Ginny pressed her lips together. She should leave poor Lena in peace. But there was something in the younger woman's eyes that seemed to be sincere so she nodded. 'Only if it's not a bother.'

'I could use the distraction. Come in and tell me what Dad's done now.'

'Nothing, exactly,' Ginny admitted and followed her into the apartment. Lena gestured to a velvet lounge chair and disappeared into the kitchen.

Ginny sat down and studied the room. Like Sylvie's place, there were several stunning oil paintings on the wall and a cabinet of exquisite porcelain. The furniture was equally lovely and not at all in keeping with what she imagined Ned's apartment would be like.

Lena returned with two teacups and must have caught Ginny's surprised expression. She let out a small laugh. 'All family heirlooms. Dad loved them, though between you and me, I prefer Ikea. But doctors thought it might help ground him. I even tried playing some of his old records, thinking it would help, but he kicked off. He's never had a great temper, and recently it's just got worse.'

'I've heard that can happen,' Ginny said, her heart going out to the younger woman.

'I know he wasn't well-liked. Even at home he could be... difficult. But he's still my dad.'

'Of course he is,' Ginny said. 'And it's never easy to see someone you love going through anything like this. I feel terrible for disturbing you. I had wanted to ask Ned a few questions about the young barman who died.'

'Nathan Richardson? That was so sad. I was there when it happened.'

'You were? I didn't see you,' Ginny admitted, searching her mind for any sight of Lena. 'Were you on one of the teams?'

'No, nothing like that. I dropped Dad there because he loves that quiz team. But he missed half of it because he went out for a cigarette and then managed to get lost.' She picked up her phone and tapped it. 'I've been worried about him for a while so I set his phone to share his location.'

Ginny raised an eyebrow. 'You can do that?'

'Oh yes. It's quite easy and you can send people your location as well. I used to do it to keep track of my teenagers when they went out at night, but lately I've had to use it for Dad. Anyway, I noticed he was halfway down the high street that night so went out to retrieve him. I tried to take him home, but he insisted on going back to the pub. I went in with him and we weren't there for long when they discovered the body. So sad.'

It *was* sad. And once again Ginny realised just how wrong she and her friends had been, not just about Ned Warner, but about everyone. Whoever had killed Nathan and Callum—if, in fact, anyone did kill Nathan—it wasn't Ned.

'One more thing. Did you know anything about your father writing a book?'

'The one about Peggy Barlow? Yes, it was no secret he wanted to... but as to whether he did write it, is anyone's guess. I have certainly not found any writing. From what I could gather there isn't much information readily available on her, and he was never known for his patience. Even with the paper he used to like taking short cuts.'

Ginny recalled what Slim and Charlie had said.

It seemed easy enough to believe that without people there to help him find the information he needed to write about Peggy, the project had remained an idea.

She stayed ten more minutes making small talk with Lena before getting to her feet and apologising for taking up her time. Then she made her way back to the car.

Too much had happened today, and she felt tired and silly. Sylvie had mentioned how everyone had had spy fever back in the sixties and Ginny wondered if that was what had happened to her and her friends. But now she realised she wasn't the spy who came in from the cold, she was the widow who came back to reality.

TWENTY-FOUR

Tuesday, October 20

The sky was gunmetal-grey by the time Ginny drove away from Ashworth Court and all she wanted to do was go home and sit on her couch. She'd long acknowledged this was her preferred way of coping with all of life's ups and downs, and these days she only allowed herself to use this method in moderation. But after talking to Lena and learning the tragic truth about Ned Warner's behaviour, she felt justified in spending the rest of the evening curled up with Edgar and her book, reading aloud and pretending that Eric was still there listening along.

And of course there would be lots of tea.

Which reminded her that she needed milk. There was a row of quaint shops just down the road and while the antique store, café and florist would be shut, the corner shop would still be open so she decided to stop there, rather than waiting until she got back to Little Shaw proper.

Ginny came to a stop and went inside to get her milk and a packet of Penguins for good measure. The sky had brightened, in that ominous way it sometimes did before a storm.

Oh dear.

Shivering, she fumbled with her keys before finally unlocking the door. At least the traffic had cleared and the road was almost empty as Ginny put her keys into the ignition.

As she did so a familiar red Mini Cooper came to a slow stop across the road.

It was bright against the miserable weather and Ginny could just see a flash of auburn hair from the driver's seat as Imogen bowed down to check something on her phone.

Had she just finished work for the day? Perhaps she was organising a date with Wallace? Or she could be dealing with a work call.

As Ginny pondered it, a large black van also slid to a halt further back from Imogen and turned off their lights, as if they were about to get out and cross the road to buy something from the same corner shop.

Imogen suddenly pulled back out and drove in the other direction. Moments later, the black van flicked on their lights and eased out onto the empty road.

As it crawled past, Ginny caught sight of a man in his mid-thirties with a trimmed beard. There was something familiar about the stern face—

The poster that Wallace had brought into the pub on Saturday.

Ice skittered along her spine as she twisted to watch the retreating vehicle. It still hadn't sped up and headlights from another car illuminated the registration number. NE67 ABE.

Ginny fumbled for a pad and pencil, repeating it as she wrote, terrified of forgetting. 'NE67 ABE. NE67 ABE. NE67 ABE.'

Once it was scribbled down, adrenaline thundered in her ears.

She had just embarrassed herself with her terrible assumptions about Ned Warner. Did that mean she should ignore this as well? After all, Wallace had never told them *why* he was looking for the man. And it could be a complete coincidence that he was following Imogen.

She squashed the thought. The one thing she had always been good at was acting quickly when required, so she picked up her phone and brought up Wallace's number. Her thumb hovered over the call button before pressing the text icon instead.

She long knew he didn't answer many of her calls and at least he replied to some of her messages. Well, one. But now wasn't the time to split hairs.

Her hands shook as she tapped the screen as quickly as she could.

> Man u look for in black Toyota NE67 ABE following Imogen on Acorn heading north.

Without stopping to read it back or correct anything, she hit send. A second later Wallace's name flashed up on her screen as an incoming call. Her hands shook as she answered it.

'Where are you?' he said without preamble. His voice was filled with tension and Ginny's heart hammered in her chest.

'A-at the corner shop past Ashworth Court. What can I do?'

'Call Anita. Tell her I am five minutes away. I have Imogen's location on my phone so I can follow her.' Then, without another word he hung up. Ginny's throat went tight. She had no idea what was going on, but it was clearly important. She called the DC and passed on the message before leaning back in her seat.

Whatever this was, she needed to let the police handle it and she hoped that it would all turn out well.

TWENTY-FIVE

Wednesday, October 21

The following morning Edgar executed a lap around Ginny's legs before jumping up on her lap and nudging her. If he could speak, she was pretty sure he would be reminding her that she was late for work.

'It's okay. Slim has kindly offered to cover for me, and Cleo and Andrea are going to help,' she informed him. It seemed to satisfy the cat's curiosity, and he closed his amber eyes and pushed his head into her hand. As if by selflessly offering himself up for a fuss, she would feel better.

She patted him, letting his warm fur and familiar snore relax her.

Though truth be told, she felt a bit silly staying home, when she wasn't the one who had been in danger, and she probably wouldn't have agreed except Wallace had sent her a text message at eleven last night to tell her Imogen was safe and that he would visit tomorrow. The other reason was that she had hardly slept, as her mind went over and over what she'd seen.

Who was the man? Had he been stalking Imogen? Did she know him?

On more than one occasion Eric had treated victims of domestic abuse and while he had never broken his patient's confidentiality, she knew how upsetting he had found it.

'I just hope she's okay,' Ginny said to the room, allowing herself the rare gift of speaking directly to her dead husband. She was saved from not hearing his answer by a knock on the door.

'It's me—James. Imogen is also here,' her neighbour called out.

She carefully detached herself from Edgar's paws to unlock the door and let them in. The pathologist's face was pale and there were dark smudges under her eyes, but at the sight of Ginny, she stepped forward and hugged her.

'Thank you, thank you, thank you,' she said.

'Let's take this inside. I can see the neighbours gathering,' Wallace said in a cool voice as Ginny untangled herself from Imogen and led them both through to the living room. But despite his tone he looked just as tired, with a pale face and a two-day beard.

'They'll find out soon enough,' Imogen said but then paused to smooth away the worry lines that were covering his brow. 'It's okay. I'm safe.'

Ginny's throat went dry as she took them both in. Had she been right about Imogen being stalked?

'Would you like a cup of tea?'

'I can't stay long,' Imogen said, her hand slipping into Wallace's as they both sat down on the sofa, leaving Ginny to settle in her new reading chair. 'But I wanted to see you and let you know what happened. I gather that James was a bit... abrupt on the phone last night.'

'Not at all,' Ginny quickly assured her. 'I didn't know what was happening, but it was obvious he was worried. I-I'm pleased things seem to be okay now.'

'They are,' Wallace said, before exchanging a look with Imogen. 'Do you want me to tell her or you?'

'You do it.' Imogen nodded, face still pale.

He kissed her before turning to Ginny. 'When Imogen moved

up this way, it was to get away from Evan Devril, her ex-boyfriend. He was toxic and abusive, but she hoped the move would give her a clean break. However, not long after she started the new job, the text messages began, and because we were friends, she confided in me.'

Ginny thought of all the times Wallace had appeared distracted—his face buried in his phone. Was it because he had been worrying about Imogen? And what about her, starting again in a new place and not knowing who she could trust.

Her heart ached for them both.

'I'm pleased she had someone she could trust,' she finally said.

'So am I.' Imogen leaned against Wallace's shoulder. 'I'd been justifying Evan's bad behaviour for so long and couldn't really see it for what it was. But as you know James doesn't suffer fools and it helped wake me up to what was really happening. Plus, it brought us closer together.'

'I would have preferred you not to have gone through that for us to get together,' Wallace growled but he couldn't hide the colour creeping up his cheeks. It was strange to see him so *human*.

'You make a lovely couple,' Ginny said to them both.

'I think so.' Imogen managed a smile.

Wallace coughed. 'Thanks. Anyway, since he didn't know where she lived, we hoped it would eventually stop. But Devril saw that damn photograph Mitch posted on their social media account. When we won the quiz.'

Ginny's hand flew to her mouth. 'That's why you asked Mitch to take it down?'

'Yes, but it was too late by then and Imogen found a note on her car. It was stupid because there is already an arrest warrant out for him. But the closer he got, the more reckless he became.'

Ginny turned to Imogen. 'When I saw you the other day you were so pale. Like you had just seen a ghost.'

'In a way I had.' Imogen shivered.

'I'm so sorry you went through that.' Ginny silently berated herself. She had assumed Imogen was hiding there because of Ned Warner.

'It gets worse. Her neighbour caught someone trying to break into her apartment, which is when we discovered Devril got her address while he was working at the pub.'

'Working at The Lost Goat? I don't understand.'

'Apparently, he did a trial shift on Friday night and managed to get Imogen's address out of a local electrician while the guy was drunk. He went back on Saturday night as well to work another shift and ask more questions about her.'

No. This was too dreadful. JM had mentioned that working behind the bar seemed like a confessional, but it truly shocked Ginny that Imogen's ex would do something like that. And how hadn't Mitch recognised him? She frowned, thinking of the photograph Wallace had brought around.

'What did Mitch say? Why didn't he call you when he realised his new barman was a person of interest? I promise I left it on his desk.'

'I believe you. We think Devril saw the job advertised in the window and worked a trial on the Friday. He probably saw the poster on Saturday and threw it away, leaving Mitch and Heather none the wiser. I talked to them last night, which is when they also confessed about the break-in,' Wallace growled, sounding more like his usual self.

'You think that was Devril?' She had been so convinced it had to do with Nathan's death, but there had never been any proof.

Wallace nodded. 'Don't look so guilty. Mitch told me you wanted them to report it.' He leaned back and ran a hand through his hair. 'Sorry, I'm still processing how close *he* got to her.'

Ginny couldn't blame him. It was hard to imagine how helpless he must have felt while Imogen was being tormented by someone she had once trusted. 'I'm pleased it's now over.'

'Thanks to you. Up until then we didn't have his registration number, and Imogen had no idea he was following her—' Wallace broke off, clearly overcome.

'I didn't even see you there. But I'm so pleased you were,' Imogen said before an alarm went off on her watch. She sighed and kissed Wallace's cheek. 'I need to meet with the coroner. I promise I would rather be at work than stuck at home. And you know it's safe now.'

A mulish frown rippled across his face, but she just kissed him again. 'Okay.' His voice was gruff. 'I will talk to you soon, but first Ginny and I need to continue our chat.'

'Well, just be nice about it,' Imogen warned and then gave Ginny a warm hug before letting herself out the front door.

Ginny, who had been on the verge of following her out into the hallway, sank back down in her chair, all too familiar nerves catching in her throat.

'W-we do? What is there to chat about?'

'Let's see.' Wallace held up his hand. 'To begin with we have the two text messages you sent me yesterday about needing to speak to me urgently. Then there is the question of why you were so close to Ashworth Court last night. But I'm probably most curious about why you were visiting Lena Warner.'

Ginny stiffened. 'How do you know about that?'

'She called us yesterday to report a robbery. She had been cleaning her father's apartment and noticed several paintings were missing. During our conversation your name came up, and she said you had been there asking all kinds of questions about him.'

Robbed?

This was news to her. Lena never mentioned anything about being robbed. Her heart pounded. 'Surely you don't think I had anything to do with it.'

'Did I say that?' Wallace retorted and crossed his legs before folding his arms, making him look very uptight. 'Now, I think it's time you tell me what's going on.'

'W-which part?' Ginny said, heart pounding from his unflinching gaze.

'*All* the parts.'

After a halting start Ginny filled him in on everything that had happened since discovering the photograph of Peggy Barlow last week, including her conversation with Callum Lovelace and ending with how Ned Warner had been their main suspect. Once she was finished, she folded her hands in her lap and waited for him to speak. Or to yell. It wouldn't be the first time it had happened, but perhaps this would be the most deserved.

Instead, he rubbed his face, fatigue turning his complexion a dull grey. 'Seems I've missed a lot.'

'You can't blame yourself,' Ginny said, surprised at her own response. She had been so ready for him to rip shreds off her but instead he was blaming himself. It was a little unnerving. 'There was a lot going on and it's only natural that you'd be worried about Imogen... with that man on the loose.'

'I was, but it says something that you and your friends have been running around Little Shaw and I didn't have the slightest idea.'

'Was Ned Warner really robbed?' she ventured to ask, her mind trying to sift through what she knew. But she was drawing a blank.

'Yes, two paintings are missing. Anita's already been over there, but in light of everything you have told me, it seems to me there must be a link, and I'm on the back foot.'

'Without wanting to overstep, we could help you get up to speed,' Ginny offered, thinking of the beer mats in her handbag.

'That wouldn't be appropriate.' Standing, he pocketed his phone and rolled his shoulders.

For once Ginny didn't feel nervous. She just saw a tired man who had been far too worried about someone he loved. Then she thought of Sister Bernadette and Sylvie. If there was a killer still out there, both could be in danger. 'You were complaining that your father is too anti-social and doesn't ask anyone for help, but it seems as if you're cast from the same mould.'

Wallace's eyes turned flinty and his jaw locked. 'I'm nothing like my father.'

'That sounds exactly like something Ted would say. Though

he'd use even fewer words,' Ginny told him. 'At least let us go over our research, and then if you want to throw it all in the bin, you are welcome to do so.'

He opened his mouth and then closed it again before letting out a long sigh and sitting back down. 'Fine. I'll give you half an hour.'

TWENTY-SIX

Wednesday, October 21

'The purpose of the beer mats are threefold. Firstly, it means we can bring them with us. As you can see,' JM explained ten minutes later as she pointed to the vintage cardboard mats on Ginny's kitchen table. Wallace was in a chair, with Edgar asleep in his lap. Ginny couldn't help but think it was a good safety measure since he couldn't lose his temper while Edgar was so content.

Well, she hoped not.

When she'd called her friends to get them over, they had been power walking to discuss the case and so were now dressed in an array of bright leisurewear. Still, it did help to cheer up the kitchen.

'And we can easily move each mat around as we work through our theories.' Hen picked up the card that said *No Austen* on the top and moved it next to one that said *Windscale* to demonstrate. 'Just like if we were sewing a quilt.'

'Not that we will be turning these into a quilt,' Tuppence clarified. 'In fact, I suspect we will compost them once we are finished. Or shred them... though I don't think they'll go through my home shredder. You might have a better one at the station.'

'What's the third reason?' Wallace cut in, as if not sure how to answer the shredder question. Ginny gave him a reassuring smile. He was doing very well and since her friends had arrived, he hadn't lost his temper once.

'It's thematically pleasing, of course. You see, this all started in The Lost Goat, so the beer mats keep us connected,' JM said.

Wallace blinked, then cleared his throat. 'To clarify, you're working on the theory that Nathan Richardson was looking into the disappearance of Peggy Barlow and Mikhail Volkov, and the explanation might be hidden in an unknown priest hole. And along the way he managed to uncover three people who were all trying to write books on his great-aunt, Peggy.'

'That's correct,' JM agreed, her gaze penetrating his. 'Are you disputing this?'

'No, it's the same path I would have explored; it's where the evidence points.'

He reached out and examined some of the cards more closely, before changing the order. Then he picked up the beer mat with Ned Warner's name on it. 'We need to add that he was robbed.'

'Do you think it's connected, or a separate issue?' Ginny asked. Ever since he had mentioned the robbery, she had been trying to work out how it fitted together.

'I'm not sure at this stage.'

'What exactly was taken?' Hen asked.

'Two paintings by Peter Doig.'

'Doig?' JM, who had once owned an art gallery, straightened. 'I am a big fan of his work.'

'Me too,' Tuppence agreed.

'I suspect Ned Warner was as well,' Wallace said in a dry voice before turning his attention back to the beer mats. He studied them for several moments before snatching his phone from the table.

'Oh, who do you think he's calling?' Tuppence stage-whispered.

'I don't know but it's very exciting.' Hen leaned forward.

'I admit my curiosity has been aroused,' JM agreed.

If Wallace heard them, he didn't show it as he made a call.

'Bent, go to Lovelace's house and look for any research about a spy called Peggy Barlow. Have we heard back from the insurance company on what items were registered? As soon as that comes in, I want someone going through the entire property to see if anything was stolen, then meet me back at the station.'

Ginny and her friends exchanged a glance, but it was Tuppence who spoke.

'Should you have said please?'

'Not unless I wanted him to think he was in trouble. Now, go over everything Sister Bernadette said about priest holes, and the builder chap who made them. Did she include a map of which buildings in Little Shaw she thought would be the most likely places to start looking? Apart from The Lost Goat?'

'No map, but actually that's an excellent idea. We didn't think of asking her,' JM grudgingly admitted.

'I wouldn't expect you to.' He tapped his phone against his chin. 'I'll send someone to speak with her. And I'll get the team to deep dive into Nathan's history.'

'Just like that?' Tuppence said. 'You make it sound so easy. How do you know which things to prioritise?'

'I don't always. But in the beginning it's best to cast a wide net. Now, let's move onto the photograph. What books have you used to try and decipher the numbers?'

Ginny was beginning to feel a little dizzy as Wallace fired question after question at them, and it was hard not to appreciate his abilities. Finally, he took a step back from the beer mats that were now in a completely different sequence.

'How clever you are to understand our system so quickly.' Hen gave him a warm smile then reached for several of the beer mats that were still stacked to one side. 'Perhaps we should put them all out. It might help you make some visual connections.'

His eyebrow shot up. 'You mean you haven't shown me everything?'

'Of course we have,' JM retorted before studying the extra beer mats. 'Er... except for those ones. Let's see what they are. I'm sure they're not important.'

'Okay, we have *Next of Kin*, *Veronica Yates*, and this one is just a lot of scribbling,' Hen announced.

'Let me see that,' Wallace reached for one of the cards.

Hen frowned. 'It really is just some nonsense. I was trying to doodle a rabbit, but it didn't turn out properly. However, if you think it's important—'

'Not the rabbit doodle,' he cut in. 'The one on Veronica Yates. What have you found out about her?'

'Not that much,' Hen admitted. 'She is Sylvie's daughter-in-law and acted strangely when she saw the photographs of Peggy Barlow.'

'Which is an odd thing if you ask me,' Tuppence added.

'Yes, we thought so as well,' Hen agreed in a supportive voice.

'Why do you want to know about Veronica Yates?' JM suddenly folded her arms and studied Wallace. 'Do you have information about her, because as part of our team it's only fair that you tell us.'

'Just to be clear, I am not part of your team,' he said in a cool voice and retrieved his phone once again. 'However, in this instance I will let you know that Veronica Yates visited both Callum Lovelace and Ned Warner in the last seven days.'

JM's posture snapped straight and Hen gasped while Tuppence let out a long 'whoa'. Ginny wasn't sure how she reacted, though she suspected her mouth dropped open. She turned to her friends. They hadn't considered Veronica as a potential suspect, despite her close connection to Sylvie and that she had reacted strangely to the photographs.

Was it really possible that she had been involved?

Then she recalled her own conversation with Carol and Lizzie.

With so much going on, it had slipped her mind.

'When I went to Ashworth Court yesterday, the staff were talking about how Veronica was using Sylvie as a way to meet other rich clients. She had even taken poor Sylvie out in dreadful weather. I got the feeling they didn't like her.'

'Oh, that's interesting. Let me get that down.' Tuppence swept up Veronica's beer mat and began to write. Then she turned to Wallace, who was busy making his own notes. She leaned over his shoulder and scanned the page.

Satisfied with whatever she saw, she capped her hot-pink felt-tip and reached for a green one to underline something, before offering it to Wallace.

'I'm good, thank you.' He grimaced and turned his attention back to the other beer mats. 'So, we know that Veronica Yates is interested in getting new clients—rich ones—and that she is happy to use her mother-in-law's name to get through the door. Is it possible that she considered Nathan a threat?'

'Oh, I hadn't thought of it like that,' Hen gasped. Ginny couldn't blame her. While she hadn't found Veronica warm, she hadn't liked to think her capable of doing anything truly dreadful.

What if Wallace was right?

After all, Nathan was young and smart, and he suddenly turned up on Sylvie's doorstep claiming to be the great-nephew of a dear friend. And Sylvie had given Nathan a photograph in a yellow envelope. Would Veronica have seen him as competition for her inheritance?

Quite possibly.

She looked up at Wallace, who was still staring at the cards. 'You think Veronica was jealous of Nathan?'

'I have seen people do worse for less,' Wallace said in a cool voice. 'We know Nathan was looking for something Peggy Barlow hid in a priest hole. What if Veronica was worried about the information coming out?'

Ginny nodded. 'That's possible. When Tuppence and I first met her, she was very quick to take the photographs of Peggy Barlow from us. As if she recognised them.'

'Perhaps she did?' Wallace said and began to tap something on his phone. Then he looked up. 'I've just sent DC Singh a message asking her to bring Veronica Yates in for questioning. Can I take these with me?'

Ginny followed his gaze to the scattered beer mats but before she could answer JM made a growling noise. 'They are our intellectual property, and if we're not on your team, then I don't think it's appropriate.'

'Not unless you can assure us that they will be correctly recycled,' Tuppence added.

'You can have my rabbit doodle,' Hen offered up.

Wallace's expression morphed into an all too familiar scowl.

Ginny turned to her friends. 'It's a group decision, of course. But... I think we should let DI Wallace take them. If they can help solve the mystery, then it seems the correct thing to do. And we can't forget that Sister Bernadette might be in danger.'

'I suppose you have a point.' JM swept them up into a neat stack before passing them over to Wallace. 'But Tuppence is right about making sure you shred them afterwards. If there is one thing this business has taught us, it's that we shouldn't leave a paper trail.'

'Thank you.' Wallace took the pile and walked to the door, before turning back to face them. He let out a long sigh. 'I hope I don't live to regret this, but if you would like to come along and observe the interview, you may do so. Oh... and thank you.'

Then without another word he disappeared from the room.

Ginny and her friends exchanged a shocked glance and scrambled to their feet. She doubted he would make the offer again.

TWENTY-SEVEN

Wednesday, October 21

Ginny followed Anita down the narrow hallway of the police station and into a small room with a large glass window that looked into a second room. Except it wasn't really a window but rather a two-way mirror. Her friends trailed behind her, still wearing their exercise gear, eyes bright with excitement. And while Ginny didn't feel excited, the usual dread that accompanied most of her visits to the police station was gone.

'Okay, I'd better go. Wallace requested me to join him,' Anita said with deep pride. 'Please remember to keep your voices down, and don't touch the glass.'

'Of course.' Tuppence, who had stepped towards it, quickly held up her hands as Hen unpacked sandwiches from her large knitting bag.

'Would you like one before you go? For luck?' She offered it up.

'Better not. I'm a bit nervous so don't want to risk it,' Anita admitted.

'You will do an excellent job,' JM assured her in a confident voice, which seemed to boost the young detective constable, and Anita pushed her shoulders back and left the room.

'Look,' Tuppence said. 'They're bringing in Veronica. She looks pissed off.'

Ginny stepped up to the glass. Veronica did indeed look annoyed. Her mouth was in a tight line and her shoulders were rigid under her elegant jacket. They watched PC Bent direct her where to sit and then he disappeared. Wallace and Anita entered, their backs to Ginny and her friends.

There was a tape recorder which Anita reached for. 'This interview is being recorded,' she said then read through the rest of the statement, pausing every now and then for Veronica to reply.

As soon as the formalities were over, Veronica leaned forward. 'I still don't understand why I'm here,' she snapped. 'I have already given a statement about my appointments with Callum Lovelace and Ned Warner.'

'That is correct,' Wallace agreed in a neutral voice. 'Can you tell us about your relationship with Callum Lovelace?'

'What relationship?' Her jaw muscles flexed. 'I literally just told you that I have already given a statement about it.'

'We'll ask the questions. How do you know Callum Lovelace?' Wallace repeated.

Veronica's eyes flashed with annoyance before she sighed. 'I don't know him very well. I visited his house last week in a business capacity.'

'Ah, yes, you're an estate consultant. What does that entail?' Wallace pressed.

'I catalogue people's assets to ensure everything is in order.'

'And how do you get paid?' Anita asked.

'I get a commission of the estate when it is settled,' she said in a sullen voice before folding her arms. 'Not that it's any of your business.'

Wallace ignored her dig. 'Did Callum agree to become a client?'

Her mouth twitched. 'In my line it's not one-and-done. My

first visit was just to lay the groundwork. I planned to go back and discuss it with him further, but was prevented by his untimely death,' Veronica admitted.

'You mean his murder,' Wallace corrected before leaning back in his chair. 'What about Ned Warner? In your statement to DC Singh, you mentioned that you went to his apartment for a social visit, despite never having met him before. Was the real reason to discuss his estate?'

'I don't need to answer that.'

'No, you don't,' Wallace agreed and then fell silent. Veronica glared at him, and while it was impossible to see his expression, it was clearly aggravating the other woman.

The silence stretched on and JM let out a low whistle. 'Oh, he's good. That's a classic trick to make people so uncomfortable that they end up spilling the beans.'

'What do you think she's going to say?' Hen whispered, eyes wide with curiosity.

'Whatever it is, it's going to happen soon. Look at her mouth, she is moving from anger to irritation,' JM explained. 'You must admit that Wallace is excellent at bringing out that emotion in people.'

Ginny recalled her own early encounters with the detective. It was true, though the more she got to know him, the more she admired him not just for the job he did, but as a person. That wasn't to say there wasn't room for improvement when it came to his text messages.

Veronica shot Wallace a look of loathing. 'I met him on Friday to talk about hiring me. He was so rude and virtually kicked me out.'

'Did you discuss Peggy Barlow?' Wallace suddenly asked.

'Who?' Veronica said but colour crept up her cheeks, and she dipped her gaze.

'Oh, she's lying. I wonder why,' Tuppence said. Ginny was wondering the same thing. Veronica had acted strangely when she'd seen the photographs of Peggy Barlow, and she was still doing it now.

Wallace didn't reply, and while Ginny couldn't see his face, she imagined he was staring directly at her. After at least a minute Veronica groaned. 'Fine. My mother-in-law Sylvie lives at Ashworth Court and after her medication she gets a bit... disorientated. Sometimes she talks about people. One time she said that her friend Peggy Barlow went to Ned Warner's family farm back in the sixties and that it was full of amazing old-world treasures. In my business, clients with inherited wealth and assets are... desirable. I was hopeful I could get a look at them. But when I mentioned Peggy's name, he got very aggressive and told me to let sleeping dogs lie.'

Ginny and her friends exchanged a startled look.

If Peggy Barlow had visited the family farm, did that mean Ned Warner or his parents had known the couple? More importantly, did they know what happened to them? Was that why Ned Warner was interested in researching them?

'And the rest?' Wallace's sharp tone caused Veronica to shoot him a furious glare.

'We argued about it, okay? He was a dreadful man and look what he did.' She pushed back her jacket to reveal bluish bruises on her left wrist. 'He told me that if I didn't leave, he would kill me.'

'Why didn't you report it?' Anita demanded.

'I was hoping to change his mind. Do you know he had a real Picasso in that tiny apartment?'

'And what about Callum, what assets did he have?'

'He had an excellent collection of first editions as well as some exquisite Chinese porcelain.' She let out a regretful sigh.

'So, you didn't kill Callum Lovelace because he wouldn't sign on the dotted line?' Anita pushed.

'Of course not. Murder is hardly good for my reputation,' Veronica snapped.

'What about your bank account? It's possible you decided to

kill Callum Lovelace and just help yourself to his collection?' Wallace flipped open a file. 'According to his insurance broker, the collection was worth three million pounds.'

At the mention of his net worth, Veronica flinched, as if it was a wasted opportunity. 'I wouldn't be stupid enough to steal anything. Do you have any idea how difficult it is to dispose of high-value collections? Unless you have a black-market buyer, it's virtually impossible.'

'You seem very well informed on how it works?' Anita said.

Next to her, Wallace shifted in his chair and then leaned forward, as if studying Veronica intently. 'Was Ned Warner the only client you approached after hearing your mother-in-law talk about his family assets?'

Veronica had the good grace to blush. 'Not exactly. But that didn't mean I went in there blindly. I did my due diligence on each potential client. At the best all she gave me was cold leads. It was up to me to activate them. Anyway, it's the least she can do. She's loaded and after Louis, my husband, died, she refused to give me any of what would have rightfully been his inheritance.'

'What a terrible thing to say,' Hen gasped before pressing her hand to her mouth. 'Poor Sylvie. No wonder they don't get on.'

Ginny nodded in agreement. It was hard to feel much sympathy for Veronica, who seemed to think it was her right to take advantage of an old lady who was simply sharing some of her memories. After all, what had Sylvie told them? That memories lived in the heart, not in photographs.

'What about Nathan Richardson?' Wallace suddenly asked, and Ginny snapped back to the conversation. He clearly asked his questions in such a manner to throw people off guard.

'The barman?' Veronica frowned. 'What about him?'

'How well did you know him?'

'I didn't.'

'Even though he visited your mother-in-law?' Anita flipped open her notebook. Wallace gave her an approving nod and Ginny couldn't help but be proud of the young DC. 'Because according to the staff at Ashworth Court you visited on the same day he did.'

'You two are *very* irritating. Fine. He came to see Sylvie and if you ask me, he fed her a load of bullshit. It was clear he was trying to get into her good graces by feigning interest in his great-aunt. I wasn't buying it for a minute.'

'What did he have to gain?'

She snorted. 'My mother-in-law is a piece of work. You hear stories of young men romancing older women for their money. What's it called? May and December or something like that? I could tell he had an agenda.'

'That's rich, coming from her,' Tuppence retorted in a low voice. 'She just didn't want to lose her access to Sylvie's friends... and any inheritance she might receive.'

JM made a disgusted sound and then they all turned back to the interview room.

'Where were you on Sunday the 11th and 18th?' Wallace asked.

'Are you seriously trying to accuse me of pushing some kid over a beer keg, and then the following week going and killing Callum?' Veronica snapped before pausing. She closed her eyes, as if trying to recall her movements. 'On the 11th, I was in the Cotswolds with friends and last Sunday I was with Sylvie.'

'We will need your friends' names and contact details,' Anita said in a calm voice as Veronica rattled off several names and phone numbers. Once she was done, she tapped the table with her fingers, signalling she would like to leave.

Wallace dipped his head and extracted his phone from the pocket of his jacket. It must have been set to silent. He didn't speak as he read the screen, then he pocketed it again and got to his feet and signalled to Anita to finish the interview.

'We're done here, but please don't leave the area.'

Wallace walked out and several minutes later he appeared in the viewing room.

'Why didn't you push her further? That silent treatment you

did was totally working. And when you suddenly asked her probing questions. You were so close,' JM bristled.

'No, I wasn't. She knows as well as I do how difficult it is to sell valuable items without getting caught. Until I have a motive there's nothing I can do.'

'So, what, you're giving up?' Tuppence demanded. 'That just means we need to find out what her motive is.'

'I couldn't agree more,' Wallace said and glanced at his watch. 'Which is why I need to leave. I'm due at court for another case, but will be talking with our forensic team. Can I trust you to not do anything behind my back?'

'As if we would,' JM said with dignity. 'I take it you're not going to warn us not to leave the area.'

'I might if I thought it would work,' he retorted and then gave them a ghost of a smile. 'Thank you for your help today. I appreciate it.'

'That's what teams are for.' Tuppence patted his arm. 'I wonder if we should get a group handshake?'

'Don't even think about it.' Wallace's smile faded and he led them down the corridor and out of the building before disappearing back inside. Once he was gone, they all stared at each other.

'Well.' JM sighed. 'That was anti-climactic, though at least we will now have time to finish our power walk.'

'Excellent idea. We can go over the rest of the case as well. Just to make sure we didn't miss anything,' Tuppence agreed.

'Finish it? Surely we have done enough,' Hen protested, but it was met with a dismissive wave.

'Nonsense, we only got halfway around the park when Ginny called us in,' JM said. 'Now, let's get going.'

Ginny bit back her groan. Power walking was the last thing she wanted to do, but JM was right. There was something very anti-climactic about passing the case over, and the idea of going home seemed flat and uninviting.

She forced a smile. The sooner they started, the sooner it would be over.

190   AMANDA ASHBY

TWENTY-EIGHT

The dull afternoon sky threw a blanket of gloom over Ginny and her friends as they came to a panting halt in the park. They had discussed the case the whole time they'd been power walking, which hadn't helped her lung capacity.

'It still feels strange that we can't update our beer mats.' Tuppence leaned against the trunk of an old oak and started a series of stretches. 'I do hope Wallace won't use anything boring like a blue biro when he fills them in. I should have given him my felt-tips.'

Ginny was almost certain that Wallace had no intention of adding to the information on the beer mats, though she supposed it was a compliment that he had wanted to use them for his own investigation. She sat on the bench, willing her breath to return to a normal speed.

'I know what you mean.' Hen dropped down next to her and toed the pile of autumn leaves that covered the ground. 'It seems extraordinary that Ned Warner wasn't behind it all. It all fitted together so nicely. And those eyebrows.'

'Until we discovered he was with his daughter when Nathan

was murdered. Nothing like an alibi to kill a theory.' JM put her long arms behind her neck and twisted at her torso. 'But that location trick is a jolly good one. I think we should all practise using it. We never know when it might come in handy.'

'Good idea. I'll do it tonight when I get home,' Tuppence announced and frowned as she ran her hand across the thick bark of the oak. 'You know, I really wish people would stop carving their initials into trees. Look at them all.'

Ginny obediently glanced over to an array of love hearts, arrows and initials as well as numerous dates. 'It's not a custom that I like either,' she admitted before something akin to déjà vu skittered along her skin. She shivered, not sure why the carving should have any effect on her.

Rubbing her arms to dislodge the sensation, she got to her feet.

'Is everything okay?' Hen gave her a worried glance.

'I-I don't know,' Ginny admitted as she walked over to the oak tree. 'Something Tuppence said made me feel... uncomfortable... but I can't work out why.'

'Well, you do like nature and it's not nice to see so many people carve up this lovely old tree,' Tuppence reassured her. 'It's like they wanted to leave their mark on the world and couldn't think of another way of doing it.'

Leave their mark on the world.

Mark. Maker's mark.

Of course. Why didn't she think of it sooner? She got to her feet and joined Tuppence at the tree.

Hen peered over and frowned. 'What are we looking at?'

'All the engravings reminded me of the symbol Alfred Meeks used,' Ginny said as she retrieved her phone and brought up the photograph of the carved rose that Sister Bernadette had given them.

'Oh, do you think the priest hole is in the tree?' Tuppence stared at the thick trunk. 'Like a hobbit?'

'A hobbit? I thought they only lived in New Zealand.' Hen frowned.

'Hobbits don't live in New Zealand, they live in Middle Earth,' Tuppence corrected.

'Ginny isn't talking about hobbits,' JM cut them off impatiently. 'What's this about?'

'I'm not sure,' Ginny admitted, her mind whirling. 'Hen said she was still surprised Ned Warner was innocent because everything seemed to fit.'

'Y-es,' Hen agreed cautiously. 'And now I feel dreadful for thinking it. I suppose it's because he was also writing a book about Peggy. Well, allegedly writing one. But if Lena is correct, that's not even true.'

'Exactly,' Ginny said, sifting through their evidence in her mind. It was because they thought Ned Warner was writing a book that it made sense he had broken into Callum's house and killed him, because they thought he might've stolen his research. 'If Ned *didn't* kill Callum, then why did the person responsible leave such a mess?'

There was silence as the four friends exchanged startled looks.

'Oh.' Tuppence was the first to let out an excited squeal. 'You think the killer was looking for the priest hole?'

'It's possible,' Ginny said cautiously as she told them about Callum's family house. 'From the outside it appeared to be Georgian... but one side was covered in scaffolding, with a damaged roof. Remember what Sister Bernadette told us about old buildings being renovated.'

'We need to find out,' JM said. 'Because Ginny's right. The priest hole is at the heart of this riddle. If it's at Callum's house, we are duty bound to look for it.'

'Don't you mean that Wallace is duty bound to look for it?' Hen said in an uncertain voice. 'He was very clear that our part in the case is over.'

'He was also very clear that he had to go to court and then talk to forensics about something,' JM retorted. 'He could be gone for hours.'

'True, but PC Bent should be there,' Hen pointed out. 'We

heard Wallace send him there. What if we talk to him? I'm sure he will agree to let us look around.'

'Wallace could hardly argue with that,' Tuppence added. 'And if we do find it, think of what a lovely surprise it will be for him.'

Ginny rubbed her chin.

She doubted Wallace would see it that way... but her friends were right. If the young PC or even Anita was at the house, then it wouldn't be difficult to explain their theory, and if they were to find the priest hole, Wallace could hardly accuse them of going behind his back.

It made so much sense that the priest hole *might* be there.

Callum's father was the curator of the shoebox of newspaper articles about Peggy Barlow, as well as being her doctor. Did that mean Peggy had visited the house and discovered the priest hole on her own, or had Callum's father shown it to her? Had he also been a spy? Or someone dedicated to helping her?

Either way, Ginny realised there would be no sleep for any of them until they searched the house.

It didn't take them long to drive over and for the second time in a week, Ginny pulled up outside Callum Lovelace's Georgian manor house.

Crime scene tape still covered the front door, but while her friends went in search of PC Bent, Ginny crossed the lawn and over to the crumbling wing that was still half buried under scaffolding. She carefully stepped around the metal uprights and over to the leaded casement windows. Small rectangular panes were held together by lead strips, and the sight of them caused Ginny's heart to race.

The windows were most definitely from much earlier than the Georgian exterior of the front of the house. She peered through the thick glass, and was grateful for the late afternoon sun, which had burst to life and helped illuminate the room.

It was a library, with square wood panelling and shelving

which announced this part of the house was older. It matched the collection of leather-bound books, many of the titles faded with age. A ladder was propped against the highest shelf while to one side was a reading chair and a huge floor atlas. Next to the large fireplace was a hewn wood beam that ran up the length of the wall, and—

Ginny broke off and gasped as she could just make out what appeared to be something carved into the wooden beam. She brought up the camera app on her phone, using it to bring the wooden beam into focus. Her heart hammered as she inspected it.

It was a tiny carved rose.

They'd been right. The priest hole was here.

TWENTY-NINE

Wednesday, October 21

Ginny's excitement quickly faded as she thought of Callum Lovelace. The poor, poor man. All this time the key to what happened to Peggy Barlow might have been inside his own house. It was painful to think how many times he must have walked past the tiny rose carving, never knowing what secrets it contained.

Then she checked herself.

They still didn't know if the priest hole was in there. Perhaps it was just a coincidence. Still, at least now they had a place to start. She turned to find her friends, only to see them all walking towards her.

JM was frowning 'We have a problem. The door's locked and there is no sign of PC Bent.'

'Or DC Singh.' Hen appeared next to JM.

'Which is a jolly nuisance, because now we're going to have to wait to see if we can find it,' Tuppence concluded.

'Actually, I think we *have* found it.' Ginny gave them a reluctant smile and showed them her photograph. Her three friends immediately pressed their faces to the glass and stared at the wooden beam.

'Oh, poor Callum,' Hen spoke first, echoing Ginny's own thoughts. 'That's so tragic.'

'Yes, it's quite dreadful.' JM stepped back from the window and gave it a careful rattle. 'Which makes it even more imperative that we confirm if it's the priest hole. That way we're finishing the story for him.'

'JM, that is very touching,' Hen said with a watery smile.

'Well... I don't like unfinished business,' JM said gruffly as she looked away and tried the third window. It seemed Ginny wasn't the only one who couldn't always take a compliment. She gave her friend a fond smile, before too late realising what she was doing.

Her stomach dropped. 'You don't mean we should break in, do you?'

'Of course not,' JM assured her before poking at the frame. 'But if we were to find an open window then that's another story.'

'D-do you think Wallace would mind?' Hen asked cautiously.

Yes. Ginny was most certain that he *would* mind. 'We could call him, or Anita, and ask them to meet us here,' she suggested instead but was cut off as Tuppence, who had started helping JM, let out an excited squeal.

'Ta-da.' Tuppence pulled back the window, which opened outwards, the metal stay trailing it. Clearly the stay hadn't been latched properly.

'Oh, well done.' Hen clapped before wrinkling her nose and peering over at Ginny. 'Er, I mean, I think it's well done. Unless you would prefer we do wait for the police.'

'Nonsense.' JM joined Tuppence and inspected the window. 'It's not our fault they aren't here when we need them to be.'

'JM's right.' Tuppence dragged over an old milk crate that had been turned over and appeared to have been used as a stool for when the builders were having a tea break. 'Besides, you know what they say: When in Rome...'

'I don't think that's what it means,' Ginny protested, but she was too late and JM had already stepped up and was halfway through the window casement. Tuppence scrambled in after her and Hen gave Ginny a reluctant smile.

'Climbing through a window doesn't seem nearly as bad as power walking.'

Ginny swallowed and waited until Hen had disappeared in, before carefully following her. Besides, if they were going to get in trouble for doing it, they might as well all be together.

Their footsteps echoed as they made their way to the long, hewn beam that ran up the wall. Her heart pounded as she leaned forward to inspect the small carved rose. She held up the photograph on her phone and then turned to her friends.

They were identical.

'What now?' Hen whispered, as if worried someone might overhear them. 'How do we find the priest hole?'

'They were often under the floor or in walls.' Ginny ran her fingers further up the beam before giving a little gasp as it shifted under her touch. She pushed harder and the lower part of the beam lifted up.

A collective gasp went up as they all stared through the narrow gap into a small, bricked compartment.

Ginny shivered as dust motes floated in the air. It had an alien feel, like looking through to a different world and even though she could imagine a figure huddling in there, hiding from persecution, it was hard to accept it had really happened.

Again, sorrow filled her for poor Callum. Had he known it was here? And if not, what a terrible shame that he had been so close to it his entire life.

'What now?' Tuppence also whispered. 'Should one of us go in? It's very narrow.'

'I think JM would be best. She might be the tallest of us, but she is also the slimmest,' Hen said, patting her own belly. 'That is, if you think it will be safe.'

'I'm happy to try,' JM agreed and tentatively put one leg through and twisted herself sideways so she could slip past the narrow gap.

The light was fading and with no window in there, Hen held up her torch app on her phone, to give their friend some light. 'Here you go.'

'Thank you.' JM's back was to them as she moved around the confined space. Ginny shivered, feeling claustrophobic just looking at the tiny area. She shuddered to think of what it would have been like to be stuck on the other side, not knowing what your fate might be. 'I've found something.'

'Oh my,' Hen squeaked as JM dropped to her knees and rummaged in the far corner. Then she returned to the confined gap and carefully stepped back through, followed by a wave of dust. In her hands was a bundle of manilla folders that were brown with age.

'There was a loose brick at the back, and these were tucked behind it.' JM carried them to the reading table by the window and opened the first folder to reveal a bundle of typewritten notes, but before they could read them, there was a scuffle of feet and the door burst open.

Wallace stalked in, closely followed by Anita and PC Bent, who was clutching at a half-eaten sandwich. The three of them were grim-faced as they stared at the folders before glancing around the room.

Finally, Wallace spoke. 'Does someone care to explain why we got a call to say that four women were breaking into this property?'

'Not breaking in. The window was open.' JM pointed to the leaded casement. 'And we only did so because we couldn't find PC Bent.'

'Sorry, guv. I went and got some food. I swear I was only gone for ten minutes.'

'We pride ourselves on our efficiency.' Tuppence beamed.

Wallace ignored her and turned to Ginny. 'Why are you here?'

Her throat tightened but she put back her shoulders. 'We wondered just why whoever killed Callum also left such a mess behind. Originally, we thought that Ned Wallace had been responsible and was stealing research. But then we wondered if they were searching for the priest hole, and since we know that the maker's mark was a small carved rose, we came over here. We hoped PC Bent would allow us to look. I swear we didn't mean to go behind your back.'

'But you know how it is, when in Rome...' Tuppence said in a bright voice, which Wallace ignored. Instead, he sighed and ran a hand through his dark tousled hair.

'Am I to understand that you found the priest hole?'

'Oh yes,' Hen told him as JM walked over to the old beam and pressed it at the top, displaying how it opened up. 'Isn't it marvellous?'

Neither Wallace nor PC Bent spoke as they inspected the priest hole before finally returning to the manilla folders stacked on the table.

'Have you read the contents?' Wallace asked, his annoyance replaced by curiosity.

'No, not yet,' Ginny admitted before taking a deep breath. 'But we would like to help go through them. I-if you don't mind.'

'Put gloves on,' he instructed, gesturing to PC Bent to supply them and the last of Ginny's worries disappeared. They'd come a long way in their relationship with the detective and she would have hated to backslide. Especially when they were so close to the truth.

Once they had the gloves on, Wallace spread out the documents, brittle paper rustling under his touch.

Ginny leaned forward, eager to read the contents. It was a report about a suspected dead drop in the area and how Peggy had found it on an outlying farm.

There was no mention of what happened with the information and again Ginny shivered at how different the spy's life had been to her own.

Wallace flicked through the pages, and allowed them all to read the reports, which talked about Mikhail Volkov and several visits to Windscale. The other folders were similar, but the last one was thicker, and he opened it to reveal a slim brown diary.

A hush settled over the room as he opened it, but instead of the typewritten reports, the pages were filled with small, tight cursive. Squinting, he studied it for several minutes before looking up.

'I'm not sure I'm the best person to decipher this,' he admitted.

'Ginny's very good at handwriting. On account of being a doctor's wife,' Hen quickly announced and before she knew it, Wallace had passed the diary to her.

'I'll do my best.' She studied the page. *Hmmm.* She could understand why Wallace had a problem with it. The letters were tight and appeared to have been written in a hurry, despite the neat appearance. She scanned the first line several times, getting used to the style.

'Otherwise, we can take it back to the station and see what the software can do with it,' PC Bent suggested.

'It's okay, I think I've got it.' She scanned a few more lines before reading it out loud:

'*Twelfth March 1963. We've decided that it's impossible for us to stay here safely. Everywhere I turn there is a shadow, a whisper and the sensation of the other shoe about to fall. They don't want us to be together. Oh, that I'd never met him. How simple it would have been to continue my work, to serve my country and do my part, but from the moment I laid eyes on him, my heart was gone. He said it was the same for him, which now means we have both sides hunting for us. I don't know who I fear more, his government or mine.*

'*Seventeenth March 1963. We were followed last night. Thank goodness a bus had broken down on the high street. It allowed us to slip away and hide in the back of a van, but it's now apparent someone is getting closer. Yet still I can't see their face. They are always cloaked in darkness as if they are night itself. I need to find somewhere safe to keep my files. But where? So far, my only option is Lovelace's house. He cared for my broken arm and other wounds and doesn't know about the priest hole in his house. Yet, what if it's a trap? What if he is also my enemy? Will it ever be possible for us to be free?*'

Ginny read more of the pages out loud as Peggy's love for Mikhail increased, along with her fears that some unknown enemy was hunting them. It was unclear which government the spy worked for, or what they planned to do, but Peggy was preparing for the worst outcome.

Death.

Halfway through the diary, Ginny paused to catch her breath.

'Oh dear. This is quite shocking and the suspense is terrible,' Hen said, lowering her knitting.

'I have no time for suspense,' JM interjected. 'Go to the end and see what happens.'

'That's an excellent idea,' Tuppence agreed.

Ginny, pleased to be able to skip the increasingly panicked entries, carefully turned until she came to the final page.

'*Ninth June 1963. It is over. We are finally free. To think that after all this time I have discovered my greatest enemy is, in fact, my ally. Right under my nose, the spy who has been hunting me has been working next to me every day. Svetlana Yamilov, but I knew her as Sylvie Harris. I discovered it by accident... which is fitting since that is how she discovered my identity when I left a cipher in her raincoat pocket. In this instance I had arranged to meet Mikhail behind the pub, and who should I see but Sylvie speaking in Polish to a stranger.*

'*I don't know which of us was more shocked. I half expected her to kill me, or hand us both into her bosses, and I was almost ready for it. I am worn down from the intrigue. But I discovered she was equally tired, and so we hatched a plan to let Mikhail and I start again in Australia, and Sylvie would strike a deal with the government and in exchange for information they would protect her and let her continue her life at Little Shaw.*

'*I know I will never see her again, this woman who gave me and Mikhail a chance at happiness. I wonder if the world will ever know about the two female spies who found a different way to live. I leave this record, just in case, so that people will know of the gift we were granted by Sylvie Harris.*

'*Tenth June 1963. There is no more time. I must trust that Lovelace doesn't know about the priest hole in his house. I will hide everything here, and then try to forget that Peggy Barlow ever existed...*'

Ginny lowered the diary as the final pieces of the puzzle fell into place.

All this time Sylvie—far from being an innocent bystander—had been the one hunting Peggy Barlow. An enemy who lurked in the shadows. It seemed surreal that the tiny woman could have ever been a covert spy.

But then again, what better way to be a covert spy?

She tried to guess why Sylvie had been following Peggy. Was it to get to Mikhail? To retrieve him? Yet, if the diary was to be believed, instead of killing them, she had helped them escape, before creating a new life for herself.

It was the happy ending Ginny hadn't expected to discover. However, as she glanced over to Wallace's grim face, her hope was short-lived as his words rang through her mind.

Until I have a motive there is nothing I can do.

No. Oh no. While the diary cleared Sylvie of any wrongdoing, there was still a motive for someone else. Had Veronica Yates found out about her mother-in-law's secret past, and decided it could be damaging to her reputation? Based on what Ginny knew about Veronica, the answer was a resounding yes. It didn't make her feel any better as Wallace exchanged a glance with Anita. Moments later the DC hurried out of the room.

Ginny had a terrible feeling that it was to arrest Sylvie's daughter-in-law, Veronica Yates, for the murder of Nathan Richardson and Callum Lovelace.

THIRTY

Thursday, October 22

'I could have told the police that Veronica Yates was guilty,' Cleo announced in a loud voice, much like a street vendor trying to drum up business. The fact it was three o'clock in the afternoon and the Little Shaw library was all but deserted didn't seem to make a difference.

'It's true,' Andrea stage-whispered as Cleo stretched out her arms, skywards. 'She had another dream on Tuesday night.'

'You dreamed Veronica Yates would get locked up before it happened?' Slim put down the pumpkin he had been using for the Halloween display he was making. 'That's a handy skill to have. I know a few fellas who would pay well for a decent heads-up if trouble is on the way.'

'I can only use my powers for good. Besides, the spirits don't talk to me in simple images like a movie. Sometimes it is hard to interpret.'

'They send her snippets and sensations which she pieces together using her divine feminine intuition,' Andrea added.

'Sounds a bit havey-cavey to me.' William, who was sitting at a nearby reading table, peered at them.

'That's because you've not been granted the gift,' Cleo told him imperiously. 'My vision showed me a woman who was holding onto a balloon while she was queuing up to board a bus to Blackpool.'

Ginny, who had been pushing a trolley of Halloween-themed books to give to Slim, opened her mouth and then closed it again, not sure she wanted to find out the correlation. Though, Cleo's dubious prophetic warnings aside, it was true the arrest had indeed taken place earlier on this morning.

Unfortunately, after leaving Callum's house yesterday, Wallace thanked them and made it clear that they were no longer part of the police team. She supposed it was a step up from his usual warnings, but it meant they only had the village gossip to keep them going, and word was that Wallace had spent an hour with Sylvie at Ashworth Court while his team had searched Veronica's house, before finally making the arrest.

'Blackpool,' Andrea said, voice filled with awe. 'Isn't it marvellous the way the brain works? Cleo, you should offer up your services to the police. Think how much time you would have saved them.'

'I'm just pleased that monster is off the street before anyone else was killed—' Cleo broke off abruptly and glanced at her watch. 'Will you look at that, it's time for our tea break. Slim, I hope you didn't eat all the chocolate fingers.'

'There's another packet in the cupboard,' Ginny quickly assured the volunteers as she gave Slim the trolley-full of books and made her way to the issues counter, hoping that the rest of the afternoon would go by without anyone else mentioning Veronica's name.

I'm just tired, she tried to tell herself. And it was true. She had slept poorly last night as her mind went over all that had happened.

They'd found the priest hole and solved the riddle that was Peggy Barlow and Mikhail Volkov, which explained how Nathan and Callum had been involved. They'd also discovered Sylvie's hidden past... and the truth about Veronica's desire to keep that past hidden.

Ginny should be pleased. Except something was holding her back. As to what that was, she couldn't say. All night she'd been torn between trying to imagine fastidious Veronica brutally murdering two men, and then worrying what would've happened if they hadn't caught her. Except neither option sat easily with her. And how did Sylvie figure in it? After all, she'd lied about her life as a spy... did that mean she was hiding something else?

Hence her disquiet.

The rest of the afternoon dragged on, but finally it was over and she locked the library and climbed into her car and made the short drive to Ashworth Court.

Once it was clear that Wallace wasn't going to drag an eighty-nine-year-old woman down to the police station, the widows had debated whether they should all visit, or if Ginny should go on her own.

She had won. Or lost, depending on what Sylvie told her.

Whatever it is, I would rather know.

Dredging up her nerves, Ginny stepped out of the lift and walked up to Sylvie's apartment. She hadn't called or left a message, because she was unsure of the reception she would receive. Yet, despite the secrets that Sylvie had kept from them, she needed to find out the truth.

Sylvie immediately answered. 'Please come in, Ginny.'

'Thank you.' Ginny pushed open the unlocked door on the lavishly decorated apartment. Except now it seemed less like Aladdin's cave and more like a relic of the past. A time capsule of a life that no longer existed. 'I wasn't sure if you'd want to see me.'

'I could say the same to you. After all, I wasn't exactly honest with you. You could say it's a hangover from my old life. But I'm pleased you did come. I was wondering how long it would take for you to figure it out.'

'I'm almost sorry I did,' Ginny admitted as she took Sylvie in. She was dressed in an exquisite white suit with a huge diamond brooch on it. 'I take it Wallace was here yesterday. I hope he wasn't too... aggressive.'

Sylvie's lip twitched. 'I've faced worse than him. Though I didn't let him know that. It never works to let them think you're humouring them.'

Ginny wasn't sure if she was joking or not, so didn't answer as she walked to the kitchen. As expected, two porcelain teacups had been arranged on the countertop, along with an empty serving plate. Ginny almost smiled as she transferred the delicate sugar biscuits that she had made onto it. The kettle was already warm and didn't take long to boil.

'Did he tell you about Veronica's arrest?' She carried the tea and biscuits back out.

Sylvie closed her eyes, appearing frailer than last time they'd met. 'He called this morning. Veronica admitted to knowing about my past, after I let it slip.'

'Was it because of one of your medications?' Ginny guessed, based on Veronica's reluctant confession about how she got the names of potential clients from Sylvie after she had taken certain pills.

'Turns out that eventually, one's mind can betray you. I have no memory of it happening. Veronica hoped my dark secret would die with me, but then when Nathan turned up with a photograph of Peggy, she panicked—worried that if the truth came out her reputation would be ruined. She spoke to Nathan, but when he refused to let it go, she started following him and watched him meet with Callum. But she's denying murdering them.'

Ginny's skin prickled but she tried to hide it. After all, Veronica wouldn't be the first person to claim they were innocent, even if they weren't. 'Do you believe her?'

Sylvie gave a weary sigh. 'The world likes to think things are black and white. This person is bad... that person is good. Only a killer can kill. But this is not how it works. I am capable of all things, good, bad, beautiful and cruel. So was Peggy and so are we all.'

Ginny was silent as she let Sylvie's words settle in. The hint of Frenchness had fallen away, though it was hard to place the accent. Perhaps that was the whole point of Sylvie's argument? She was good and bad, old world and new world.

Yet, part of her had hoped Sylvie would insist that Veronica was innocent and that the police had got it wrong. Just like part of her had hoped Sylvie hadn't been a foreign operative. What things had she done on behalf of her country? For every Peggy Barlow she had saved, how many others had she betrayed? But was Peggy any better?

'I'm sorry it ended up like this.'

'Being sorry for what has come to pass is pointless,' Sylvie said, though it didn't seem to give her much reassurance. She let out a sigh. 'I would like one of those biscuits if you wouldn't mind.'

Ginny put one on a side plate and passed it over along with a cup of tea. She took a sip of her own. 'What made you decide to help Peggy and Mikhail?'

'Would you believe it was because I heard them bickering about a photograph? It was that one that led Nathan to me—of Peggy standing in front of her car. If you look very closely you can see Mikhail's outline reflected in the window. It was his camera, you understand, and his joke that made her laugh. She wanted him to destroy the photograph, but he refused. It was precious to him.'

'I hadn't noticed it,' Ginny admitted. To think that such a simple photograph had been their downfall, yet it had also been their new beginning.

'To bring Mikhail back was the last order I ever received.' She let out a small sigh and shook her head. 'Stupid man. He was brilliant but when it came to love, highly silly. And yet... I couldn't complete my mission. There they were together, bickering over a photograph with no idea I was standing there. All I had to do was make my report and someone else would have come in and finished the job. But I couldn't.'

'That was very brave of you.'

Sylvie let out a bark of laughter. 'It really wasn't. I was just as foolish as Mikhail. And Peggy. But I was also tired. Nothing I did really mattered. I would strike. They would strike and everything would reset and start again. So together we worked out a plan. We created a fight scenario and I was left with broken ribs. By the time the nearby operatives arrived, Peggy and Mikhail were long gone. I was taken into custody as a spy, and as far as my government knows, that's where I died. But instead, I cut a deal with them and told them everything I knew... well... almost everything. And then I went back to the one place no one would ever look for me. My last posting. And for sixty years my secrets had been safe.'

'Did you ever hear from them?' she asked.

'No. We decided it was too risky. But I like to think that they arrived safely.'

Ginny drank her tea and stayed for ten more minutes. Despite the many questions she still had, it was clear that Sylvie was tired and so she took her leave and promised to visit again soon.

Once down in the reception area, she checked the time.

Even though her friends hadn't come with her, they had promised to wait at the nearby café. It was in the row of shops where Ginny had bought milk the other day, and she knew they would be eager for the full story. It was a short drive and unlike the other night, the shops looked quaint and inviting.

She parked up and hurried past a lovely florist, which she suspected did a lot of business from people visiting Ashworth Court. The café was equally charming and she joined her friends by the window.

'Perfect timing.' Tuppence held up a rose-patterned teapot and poured the steaming liquid out into a delicate porcelain cup.

'And we saved you some chocolate slice,' Hen added, pushing across a small plate. 'It looks like you need it. Was it dreadful? How is Sylvie taking the news?'

'As well as can be expected.' Ginny gratefully took the tea and slice and filled them in on the conversation. Once she'd finished, they were all silent as if trying to make sense of the decisions that had led three people to turn their back on politics and the demands of their countries, to achieve personal happiness.

'I suppose we will never know what really happened to Peggy and Mikhail.' Hen retrieved her knitting. 'Though it does seem sad that the three of them went to so much trouble to escape from the clutches of international intrigue, only for Veronica to do something diabolical because of her reputation.'

'The irony is hard to ignore.' Tuppence sighed before wrinkling her nose. 'Or do I mean pettiness?'

'Both?' JM suggested and got to her feet. 'I for one have had enough of sitting down. Wallace is meant to be giving a press conference this afternoon, and I suggest that if we want to be within viewing distance, we get moving.'

'A press conference?' Ginny shuddered. 'I wonder if he will include Sylvie's part?'

'It's probably impossible to keep it hidden.' Hen tucked her knitting away and also stood.

'The news of the priest hole will be good for tourism, but it does seem a high price to pay. Poor Sylvie,' Tuppence added.

Outside the scent of late-blooming roses drifted over and Ginny stopped at the florist. 'I might get a bunch of flowers for Sylvie to let her know we're thinking about her.'

'That's a lovely idea,' Hen agreed as someone hurried past them. 'Oh, look, there's that kind nurse.'

Ginny turned in time to see Lizzie Foreman disappear into the antique store next door.

'She's brave, that place has wonderful pieces but it's *so* expensive,' Tuppence said.

JM used her height to peer around Hen's shoulder and into the shop itself. 'Looks like she's selling, not buying. Oh my, she's offering him a Faberge egg.'

Ginny's head jerked forward, and, flowers forgotten, she turned to the store entrance. However, without JM's extra inches, all she could see was Lizzie's back.

'Aren't those things worth a fortune?' Tuppence said then frowned. 'Is everything okay?'

Was it? Ginny pressed her lips together, her mind going back to Sylvie's Faberge egg. It was a stunning piece and while she knew the prices varied depending on how each one was made, they were highly collectable and not something that turned up every day.

It could just be a coincidence. She tried to remember if she had seen the egg during her visit, but she had been distracted by the shocking news about Veronica. Though the place had seemed less bright. Was it possible that the egg wasn't there?

Then she thought of Lena Warner's discovery that two paintings were missing from her father's apartment. It had been so easy to assume that Veronica Yates, an expert in antiquities, was behind it... but had they been wrong?

'JM, can you see if the egg is green and gold?' she said as her heart pounded an urgent beat.

'You think it's Sylvie's egg?' Hen gasped—clearly, she had also noticed it at their first visit.

'I can confirm the colours are green and gold. Oh, and look, he's giving her money, which means it must be authentic. *Hang on.*' JM abruptly leaned forward and swept her friends into a huddle.

'What's going on?' Tuppence said in a muffled voice, her mouth pressing into JM's chest.

'She's coming out,' JM whispered, her arms taking on octopus-like qualities as she cocooned Ginny and Hen from sight.

'How dreadful,' Hen whimpered as the sound of footsteps hurried past them.

The four friends stayed like that for several moments, frozen together. Was this what priests had felt like while hiding in those confined spaces? Ginny's heartbeat echoed in her ears and eternity seemed to pass before JM stepped back and released them.

'She's looking in the other direction, but I suggest that Ginny and Hen stay behind me. Tuppence, you can keep us posted.'

'She's about to get into a yellow van,' Tuppence announced, peeking around the side of JM's arm. 'But what's going on?'

Ginny calmed down her racing heart, grateful that her friends trusted her and Hen enough to act first, ask questions later.

'Sylvie Yates owned a beautiful Faberge egg when we visited her last week, but I don't remember seeing it when I was there today. And they are quite rare.'

'Surely it can't be true,' Hen fretted before daring to look back into the antique store. She let out a gasp. 'It *is* the same one. What does it mean?'

'More importantly, why is she selling it?' JM growled. 'I think we need to have a chat with this Lizzie.'

'No.' Ginny stepped in front of her friend. She longed to turn and follow the nurse's progress but didn't want to be recognised. She also knew that they couldn't confront her without any proof. 'We will only make things worse if we run in guns blazing. We don't even know if Sylvie's egg is missing.'

JM reluctantly sighed. 'You're right. But we don't want to let her get away while we're doing our due diligence. Tuppence, has she started the engine?'

Tuppence stepped away from the huddle for a better view. 'No, she's talking to someone on the phone. It looks like they're arguing.'

'Why don't you all get in the car and keep an eye on her? If she leaves, follow her. Hen, you should drive.' JM, whose car they had come in, retrieved her keys.

'Okay.' Hen, who was usually calm and mild-mannered, and by far the best driver out of them, took the keys and thrust her knitting bag at Ginny.

'What are you going to do?' Tuppence frowned. 'We can't just leave you behind.'

'I'm going to speak to the chap who just bought the egg and see what else I can find out. But don't worry about me. I can always follow in Ginny's car.'

'Ask if she has recently sold him any paintings.' Ginny passed over her car keys then clutched at the knitting bag as they allowed Tuppence to shepherd them towards the little silver car.

JM gave a sharp nod in acknowledgement and disappeared into the antique store as they scrambled into the car. Hen started the engine and then slunk low, as did Ginny.

'She's still on the phone,' Tuppence announced. 'Oh, wait. She's finished the call and is putting on her seatbelt.'

'Then I suggest we do the same,' Hen said as the back door opened and JM clambered in, her long legs pressing up against Tuppence's seat. 'You made it in the nick of time.'

'What did you find out? Did he tell you anything?' Tuppence demanded.

'Only that Lizzie had been selling lots of items over the last six months. Told the man that her father died and she was disposing of his estate, but that she was about to move and wouldn't be coming back.'

'It could all be true,' Tuppence pointed out.

'Then tell me why there were two Peter Doigs on his wall?' JM arched an eyebrow and thumped the driver's seat. 'It's time to follow that van and don't let her out of your sight.'

THIRTY-ONE

Thursday, October 22

Ginny was still clutching at Hen's knitting bag as the yellow van turned out onto the main road and sped in the direction of Little Shaw proper. Several cars beeped, but Lizzie didn't seem to pay attention as the van continued to weave through the traffic.

The October sky that had been bright only moments ago began to darken as the yellow van came back into view. Hen adjusted her speed accordingly and Ginny let out her breath, grateful that she wasn't the one driving, especially as the storm clouds continued to gather.

Was it really possible that Lizzie was behind the thefts *and* the murder? But why? Was she somehow related to Peggy Barlow and Mikhail Volkov? Or had it only ever been about money? Had she been stealing from the residents of Ashworth Court to line her own pockets? Either way, Wallace needed to know.

'I'm going to call the police.' Ginny retrieved her phone and brought up his number. There was no reply.

Then she remembered the press conference. Oh no. What terrible timing.

Not only did it mean they were on their own, but that Wallace would be announcing Veronica's arrest. She had to let him know that he might have the wrong person. She followed up with a text message, this time ensuring it made sense, without being too formal.

> Lizzie Foreman works at Ashworth Court and has been stealing from residents. We're following her in JM's car. Will share my location with you. If I can remember how to do it. Lena Warner told us about it but I still need to practise.

Once the text was sent, Ginny turned on her data. At JM's suggestion, they had all tried it out at home, but Ginny wasn't certain if it worked. *Now... what is it I do again?* She took a deep breath and brought up her location before sharing it with Wallace's number. As an afterthought she tapped Anita's number in there as well.

Now she just had to hope she'd done it correctly.

Ginny stared at the blank screen as Hen continued to stay at least one car behind Lizzie the whole way. They had soon passed through the main part of the village and out towards Walton-on-Marsh.

JM groaned. 'Please don't tell me that's where she lives. None of us operate at our full powers when we are there.'

'It's okay, look, she's about to turn off at Halton Park,' Tuppence said as the housing estate where Connor had grown up came into view. It was a rougher area and Hen slowed down.

Ginny closed her eyes, not sure whether to be pleased or disappointed that Lizzie lived there. It was a poorer area and she knew a lot of people were struggling. Was that why she had stolen from the residents? Not that it justified what she had done.

The wind had now picked up as the yellow van finally pulled into a cul-de-sac. Old trainers dangled from the power lines and the street sign was twisted where someone had knocked it over. She could just make out the name. Presbury Crescent.

Hands shaking, Ginny sent another text to Wallace letting him know the location in case she had messed up the mapping app.

Lizzie pulled up outside a red brick terrace house and disappeared inside.

'That must be where she lives,' Tuppence decided as Hen came to an abrupt halt further down the street, so they wouldn't be seen.

The house needed repair and weeds were pushing through the concreted area where a grass lawn would have once been. There was an abandoned swing set on it, lying upside down like a beached whale, and next to it was an overturned wheelchair, red ribbons catching in the wind.

Ginny's skin prickled. She knew that wheelchair.

A moment later the door opened and Lizzie marched out of the house, dragging a suitcase behind her as the wind continued to blow. She was followed by Charlie, navigating his new wheelchair down an accessibility ramp. His long hair blew around his face, making him look as if he was in a heavy metal band.

He was yelling something as he went down the ramp, but whatever it was, Lizzie seemed to be ignoring it. Were they arguing?

'What's he doing there?' JM demanded. 'Do you think they're related?'

'She could be his daughter,' Ginny said, as she tried to piece the new information into the puzzle. Slim mentioned that Charlie's daughter drove him to and from the pub for quiz night. Did that mean Lizzie had turned up to The Lost Goat the night that Nathan had been killed?

The hairs on Ginny's arms prickled and she checked her phone again for a reply. Still nothing. On cue, large raindrops began to fall.

They watched Lizzie thrust the suitcase into the back of the van then march to the driver's side and reach for the handle.

'Seems she is following in Charlie's footsteps... so to speak,' JM amended as her eyes fixed on the wheelchair. 'Do you think he's in on it?'

'According to Slim, both he and Charlie have turned over a new leaf,' Ginny said, reverently hoping that was true. 'I wish we could hear what they are saying.'

'Me too,' Hen agreed. 'But it's probably not safe to go up and confront her. Should we wait until she drives off and keep following her?'

'Like a stakeout?' Tuppence said.

'I have no time for stakeouts.' JM retrieved an umbrella from her handbag, untangled her long legs and stepped out into the rain.

'Well, you can't go alone.' Tuppence threw open the door and joined JM, who was marching up to the house.

On seeing them, Lizzie let out a snarl, as the rain plastered her hair to her face. Veins showed on her neck and her eyes flashed.

Oh dear. Why hadn't Ginny stopped JM and Tuppence from putting themselves in danger? Lizzie took several steps forward, and then stopped, as if deciding it was best not to engage. Instead, she yanked open the driver's door.

'She's going to get away,' Ginny said, voice breathless.

'Not if I block her in,' Hen suddenly said and before Ginny could reply, her friend slammed her foot down on the accelerator.

Ginny had expected Hen to pull forward so they were parked across the driveway, so was surprised when Hen arced out in a wide circle before speeding directly towards the back of Lizzie's yellow van. At the last moment she slammed her foot on the brakes, stopping only inches from the vehicle in front.

Lizzie, who was half in, half out of the van, twisted to face them. 'Move, you stupid idiots. You can't do that.'

'Seems like they just did,' Charlie hollered before turning to Hen and giving her a thumbs-up. 'Nice manoeuvre. JM, you might want to shut the gate as well to stop her trying to reverse into the car.'

'Gladly.' JM passed Tuppence her umbrella and strode over to the low wrought-iron gate and dragged it across the driveway before yanking open the van door. 'You're trapped and the police are on the way. And don't think of running because I will have you know that Tuppence and I are excellent power walkers.'

'Even better when we're not carrying our weights,' Tuppence seconded.

'I think we had better get out of the car,' Hen said quickly. 'Just in case she does try to reverse.'

Ginny threw the door open and hurried out, still gripping Hen's knitting bag. She passed it back to her friend, and they joined Tuppence as JM continued to lock eyes with Lizzie.

Finally, the driver's door opened and Lizzie emerged. 'You're making a big mistake and I will sue you all for harassment. It's illegal to block me in like this.'

'We followed you from the antique store.' Ginny stepped forward, raising the hood on her sensible raincoat to stop the worst of the weather. 'We know that you stole Sylvie Yates' Faberge egg. And the two Peter Doig paintings that belonged to Ned Warner.'

'You can't prove anything,' Lizzie snapped. 'Now move that car, or I will get the whole neighbourhood down here. And they won't be on your side. Unlike my scumbag father.'

Her last sentence was accompanied by a furious look directed at Charlie. So they *were* related. Ginny rubbed her brow as several people appeared on their front lawns. Connor had told her enough stories about the neighbourhood to know that they didn't take kindly to outsiders, which Ginny and her friends clearly were.

She turned to Charlie for guidance, but he was staring at his daughter.

'Lizzie, don't do this. It's not too late. Don't make it worse. Learn from my mistakes.' He moved his chair closer, eyes full of pain. Ginny got the feeling that he hadn't known anything about it. But why wouldn't Lizzie have told him? After all, he had once been a thief. Was it because she didn't want him to worry? Or was it something else?

'You can talk,' Lizzie snapped before holding her phone up to her ear. 'There's been a complication. You need to pick me up. Now.'

'Who did you call?' JM said in a cautious voice.

'Someone you won't enjoy meeting. Thankfully they only live around the corner,' she retorted as the low rumble of an engine sounded through the growing storm. Ginny turned, hoping to see a police car but it was a navy BMW with a huge man in the driver's seat.

'Let's go,' he hollered and honked the horn. More people emerged from their houses to watch the drama unfold.

Lizzie dragged her suitcase out from the back of the van, then winked. 'Looks like my ride is here.'

No. Ginny's heart pounded as she tried to work out how to stop her leaving.

She needed to get her talking. At least if they could get the truth, it would make it easier for the police to catch her. But so far Lizzie didn't seem interested in discussing anything. Ginny turned back to where a distraught Charlie was sitting. It was clear that despite caring for him, Lizzie didn't have much love for her father. Then she remembered Wallace's interview technique of asking a random question. It had totally thrown Veronica Yates.

But what could Ginny say to throw Lizzie?

Ginny pushed back her rain hood and peered around before her gaze landed on Charlie and the way his hands clutched at his new wheelchair. Had Lizzie bought it for him? Then she discarded the idea. Judging by the animosity coming from the nurse, she could barely tolerate him. Feeling dreadful that she might say something hurtful, she took a deep breath.

'That was so lovely of you to use the money to buy your father a new wheelchair. Shows how much you love him.'

Lizzie, who had been marching towards the waiting BMW, spun around, green eyes blazing. Ginny winced. Had she made a mistake? Then she remembered Wallace's other trick of keeping silent long enough to make someone else want to fill the gap.

The rain increased and still the silence dragged out before

Lizzie let out a guttural howl. 'Love him? *Love* him? That man ruined my life. I only moved back to this dump of a place and agreed to be his carer after he got out of jail because I thought he had stashed money away. All the stupid jobs I had to listen to him talk about. All the stories... and where is the money? I will tell you —it's *no*where.'

'That's what happens when you get caught,' Charlie said, almost apologetically. 'But I never pretended I had any dough. Why do you think I got this new chair through a charity group? Come on, Liz, you know I'm sorry about how things were. I'm trying to make amends.'

'I couldn't care less about your amends. Or your stupid quiz nights, or that you want to write a book. All I care about is not living in a dump and working my arse off. I want better for me and the kids. And *this*'—she dragged her suitcase behind her—'is how I get it.'

'What? By stealing from the residents of Ashworth Court?' JM demanded.

'It's not like they need all that stuff anymore,' Lizzie retorted, not taking her eyes off her father. The BMW honked its horn, but the nurse didn't seem to hear it. 'They're all half dead, just waiting until their number is up. Why shouldn't I lighten their load?'

'What about Nathan? And Callum?' Ginny suddenly said.

Lizzie's head jerked around and her mouth flattened out. 'Nathan Richardson was too damn nosy for his own good. I saw him leaving Sylvie's apartment with a yellow envelope and when I asked him what it was, he said it was personal.'

Ginny froze. The photograph in the envelope *had* been personal. It was of his great-aunt. Had he been killed because of a misunderstanding?

'What did you think was in there?' she pushed.

'Think? I didn't think, I knew it. I was in Sylvie's apartment when he was looking at everything she keeps on her shelf. He was making notes of what was missing.'

'That's not true,' Ginny gasped. 'He was there to find out about his family tree. If he was looking at her treasures it was because he was a history student and had an interest in them.'

'You don't seriously expect me to believe that bollocks,' Lizzie snapped.

'What about Callum?' Ginny pushed. 'Was he also making notes?'

'Don't speak to me about Lovelace. You can blame the old man for that one. He kept going on about what a nice house he has and all the artwork. So, I went there while the pub quiz was on, when he wasn't meant to be home. But he was... and he put up a fight. It made quite the mess, but I put an end to it. Now, as fun as this has been, I need to leave—'

A loud police siren broke through the swirling storm and the BMW driver, clearly not in the mood to get caught, reversed out of the cul-de-sac while the neighbours who had been watching all disappeared back into their houses.

'No,' Lizzie screamed in fury, too late realising what had happened.

'Elizabeth Foreman,' Anita said, running forward as Wallace appeared behind her, arms folded and mouth grim. 'You are hereby under arrest...'

THIRTY-TWO

Sunday, November 8

'And we have a well-deserved win for The Village Idiots in the inaugural Nathan and Callum weekly quiz, to be known as the Nacas from now on,' Mitch said two weeks later as he handed over the twenty-five pound gift certificate for a trampoline park in St Helens.

The worry lines around the pub owner's mouth had disappeared and his tentative smile was mirrored in Heather's face as she stood next to him, arm around his back.

'Rigged,' someone called out. 'How do those dunces know what fracking means?'

'Because we went to the protests,' one of the winners responded from the podium. 'You should try it sometime.'

However, Ginny, who now accepted that banter was all part of the experience, turned back to her friends and gathered up the glasses. 'I'm going to get a round of drinks.'

'Good idea. It's nice to support Mitch and Heather.' Hen smiled as she continued to knit the rainbow-coloured wheelchair handle covers for Charlie.

'And much nicer to do it with a glass of wine, than crewing the bar.' Tuppence leaned back.

'I must admit I'm pleased they have finally hired someone. I don't like my hair smelling of beer,' JM agreed as Ginny made her way through the busy room. She passed the May the Force be With You team and gave them a friendly wave before reaching the bar where a man with salt-and-pepper hair and a neat beard and moustache stepped up to serve her.

'Ginny, same again?' he said.

'Thank you, Ted.' She put the empty glasses down on the bar and gave Wallace's father a tentative smile. He had arrived in Little Shaw three days ago and after finishing painting the bedroom, water-blasting the back patio and doing something else that required five hours of straight angle grinding, it had been Wallace who suggested his father apply for the part-time job at The Lost Goat.

Knowing that Ted Wallace wasn't the chattiest of men, Ginny had been slightly surprised. But since he had worked as a chef and run restaurants and pubs for many years, she supposed it made sense.

'How did you get on with the quiz?' he asked as he made up the drinks in a swift practised manner.

'I think we came somewhere in the middle of the pack. Though it's probably good your son's team has stopped their winning streak. The abuse has been a lot less aggressive tonight.'

'You can thank that case of yours. James has been working long hours dealing with the paperwork. His mind is probably elsewhere,' Ted explained. 'By the way, I noticed the guttering by your back door is clogged. Would you like me to fix it?'

Ginny blinked. Not only was it the most she had heard Ted speak since he had arrived back in Little Shaw, but she hadn't realised there was anything wrong with her guttering. It was the kind of thing that Eric would usually spot. And while he wouldn't fix it, he would bring it to her and they would discuss it together.

House maintenance. Yet another thing she now had to do alone. Familiar sadness travelled through her and she swallowed.

'Maybe,' she agreed before paying for the drinks. 'And it's nice to see you.'

'You too.' He gave a gruff nod and then disappeared down the other end of the bar to serve Esme and Elsie. She returned to the table and settled back down.

'Ted seemed chatty. How's he liking the new job?' Hen asked, taking her gin and tonic.

'I think he's enjoying it. The neighbours are certainly pleased he has something else to keep him busy,' Ginny admitted as she took a sip of mulled wine. It was warm and full of spices and perfect for this time of year.

'Did he let any of Wallace's secrets slip about what's happening with Lizzie Foreman?' Tuppence demanded.

'He wasn't *that* chatty,' Ginny admitted. Wallace said they were still determining the extent of Lizzie's thefts but that she'd confessed to both murders, which was helping them build the case. Ginny glanced over to where Slim and some of his friends were sitting. There was no sign of Charlie, but he had come into the library a couple of times. His smile was nowhere to be seen, but he had told her he had started going to a therapist to help him with the fallout of Lizzie's crimes, and to deal with his own guilt about his previous profession.

'I can always talk to him. See what else I can find out.' JM glanced in Wallace's direction, eyes gleaming. But before she could stand up, Veronica Yates joined them. She was carrying an old-fashioned hatbox, much like Ginny's mother had once owned.

'Good, I was hoping to find you all here,' Sylvie's daughter-in-law announced as she thrust the hatbox at Hen and pulled up a seat.

'Clearly, you're in too much of a hurry to indulge in social niceties,' JM said.

Veronica fixed her with a penetrating glare then shrugged. 'Hello, JM. I do hope you're enjoying a pleasant evening.'

'As it happens, I am,' JM assured her and then made a rolling action with her hands. 'Now, what's this dramatic entrance about?'

'Dramatic? That's a bit rich coming from you,' Veronica retorted.

'How's Sylvie?' Ginny quickly asked before things could escalate. They had spoken with Veronica several times since her release from custody, but she did seem to be an acquired taste. Still, she and Sylvie had repaired their relationship, which was a positive.

Veronica's expression softened. 'She's very well and wanted to come here to see you all, but we have an early start tomorrow so I've convinced her to rest.'

'Is it for another photo shoot?' Hen asked cautiously.

Veronica shook her head. 'No more of them until we're on the cruise. Which is why she needs her rest.'

'Cruise?' Ginny raised an eyebrow, trying not to think too much about Sylvie's frail health. 'Is that wise?'

'I was worried about that, but her doctors all agree that as long as we get assistance and don't do too much, she will be fine. We all went on one together, you see, before Archie and Louis's deaths.' She paused and let out a shuddering breath. 'I don't think we realised how much we needed each other until this nasty business started.'

There was silence as Veronica dabbed at the tears that had started forming.

It was something Ginny and her friends could all understand and JM even reached out and patted Veronica's hand.

'I think it's a lovely idea,' Hen said. 'Please give Sylvie all our love.'

'I will. Speaking of which, Sylvie wanted me to bring this to you.' She waved at the hatbox and gestured for Hen to put it on the table. 'And before you ask, no, I don't know what's in it. Once a spy, always a spy. Would it kill her to be a little bit less mysterious?'

'Okay, well, thank you,' Ginny said, taking Veronica's change of conversation as a cue that she was ready to leave. 'Have a lovely cruise.'

'I intend to.' Veronica got to her feet and handed Ginny another business card. 'When we're back, we must talk about your estate.'

JM made a growling noise and Veronica hurried off.

'She's certainly focused,' Tuppence commented as she cautiously touched the hatbox. 'What do you think is in here?'

'Let's find out,' Ginny suggested, not wanting any more mystery in her life. She flipped open the locks and lifted the lid. She had to stand to peer in properly.

It was beautifully lined in pale silk and there were hundreds of photographs and postcards nestled inside. On top was a heavy envelope that smelled of vanilla. Ginny's name was written on it, in shaky handwriting.

'Oh, goodness. It's the two of them together.' Hen picked up a photograph and examined it.

It was indeed a much younger Sylvie and Peggy smiling as they each held a glass of wine.

'How lovely to see them both,' Tuppence agreed. 'I wonder what the letter says?'

'She might have used code,' JM warned.

'I hope not,' Ginny said, knowing her brain wasn't up to much after sitting through the pub quiz. The parchment was heavy beneath her fingers as she eased it out of the envelope. She quickly scanned it and then read it out to her friends:

'Dear Ginny, Hen, Tuppence and JM,

'Please excuse an old woman for not being entirely honest with you about Peggy and Mikhail's disappearance, and the part I played in it. I suppose you could say it's been an occupational hazard and now it's too late to change. Though to be fair, I can't say I'm particularly motivated. The world has changed around me so it seems only fitting that I do my best to stay the same.
'Enclosed are the photographs and postcards I received from them

over the years. They are both pushing up daisies now, but I like to think they would approve of me passing these on.

'*I have spoken with Sister Bernadette several times since Veronica was released. She is very interested in telling Peggy's story... and my own, and if you feel it's right, please pass this ephemera onto her. Now, I'm an old woman who is tired and more than a little grumpy from too much nostalgia.*

'*Yours truly,*
'*Svetlana Yamilov*

'*p.s. I expect you all to visit me as soon as I return, since I presume I will be heartily sick of Veronica's company by then.*
'*p.p.s. Please find a copy of* Pride and Prejudice. *I think you might enjoy it.*'

Ginny gasped as she remembered the book cipher that had been written on that first photograph. 147-3-2, 89-12-7, 23-8-4, 156-15-3.

Was it possible that Sylvie had kept Peggy Barlow's original book all these years?

Tuppence plunged her hand through the photographs, much like Edgar would do, when he was exploring something new. She swished her hand around before grinning and lifting out an old book. It was battered with a dark leather spine and a pale yellow and brown board cover.

'Got it. Do you think this will help you decipher the message?'

'There's only one way to find out.' Ginny turned over the envelope Sylvie had used and wrote the code down, before reading each piece of the cipher out to her friends. Word by word they built it up until they got to the end.

Ginny smiled as she held up the envelope so they could all see what it said.

Have a wonderful life.

'Well, if these photographs are anything to go by, they definitely did.' Hen beamed and waved a shot of Peggy and Mikhail swimming at the beach. 'I think we should have a toast.'

'About time,' JM grumbled as Hen put down the photograph and untangled the wool from around her own glass. Tuppence grinned and tucked a small cocktail umbrella behind her ear as Ginny raised her wine and smiled at her friends.

'Here's to a wonderful life.'

A LETTER FROM THE AUTHOR

Huge thanks for reading *The Widows' Guide to Last Orders*—I hope you were hooked on Ginny's journey. If you want to join other readers in hearing all about my new releases and bonus content, you can sign up for my newsletter.

www.stormpublishing.co/amanda-ashby

If you enjoyed this book and could spare a few moments to leave a review that would be hugely appreciated. Even a short review can make all the difference in encouraging a reader to discover my books for the first time. Thank you so much.

Ever since I started this series, I knew that one day I would set a book in Little Shaw's local pub, The Lost Goat, and that it would be called: *The Widows' Guide to Last Orders*. Unfortunately, that was all I knew, and while it didn't take me long to come up with a murder in the cellar, it took quite some time to figure out why it had happened.

Who said writing was easy? But it finally came together, and I hope you all enjoy it. And one fun fact is that The Lost Goat's cellar is based on the pub I worked in when I first moved to London in the early nineties. It was dark, damp and creepy, and proves that nothing is ever wasted when it comes to having a checkered work history!

Thanks again for being part of this amazing journey with me and I hope you'll stay in touch—I have so many more stories and ideas to entertain you with!

KEEP IN TOUCH WITH THE AUTHOR

www.amandaashby.com

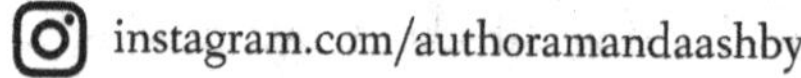 instagram.com/authoramandaashby

ACKNOWLEDGMENTS

A big thank you to the usual suspects! Sally Rigby and Christina Phillips, I am still so grateful to always have you both in my corner. To Rachel Bailey and your brilliant mind. You can always follow my half-baked ideas and then make them better. Plus, thank you for the Shakespeare quote. I told you I'd get it in there, even if I did have to add an entire scene!

To Emily Gowers, you continue to amaze me with your insightful and completely brilliant edits, and the fact you push me to go both bigger and sillier at the same time is a talent indeed! Thank you to Oliver Rhodes, Kathryn Taussig, Alexandra Begley, Dushi Horti, Amanda Raybould, Emily Courdelle, Versha Jones and the entire Storm team for all their hard work, and to Audio Factory Productions and Diana Croft for the wonderful narration that brings Ginny and her friends to life.

www.ingramcontent.com/pod-product-compliance
Lightning Source LLC
Chambersburg PA
CBHW011933050726
47590CB00011B/3272